HENRY FREY
AND THE
ELF KING

JASON RYBAK

To Amy,

Happy Christmas.

Rybak

CHAPTER ONE

Grimnir hated Christmas. He trudged through the snow, ignoring the noise, music and laughter of the party raging around him. Leaving the sloping avenue, he started along a low branch of the giant fir tree, which rose over half a mile into the freezing cold air.

A minute later, he was inside the house-sized star at the top of the fir tree, his eyes burning into the back of the one the world knew as Santa Claus. Not for much longer if he had his way. How he hated him. He realised they weren't alone and forced his face into a more pleasant expression.

"Anything to report?" The Great Santa Claus said, without turning round.

"It is as we suspected," Grimnir replied in a grave tone. "They have been lost for good. The New Year has not even begun and we are behind already."

The Great Santa Claus did not bother to reply. Just like him. He didn't care what anyone else thought anyway. He sat at his desk, staring into his LagFyurring, the glowing gold globe, three feet in diameter, which hovered in front of him.

Grimnir peered over The Great Santa Claus' shoulder. Through the LagFyurring, he could see a ten-year-old boy watching the high street below through his bedroom window. He had woken up early, too excited to go back to sleep, so he was already dressed with his fair hair combed into the side parting his mum liked.

Grimnir knew just what The Great Santa Claus was thinking.

"We already have a new Glondir," he ventured.

"I know, I know," The Great Santa Claus said dismissively.

There was a knock at the bedroom door. The boy's mum peered around it and beckoned to him.

"Watch this," said The Great Santa Claus, his eyes fixed on the LagFyurring.

The boy sat on the floor around the Christmas tree with his mum and dad, steaming mugs of hot chocolate in hand, eyes fixed on the small pile of colourfully wrapped gifts lying under it.

After discovering chocolate, books, a couple of t-shirts and a computer game, the boy had just one present left.

"Here it comes," The Great Santa Claus said, his voice thick with anticipation as he leaned forward in his chair.

The boy turned the gift over in his hands - a box covered in gold wrapping paper. The gift tag, inscribed in gold pen, read:

"To Henry, from Santa Claus."

The boy's trembling fingers tore apart the wrapping paper, then ripped open the box, his eyes and mouth wide open with excitement.

A flicker of disappointment crossed his face.

The look was mirrored in the features of The Great Santa Claus.

Grimnir wanted to burst out laughing, but he reserved that pleasure for later.

The boy examined the camera in his hands. It was bulky and old-fashioned, much bigger than the sleek, modern digital cameras and mobile phones his friends would be unwrapping. It looked like a black plastic box with a lens at the front. There was no screen at the back, just a tiny viewfinder to look through and one button to push to take the picture – the shutter. There wasn't even a slot for batteries or a memory card.

"Is it a real camera?" the boy said doubtfully.

"That looks lovely," his mum gushed. "You're going to have a lot of fun."

The boy forced a half-smile. He aimed at his parents and clicked. They posed together for him. He took a few more, pausing each time in case something happened, but nothing did. Eventually he put it down.

Once Mum and Dad were busying themselves with Christmas dinner, the boy slipped into his bedroom. He slumped on his bed, staring at the camera. It was the one thing he'd wanted and the sole item in his letter.

"Here it comes," The Great Santa Claus chuckled.

Grimnir stared open-mouthed. Something dawned on him. He hadn't known. There would be four more identical cameras out there somewhere. The treacherous old dictator.

A burst of bright light streamed from the camera. It filled the room.

The boy climbed off the bed.

In front of him was a giant, sharp picture of Mum and Dad smiling at him, sitting on the floor with their presents. It was the first photograph he had taken. The others were of smaller size, emblazoned around him against his bedroom walls.

Moving his hands the right way made the first photograph bigger or smaller. He swept it to one side and the second he had taken hung in the air in front of him. He flicked through them and back to the first. The more he looked at it, the more he liked it. If only he could print it and stick it to his bedroom wall.

Something shiny on the wall next to the bed gleamed in the camera's light. It was the photograph, positioned exactly where he would have placed it himself.

The boy grabbed the camera and ran out of the room.

"I knew it," The Great Santa Claus breathed, his voice riddled with excitement. "The boy is a Valdir. It reacted to him. He has the Affinity for Madjik."

Grimnir's eyes were fixed on the LagFyurring, an excitement of a different kind coursing through his veins. He knew what would happen next.

The boy raced to his mum, the words spilling out of his mouth like a burst dam. The expression on her face was one of confusion. The boy stopped and looked down at his camera. There was no light. Try as he might, he could not make it work. It was just an old toy camera again. He turned away, disappointed.

"That's very nice, dear," his mum said, turning back to her turkey as if she hadn't heard or understood a single word.

The boy slumped on his bed.

The light shone from the camera and filled the room. His photographs beamed around him and emblazoned the walls.

The boy sighed.

Grimnir swallowed the urge to laugh. The Great Santa Claus might think he had given the boy the greatest gift on Earth, but he knew better. The camera would never reveal its Madjik to anyone but its owner, yet the boy wanted nothing more than to show his parents and friends. By next Christmas, the boy would be writing to Santa Claus for a new camera - Madjik or no Madjik.

CHAPTER TWO

It was early December, nearly a year later. Grimnir crunched through the snow with a spring in his step. He couldn't get there quickly enough. He had accomplished things, which no one around him would have believed possible. The ValdFyurring, the Epicentre for their Madjik, was failing. He had made it happen and none of them had any idea.

He entered the Star and adopted his saddest demeanour.

"I am afraid the news is the worst imaginable," he announced gravely. "Some of our most popular gifts have been lost forever. With it being so close to Christmas, we will never be able to make up for lost time."

"What was the cause?" The Great Santa Claus replied, sitting at his desk with his head in his hands.

"It is difficult to say for certain," Grimnir replied, wishing he had a camera. "But it looks as if the ValdFyurring cannot cope with the growing population and its demands. The ever-increasing complexity of human technology is just too much for it."

"It doesn't make sense." The Great Santa Claus said it more to himself than anyone else. "The ValdFyurring is all-powerful. It is of the world and should be able to cope with whatever the world throws at it."

"Perhaps its powers are finite," Grimnir suggested, as if he had just thought of it. "And we are now seeing what those limits are. It is no longer strong enough."

"Impossible," The Great Santa Claus snapped.

"The Council believe it to be." Grimnir said it slowly so he could enjoy every word. "We are to bring in the Black List."

The look of horror on The Great Santa Claus' face was worth savouring.

"The Craft of Education has already begun putting it into practice," Grimnir announced. "They will use school league tables combined with empirical evidence."

"No." The Great Santa Claus thumped his desk with his fist. "That must never happen. Where is Yohann?"

"He is hard at work," Grimnir said solemnly.

The Great Santa Claus took in a deep breath.

"Do you think he is meant to be Glondir?" he asked quietly, showing a rare vulnerability that Grimnir couldn't wait to exploit.

Yohann had been The Great Santa Claus' special helper for over a year and Grimnir knew full well just how useless he was.

"I think he does an excellent job," Grimnir said as seriously as he could, struggling to keep a straight face.

"The ValdFyurring's decline coincides with his arrival," The Great Santa Claus shot back at him.

"But I think that is all," Grimnir replied, doing his best to keep his temper under control. "A coincidence. It has escaped nobody's attention that he has yet to be fully instated as Glondir. You have not given him the Hafskod. That might be all he needs."

"I don't know." The Great Santa Claus dismissed his suggestion with a wave of the hand and turned back to the LagFyurring hovering over his desk. !

An image appeared. The same boy, now eleven years old, stood in his bedroom studying the photographs plastered over his bedroom walls. Starting with the first he'd taken of his parents last Christmas Day, they covered the wall over the bed, surged around the window and nearly reached the door. There were lots of his parents and lots of people on Camberwich High Street taken from his bedroom window. All the natural kind. People going about their lives. Nothing set up or posed. Unique moments in time, never to be repeated.

His favourite was one of the first from Christmas Day a year ago. It was in black and white, of Mum sitting at the dinner table as they finished their turkey. She stared ahead of her, sipping her champagne, looking blissfully happy and content.

What made the picture so special was something he hadn't noticed at the time. It was Dad sitting in the background, glass of champagne in hand, watching her with a faint smile on his face. It was a perfect moment.

"Yohann was never one of the Valdiri," The Great Santa Claus said, smiling at the picture. "I believe in giving second chances to everyone, especially children, but he will never have the Affinity. Madjik will never react to him the way it would to a true Valdir. Maybe it is time for a change. I would still allow him to stay on in a helper capacity."

Grimnir scowled. Time to thrust the knife.

"I have one more piece of bad news," he said. "Henry Frey will be on the Black List."

The Great Santa Claus slumped ever lower in his chair and sighed. There was despair, but no surprise.

The boy sighed as well. He moved from the pictures over his bed to the most recent ones by the door. Mum and Dad weren't happy celebrating Christmas anymore. They were fighting, shouting and arguing. Their faces were angry. Their eyes were hurt, filled with pain and sadness.

It had been the worst year of Henry's life. The news on TV told how times were hard, that banks and economies were collapsing. And Henry's parents had run out of money. Every day was a struggle and the harder it got, the more Mum and Dad argued. They shouted at each other for hours nearly every night.

Desperate to escape, Henry would grab his camera and stare through the viewfinder at Camberwich High Street below his bedroom window where everything was peaceful.

Sometimes he would open his bedroom door a crack and watch them argue through his camera as if he was watching just another couple, taking just another photograph and he wasn't really there at all. It was like watching TV. Seeing his parents argue through the camera was always much easier.

When the shouting became really loud, Henry would shut his bedroom door and sit on the floor, hold his hands over his ears and hum to drown it out.

One really bad argument started after Henry asked for money for a new pair of trainers and a class trip to France. He hid in his room, wishing he'd never said anything.

The next day, he snuck back into his classroom at lunchtime. He didn't know why, but he wasn't in the mood for playing outside. Everyone else was happy. Life was easy for them. It wasn't fair.

He stopped and looked around him. He knew where it was. In the top left-hand drawer in Mrs. Leimann's desk. The bag filled with the money she had collected for the class trip to France.

Quick as a flash, Henry glanced towards the door. Nobody there. He opened the drawer, snatched the bag and shut the drawer. What to do with it? What if they check their pockets or their bags? Or their desks?

He opened the bag, grabbed the wad of notes and stuffed them in his underpants. They'd never look there. He opened the window next to Carl Wright's desk and dropped the bag of coins onto the soil outside. He snuck out of the classroom without being seen.

Mrs. Leimann knew just where she'd left the money. Her furious glare made the hairs on the back of Henry's neck stand on end.

She kept them all back for two hours after school, but nobody knew anything. Henry watched her shoot glances in Carl Wright's direction. He was the obvious choice. He was a bully and a thief. Everyone secretly hated him.

Henry walked home as casually as he could. He knew he couldn't spend the money in a hurry. He couldn't use it for the trip to France either, but now nobody else could. The gardener found the rest of the money that night. They all thought it was Carl, but nothing could be proven.

A month later, after a furious shouting match at home when Mum swore at Dad and said she hated him and Dad threatened to divorce her, Henry hid in bed with the quilt over his head. The next day, he set off a fire alarm in the school corridor. Carl's mum was brought in to see the headmaster. He didn't expel him, but now Carl was on his last warning. Nobody was as scared of him after that. Henry told himself he had done everyone a favour, but he didn't sleep that night.

After the money for the class trip was never found, most parents paid again and their children went to France anyway. Henry was left behind.

He wasn't included in anything anymore – not since his friends from school had laughed at his camera. It had never worked around anyone else. There were lots of photographs near the door of his friends riding their bikes along Camberwich High Street without him. They were right next to his parents shouting and screaming at each other.

Henry stared miserably at them and sighed. If that was what a magic camera brought, then he needed a nice normal one like everyone else. He took his camera, his favourite thing in the whole world, and shoved it in the back of a drawer.

Grimnir wanted to laugh. He pressed his lips together until the urge to roar with laughter subsided. He couldn't have planned it any better. He had followed Henry Frey's exploits with delight, waiting for the day when he could deliver the wonderful news to The Great Santa Claus – that his star child was on the Black List. It had turned out better than he had dared hope.

"I am very sorry," Grimnir said, putting on his most sympathetic and desolate tone. "It seems as if Henry Frey will not be able to fulfil his potential as a Valdir. After all, just consider the blow to his belief in you when he receives nothing from you this Christmas. And without belief…"

The Great Santa Claus said nothing.

The stubborn old fool.

Time to twist the knife.

"It is time to face the reality of the Black List," Grimnir said, as if he himself were resigned to such a terrible fate. "Such a shame that his recent misdeeds are undeniable. We should look elsewhere."

"I don't know." The Great Santa Claus stared into the LagFyurring as if he expected the answer to jump out of it. "I believe in second chances - and hope. There is always hope."

Grimnir trudged home through the snow, his blood boiling with anger. He took the stairs down to his wood-panelled basement. He pushed a wood panel in the wall and a door opened, revealing a hidden flight of stairs. As he marched down them, the door swung shut and locked in place behind him.

Entering his hidden base of operations, he picked up the Omnitec Neon tablet lying on the worktop next to him and tapped out the security code on it. A face appeared on the giant screen on the wall in front of him.

"The time has come," Grimnir said. "Kill the Valdiri. And most importantly of all, kill Henry Frey."

CHAPTER THREE

Henry awoke early on Christmas morning. He jumped out of bed and crept to his bedroom door. He eased it open. The living room was dark. His eyes trained on the shape of a tiny Christmas tree on top of the coffee table next to the TV. Around it was the smallest, most meagre pile of presents Henry had ever seen.

He watched every parcel clarify through the darkness. His eyes flitted over each one and fixed on three presents in gold wrapping paper. He had asked for three things in his letter to Santa: an Omnitec Flash camera, an Omnitec Neon tablet and the Omnitec Quickfire games console, which everyone at school was talking about. And there they were. He closed his bedroom door and breathed a sigh of relief.

None of his friends believed in Santa Claus. He knew he was too old, but where else could a magic camera have come from?

The stories couldn't all be wrong, could they? Santa Claus had to be old, jolly and fat with a big white beard. And if he was real, then there had to be elves and flying reindeer. Santa Claus had to be the kindest man in the world who loved every child.

But Santa didn't love every child, did he? He only gave to the good ones. What if the bad things Henry had done meant he received nothing? Mum and Dad couldn't afford presents. Would Santa Claus turn his back on him?

No. There were three presents in gold wrapping paper under the Christmas tree. He was fine.

He opened his curtains, leaned on the window sill and stared through the window. Camberwich High Street was in semi-darkness. It was still and quiet, but there were a few people out and about.

His eyes were drawn to a man lingering on the opposite side of the street who leaned against the wall, his hands in his leather jacket pockets. Henry recognised most people who passed his bedroom window, but the man didn't fit. He was tall and wiry. His long, brown hair was tied back in a ponytail. What was wrong with his ears? They looked like they had been bleeding.

The man didn't move. He didn't look left and right like he was waiting for someone. What was he doing? Something about him made a chill surge up Henry's spine. He backed away from the window.

"Henry."

Henry jumped. Mum peered around the door and beckoned to him.

"It's time for presents," she whispered.

Henry hurried after her, laughing with excitement. He sat on the floor around the Christmas tree with Mum and Dad, steaming mugs of hot chocolate in hand. He tore into his presents, opening chocolates, games and clothes, until there were just three left.

He picked up a gold-wrapped gift the shape of a flat box. It was lighter than a tablet should have been. He tore open the gold paper and pulled apart the plain, flat box. Inside was a pile of tatty brown pages bound together with string. They were covered in a handwritten inky scrawl.

Henry's heart sank. He prodded the other two presents. They were big and soft. None of them contained a new camera, a tablet or a games console. Santa Claus had abandoned him after all.

"Ooh," Mum cooed, watching over his shoulder. "That looks interesting."

"It isn't," Henry muttered.

"What's all the writing?"

"Some kind of story."

"Who wrote it? What's it all about?"

"I dunno."

Henry tossed the tatty pages aside in disgust. He grabbed one of the two soft presents and checked the gift tag. It read as Santa's always did - inscribed in gold pen:

"To Henry, from Santa Claus."

He pulled the paper apart. His heart sank even lower. Pyjamas.

"Ooh." Mum pulled the pyjamas to her, then held the jacket up against Henry. "They are lovely and warm. Blue and white stripes. They will really suit you."

Henry didn't want to know what the last one was, but he opened it anyway. It was a purple blanket.

"Ooh. That's wonderful." Mum draped herself in it. "I'm very jealous. It's just what I need. And it's my favourite colour. You know how cold our bedroom gets."

Christmas dinner was delicious. Mum and Dad were happy just like last Christmas, but Henry knew they were trying extra hard because he was so disappointed.

Once they were settled down for the afternoon film on TV, Henry grabbed his presents and skulked off to his bedroom. He shoved the blanket in the back of his wardrobe. Mum kept dropping hints about how much she loved it, but it was Henry's and she wasn't having it. He slumped on his bed and grabbed the tatty pages. He had nothing else to do.

Klasodin, Warrior and Overlord of Vanahame, led family and followers in search of a new home. His instincts led him north, to the top of the world. At the very top, hidden in an unexplored realm and nestled among the snow-covered mountains, was a basin-shaped landscape. He descended to the very bottom where he discovered the one thing he needed: a sign of life. A fir tree, the height of a man, stood at the exact centre of the basin. Among its roots under the ground was a trove of purest gold, which could serve as the Epicentre for the Madjik of Klasodin's new race, the Aesir.

Henry discarded the pages in the drawer with his old camera. He got up and gazed out of the window. Revellers piled into the Fox and Foil pub. Harvey's Fish and Chips directly below Henry's window was already open. The queue stretched back along the high street. Fish and Chips was a Christmas Day tradition in Henry's part of London.

Henry jumped. He drew a sharp intake of breath.

The man with the ponytail stood on the opposite side of the road. He showed no interest in fish and chips. The longer Henry watched him, the more certain he was that the man was watching him and knew just where he was. He backed away from the window and drew his curtains.

Bedtime came and Henry climbed into his new pyjamas. They were very comfortable and warm, they just weren't a new camera or a laptop or a games console.

There was one more thing he had to do. He peered carefully through his curtains.

Ponytail was still there.

Henry scrabbled around in the drawer and pulled out the camera. He ducked down below the window, held the camera over his head, aimed it through the gap in the curtains at Camberwich High Street below and clicked away.

He set the camera down on his desk. Bright light burst from it and filled the room. Henry's photographs hung like holograms around him. The biggest picture was the last one he had taken.

Ponytail's eyes gazed right at him.

Henry's spine tingled. He lunged for the camera. The photographs vanished. Henry shoved the camera back in its drawer.

Once in bed, Henry relaxed. It was as if the pyjamas took away every worry. He fell asleep, only to dream of Ponytail chasing him down Camberwich High Street, hurling chips at him. The chips were burning. Smoke billowed from them. Henry ran, taking in gulps of fresh air. The towering smoke surrounded him, encircling him, closing in around him. The smell filled his nostrils.

He tried to wake up. He thought he had woken up. He could still see smoke everywhere, but he wasn't outside anymore. No. He was still dreaming. Why was he lying down? Where was he?

There was a bang. Henry jumped. There was another bang. A gunshot. It came from somewhere inside the flat. Someone was shooting at him. He couldn't see anything. He must still be dreaming, but he was sure he was awake. He lay back, waiting to wake up.

Why couldn't he see? It looked like smoke, but he wasn't coughing. He was breathing fresh air. He wasn't hot. There was no burning.

There was a bang. A crash. Something splintered and broke. He heard shouting. Muffled voices. Men. They were under attack. Why couldn't he wake up?

There was another bang - much nearer this time. Another bang. A crash. A tunnel of light shone through the smoke straight into his face. A second light beamed at him. They were like torches, worn on strange, plastic, mutant heads. He couldn't see their faces. They weren't gunmen. They were invading aliens.

Two firemen emerged through the smoke and stood over him in masks with oxygen tanks on their backs.

"What's happening?" Henry blundered.

One fireman grabbed Henry and threw him over his shoulder. Henry left his room backwards.

He was flying backwards through his flat, but it wasn't the flat he knew. It was filled with smoke. Flames licked the walls.

He was outside, lying on his back on a stretcher and covered in a blanket, staring up at the night sky. Flames rose and were quelled by jets of water shooting up to meet them. Smoke billowed everywhere. Blue lights flashed. Sirens blared. People watched from behind a barrier. Why couldn't he wake up?

Second by second it dawned on him. His heart pounded. He wasn't asleep. His home was on fire.

Firemen carried out large, lifeless black shapes over their shoulders.

An ambulance materialised around him.

"MUM. DAD."

The doors slammed shut. He was trapped. It took off. A siren wailed.

A hand pushed him down gently onto his stretcher. Another hand held his. They belonged to a young woman in a green ambulance crew uniform. She smiled at him, but that was never going to help.

"My name is Ann-Marie."

As if that made any difference.

"Where are they?" Henry demanded. "What happened?"

"Let's get you to the hospital and make sure you're okay."

"Where are they?"

"We'll look after you first, then we'll find out about your parents."

"I'M FINE."

He was fine. He wasn't burned or coughing, he just wanted to know what was happening.

"We need to check you over," Ann-Marie said gently. "You've been in a fire."

He wanted to shout at her. She would act differently if it was her parents. An oxygen mask was placed over his face. A wave of exhaustion swept over him.

Everything blurred into one. Flashing lights, sirens, smiling faces. He was on his back, flying feet first down one white corridor after another. Strange faces hovered over him. Voices echoed in the distance. There were scissors and needles.

He was in a hospital gown, lying in bed.

"My name is Doctor Patel. I can't believe it, there is nothing wrong with you at all."

"I told you. You wouldn't listen."

"I don't know what your pyjamas are made of. The nurses couldn't cut them off you no matter what they tried."

Doctor Patel was trying to be funny. He was trying to smile, but his eyes weren't smiling. Henry had taken hundreds of photographs of people. He had studied them all - their faces, their expressions. Every minor detail was significant.

Henry knew something was very wrong. He glanced around him. He and the doctor were alone. He didn't want to say it. He didn't want the answer, but he had to force it out.

"Where are my Mum and Dad?"

Doctor Patel took a breath. The fake smile vanished. He cleared his throat. Henry knew the truth before he even said it. He had known it all along.

"I am very sorry, Henry, but your parents are dead."

CHAPTER FOUR

Time blurred. It didn't matter. Nothing mattered. Henry wasn't certain he was even alive, just floating somewhere, hidden deep within his own shell, unable to feel his body or anything happening outside of it. He was vaguely aware of events taking place out there. He was in hospital and then he wasn't. Voices echoed vaguely in the distance. Faces melted into the background.

The name Mrs Mcready floated in and out of his head. That must have been the name of the foster mother. His foster mother. It didn't matter.

He was in church, then he was at the cemetery, watching two coffins being lowered into the ground. The gravestone was indelibly etched on his mind:

"Julia and Daniel Frey. Gone before their time."

Now it was there every time Henry closed his eyes. He saw them whenever he slept, but then, he didn't sleep much anymore. He could see their faces - forced smiles, loving eyes masking their hurt and disappointment. That was their last day together. The items hidden under layers of paper didn't matter anymore. He wished he could go back and make the faces happier, but he couldn't. If anything, they just looked sadder.

After a while, he didn't know how long, a desire burned inside him. He wanted to see his home again.

The date was marked on the calendar in the attic room Henry stayed in.

The day itself arrived.

After weeks of nothing but blurs and echoes, life slowly came into focus. It was like rising from the dead. The world around him was tactile. He was actually there again. Henry and his body were one. No longer was he looking out from deep inside it.

At a single and distinct point in time and space - Tuesday February 15th at 2pm on Camberwich High Street, directly in front of the only home he had ever known, which underpinned everything before and everything after - Henry stood with the fire officer and a couple of policemen. They had told him their names, but he had forgotten them the instant the names left their lips, disappearing like wisps in the wind.

"What happened?" he asked.

"Well," said the fire chief. "It started in the fish and chip shop. We think someone must have left the deep fat fryer on. It exploded and the fire spread upstairs to your flat."

Two of his words rang like alarm bells in Henry's head.

"You think?" he blurted out.

"I'm sorry?" The fire chief blinked.

"You said you think," Henry pressed. "Does that mean you don't know?"

"It's the best explanation we have. The initial explosion blew out the doors and windows. Any forensic evidence was destroyed."

Henry edged forward. His eyes took in every square centimetre. He hadn't lost his photographer's eye for detail. Something was wrong. There it was, lying in sharp, glittering fragments among the ashes and rubble on the chip shop floor.

"Wouldn't an explosion blow the doors and windows out, not in?"

He'd seen a lot of CSI recently. It was the one thing he watched every night when he wasn't sleeping.

"What do you mean?" the fire chief said.

"The glass from the window is on the floor inside the chip shop, not outside." Henry pointed to the glass fragments. "Someone smashed it in."

Silence.

"I'm sure there's a good explanation for that," the fire chief spluttered.

"Like what?"

The fire chief took a moment to gather himself.

"What are you trying to say?"

"Someone broke in. That means it wasn't an accident. It was done on purpose."

"And why would they do that?"

"I don't know," Henry said angrily. "That's your job, not mine. But there was a guy with a ponytail. He was standing over there on Christmas Day. He wasn't doing anything. He was watching us, waiting to start the fire."

"There's no evidence of arson."

"He looked really suspicious."

"Did he have scars on his face and some missing teeth," one of the policemen chuckled. "Maybe an eye patch over one eye?"

"Will I laugh like this when your parents die in a fire?" Henry snapped.

That shut him up, but Henry knew they would never listen. He was a boy. They would never take him seriously when it was easier not to.

"Did you find anything in the flat that wasn't destroyed? If you bothered to look."

"Yes, we did actually." The fire chief opened the boot of his car and pulled out a cardboard box. "I can't believe this stuff survived."

Inside the box were Henry's camera, the purple blanket, the tatty, handwritten pages and every photograph from Henry's wall.

He remembered the pyjamas he had been wearing the night of the fire. They had saved his life. They were the reason there wasn't a trace of smoke in his lungs. Touching his fingers to the purple blanket, the one his mum had loved the second she'd laid eyes on it, an idea arose in the back of Henry's mind, a horrible idea, which made him want to be sick. He stuffed the blanket back in the box and let the fire chief drive him back to the foster home without saying another word.

He climbed the creaking stairs to the attic room in Mrs Mcready's Victorian home in Blackheath. There were other children living on the first floor, but Henry had the attic room all to himself. He wasn't interested in any of them.

For the first time, Henry looked around and realised how much he liked Mrs Mcready's attic room. Everything in there was really old. The floorboards creaked. Part of the wood-lined ceiling slanted and looked like it might collapse under the next snowfall. The pine bed and wardrobe were both bigger than his old ones.

The window next to the head of the bed overlooked Cadogan Road. It was quiet - too quiet. The opposite window, a wood-framed sash window, had a door either side of it, one leading to a cupboard and the other to a small shower room with a sink and toilet crammed in for good measure, which meant he didn't need to leave his attic for anything but food.

He heaved open the sash window. There was a small balcony outside. He clambered out and looked out onto Main Street. It was busier than Cadogan Road, but nothing like as good as Camberwich.

The roof covering the rest of the terrace of Victorian houses was flat – and in easy reach. Henry climbed up and away from his attic room, shoving his hands and feet into cracks and fissures in the brickwork, then jumped up and looked all around him. The view over the rooftops to Greenwich and central London was the best he had ever seen.

He lay down and gazed up at the sky. It was like being on top of the world. Right then, the rooftop became his favourite place. And it was all his.

Back in the attic room, he picked up the stack of photographs. They were in perfect condition. He wanted them on his walls in the exact same order as before, but the firemen hadn't been that careful. He passed hours sorting them into the right order and sticking them on the walls. The camera stayed in a drawer.

Winter became spring, then summer. Mrs Mcready taught Henry from home so he rarely left the house, choosing instead to spend every moment possible on his rooftop. He ate up there and even fell asleep up there. He liked to lie on his back and look up at the sky on clear nights. He wore his pyjamas under his clothes. They always kept him warm. When he did sleep, it was never for very long, so he watched CSI or NCIS on the small TV Mrs Mcready had set up on his chest of drawers. He wished he'd photographed his own crime scene.

His thoughts turned to Santa Claus. Was he out there, looking up at the same sky? What happened? Did he put Henry on a naughty list? Maybe he'd lost interest. Maybe everyone else was right and he wasn't real at all.

By the autumn, Henry decided Santa Claus didn't matter anyway and did his best to forget all about him. Christmas had always been a bright light at the end of a dark tunnel, but not anymore. Now there was no light anywhere. Nobody loved him anymore. He really was alone.

CHAPTER FIVE

It was the second Saturday in December. Henry slouched on his bed, eyes fixed on his TV, determined to stay in his room. Two pairs of tiny hands knocked on the door.

"What?"

The door creaked open. Tabitha peered in.

"Are you coming?"

She received a nudge in the back. Emily burst in behind her. Archie ducked under their arms and started bouncing on Henry's bed.

"It's Christmas," he laughed. "It's Christmas."

"No it isn't. Get off my bed."

"We're decorating the tree and writing letters to Santa," Emily announced.

"I was going to tell him that," Tabitha complained.

"I'm not coming."

After several minutes of pestering and pleading, the two girls gave up and skipped downstairs, dragging Archie with them.

Henry scowled, ignoring the sharp stab of guilt to his abdomen. The girls were both six. Archie was three. Mrs Mcready's was all they had known and it was hard not to like them, but Henry tried anyway. What was the point? He didn't belong there.

The wooden stairs groaned under a much heavier set of footsteps. Mrs Mcready darkened his doorway. She was a big woman with a warm personality and sad eyes. She wore a lot of dark blue and usually tied back her wild, dark hair.

"Come on. We're putting up the tree."

"I'm staying here," he insisted.

"Henry. I wasn't asking."

Her tone was quiet but firm, as it always was when she insisted on getting her way. She was like a steel bar wrapped in layer upon layer of cotton wool.

Henry lumbered down the creaking stairs to the first floor. He peered into the fluffy pink bedroom shared by Tabitha and Emily. There was a bunk bed against one wall, while a tea party attended by dolls and teddy bears dominated the centre of the room.

Oliver was eight. His half of his bedroom was dark blue, decorated with posters of the fantasy warriors from his favourite computer games. Archie's half was covered with Thomas the Tank Engine and Friends. The last door overlooking the stairs was shut, with a sign saying "Rosie's Room - Keep Out".

There were two large rooms on the ground floor - the communal sitting room and Mrs Mcready's bedroom, which was off limits to all children, but secretly open to nightmare-prone little girls.

Mrs Mcready's spectacular eight-foot Christmas tree already glittered with multi-coloured lights. Oliver, Archie, Tabitha and Emily dived into a giant cardboard box filled with tinsel, baubles and other decorations. Rosie stretched out on the sofa, listening to her MP3 player.

Henry felt a pang of disappointment. No. He was glad they'd already started. He hated Christmas. He was too old anyway.

"We've got the tree in the kitchen to do as well," Mrs Mcready said without looking up. "We thought we'd save you some work on this one."

Tabitha emerged from the box with an armful of tinsel, her eyes sparkling.

"Are you going to help us?"

"No."

Henry's insides screamed.

"Rosie," said Mrs Mcready.

No answer.

Oliver heaved Archie up onto his shoulders to reach higher branches and nearly toppled into the tree. Henry grabbed them both just in time and held on to steady them.

"Rosie."

Rosie took out her earphone with a scowl on her face.

"You're taking up Henry's place on the settee."

"He's taking up my bedroom."

Rosie didn't move. The part of Henry screaming to stay and help breathed a sigh of relief. So he stayed where he was, holding onto Archie with one hand while the other was fed new decorations.

He would never admit it, but it was the most fun he'd had in ages. As everyone filed out, he took one last admiring look at their handiwork, before a pair of tiny hands dragged him away.

The last flight of stairs led down to the open basement area, with the kitchen to his right and another living area to the left complete with TV and its own Christmas tree. Henry let Archie haul him towards the tree. Rosie had draped herself on the settee, but she left her earphones out.

Soon Archie was standing on his shoulders while Mrs Mcready held him in place. Rosie fed them decorations and the others buzzed around them, covering the tree with everything they could find. Once they had run out of decorations, they used teddy bears, a tea cup, toy trains, a Transformer, a toy gun and a plastic sword.

"I don't think Santa Claus likes weapons," Mrs Mcready said doubtfully.

"What if someone tries to steal the presents?" Oliver suggested.

"There might not be any," Henry grumbled.

"What?"

"No presents?"

"But I've been good."

"I was very good."

"I knew it," Rosie muttered, looking as aghast as the others.

Mrs Mcready ushered five alarmed children to the dining table and pushed papers, pens and envelopes in front of them, shooting an irritable glance at Henry.

"Well, you'd better make sure your letters get to Santa in good time, hadn't you," she suggested, sliding a paper and pen towards Henry.

"I'm too old," he said, pushing his away.

"I think we both know you're not."

Henry scowled and folded his arms, watching the others scribble furiously.

"Are you sure?" Mrs Mcready said, once they'd finished.

Henry nodded, secretly annoyed with himself for scaring the others, but they may as well get used to the idea. He listened to the four younger children chatter excitedly about all the toys and games on their lists and hoped they wouldn't be as disappointed as he was last year. Even Rosie seemed quite excited once they had persuaded her to reveal what was on her list. She wanted a new Omnitec Quickfire just like Oliver.

It was late when Henry eventually made it upstairs. Something exploded inside him, shouting about how much he'd enjoyed himself. No. His family was dead.

Still, he allowed himself to be more involved as Christmas neared. The following Saturday, he queued with the others to meet Santa in Hamleys toy store on Regent Street. He could hear the fake booming laugh through the crowds, but he refused to speak to the old man no matter how much they all tried to persuade him.

That night, he lay back on the roof for a while with his pyjamas on under his clothes, scanning the night sky for letters flying magically towards the North Pole, but like every other night for the past week, nothing happened. He heaved himself up and went to bed. He felt more tired than normal and before too long, he drifted off.

A floorboard creaked. There was a squeak and a groan, like a door opening. The floor creaked again. Henry awoke with a jump. He blinked in the light of his bedside lamp. An ice cold breeze blew into his face.

A dark silhouette of a giant, bulky figure loomed in front of the far window. He advanced on Henry with head bowed forward so it didn't bang on the ceiling.

Big brown leather boots stepped into the light. Red trousers. A thick, fur-lined red coat. A thick white beard spilled out from under the hood. Calloused hands pulled the hood away. The face was old and familiar, but the worry lines on the ancient features and the deep sadness in the eyes told Henry something was very wrong.

"Santa Claus?" he whispered.

"No letter this year, Henry?" the visitor said quietly. "I think you and I need to talk."

CHAPTER SIX

"You're really Santa Claus?" Henry said in a low voice, staring wide-eyed.

"That's right."

Henry felt his end of the bed elevate as his visitor sank down on the other end.

"What happened to your letter?" the visitor asked calmly, as he leaned forward and clasped his fingers.

Henry's jaw dropped.

"You know about that?"

"Of course," Santa Claus replied, like it was the most normal thing in the world. "The letters arrived in Alvahame the minute you went to bed."

Henry frowned. Why did that sound familiar?

"Parents don't ask questions," Santa Claus continued. "Our Madjik has a way of remaining unseen by those who don't believe. Your mother never even thought to ask where your letters went." He paused and looked at Henry. "So you thought I'd forgotten you? Maybe decided I didn't exist anymore?"

Henry didn't have an answer.

"I gave you three gifts last Christmas. I chose them myself." Santa Claus shot him a sideways glance, a faint smile on his face. "But they weren't the gifts you were hoping for, were they?"

"I just…" Henry spluttered.

"I know," Santa said calmly. "But I don't do this to give you everything you want. I think about what is best for every child."

A knife of guilt plunged through Henry's stomach.

"I do like to give the gifts they love as well." Santa Claus sighed. "But something did happen last year for the very first time. We brought in the Black List."

"Like the Naughty List?"

"Exactly. And after your shenanigans at school, you weren't supposed to receive anything. I added your gifts myself."

Henry groaned inside himself.

"You never used the Black List before?" he asked.

"Never," Santa replied - with force.

"But all the stories. . ."

Santa snorted.

"A way to blackmail children into behaving themselves. Nothing to do with me. But the previous Christmas, when you received your camera, we failed to provide every gift we set out to give. That had never happened before. Some say our Madjik is failing. Some say we just can't cope with the increasing demands of modern-day children. I'm not so sure. I believe I am being sabotaged."

"Sabotage Santa Claus?" Henry was horrified. "Who would do that?"

"More people than you might think," Santa replied. "When Omnitec bought up every large technology firm, I became their last major competitor. There are those within Alvahame who believe we should change our ways and do business like them, rather than sticking to how we've always done it."

"But you're Santa Claus."

"To some I'm the enemy. Things are so bad now that the Council of the Aesir has already decided to implement the Black List again this year."

"Who are the Aesir?"

"Elves. Those stories of yours are based on some truth."

"There really are elves?"

"Of course."

"They tell you what to do?"

"They can outvote me on some issues."

"And they really are elves?"

"Every last one of them."

"But they're your helpers." A swell of anger surged inside Henry. "They should do what you tell them."

"My boy," Santa replied firmly. "I am their leader, not a dictator."

"But they're your elves."

"They are my kin."

Santa pulled back his hood. A pointed ear protruded from long, grey-white hair. Another good look told Henry that the thick coat accounted for a lot of his bulky size. Santa's face was less jolly and fat, more angular, with high cheekbones and green eyes.

Henry stared in amazement.

"You're an elf too?" he whispered.

"Of course," Santa said. "What - you thought some kindly human happened to stumble upon a race of elves and decided to give out presents?"

"I don't know," Henry shrugged. "I've seen a film where that happens. He's always human on TV. And the elves are always these tiny little things with squeaky voices."

"Pah!" Santa dismissed it with a wave of his hand. "All rumours started by Omnitec to make me look ridiculous. The naughty list was their idea too. Some executive doesn't have enough time to bring up his children properly so he decides to resort to threats and bribery instead."

"What about you wearing red?" Henry asked.

"It started with the adverts. After so long, the Aesir Council decided I should wear red to go along with popular opinion. Ridiculous. No elf wears red. I only ever wear it when venturing into human territory. Not that I used to." He looked down at his coat. "I was once the greatest warrior of my race. To me, the colour red means something quite different. But what do I know?"

Henry frowned. That sounded familiar as well.

"This is the trouble, you see?" Santa sighed. "Some think I'm old-fashioned. What they really mean is I'm not business-minded and I don't do it for the money. Such a concept is virtually unheard of nowadays." He gave Henry a knowing glance. "You haven't read my memoirs."

"Memoirs? You mean like the story of your life? A biography?"

"The handwritten pages currently lying discarded in your bottom drawer. The ones you dismissed as rubbish when you first opened them."

Suddenly Henry wished the floor would swallow him up. He stared at his quilt. He couldn't look Santa in the eye.

"You were watching?" he said in a small voice.

"Of course," Santa replied. "Who doesn't enjoy watching children open presents? Who doesn't take delight in seeing the joy their gifts bring? Usually at least."

"I read a paragraph."

"A whole paragraph?"

Henry's face burned with embarrassment.

"I'm sorry." He looked up. "I will read it."

"Good." Santa's expression was serious, but there was no blame or judgement in it. "Yours are the first human eyes ever to see it."

"Me?" Henry felt his jaw drop. "Why?"

"I have high hopes for you, Henry Frey."

"Really?"

"Not every child could have operated the camera. And I have never seen it react the way it did to you. To me, that is a sign of what you might become."

"Like what?"

"Well, Henry, I always have human helpers. I need them. Some humans possess the Affinity for our Madjik and they make it stronger. These humans are special. There are five in every generation. We call them the Valdiri."

"So I'm a ...?"

"Valdir," Santa said for him. "Yes. And right now, I think Alvahame needs a new Valdir more than ever."

Henry desperately wanted to be Santa Claus' helper. But it wouldn't be that simple.

"So you might choose someone else?" he asked, as a sudden vision of Charlie in the Chocolate Factory flashed before his mind's eye.

"No." Santa took a deep breath. "The night your flat burned down, the other four Valdiri were killed."

CHAPTER SEVEN

"The others all died?" Henry gasped. "How? What happened to them?"

"Their homes burned down."

"Like the fire in my home?" Henry looked at Santa, open-mouthed. "So that was on purpose? Someone was trying to kill me?"

Santa nodded.

"Did anyone survive?"

"Of all five fires, you are the sole survivor," Santa replied.

"Why did I live and not them?"

Santa gave a faint smile.

It dawned on Henry.

"The pyjamas. But you only gave me them because I was on the Black List."

"You were the only Valdir on the Black List," Santa said. "The others received bikes, computer games and the other things they asked for. Never did I think someone would try to kill you. I just gave you the best pair of pyjamas we had, which, of course, were made with Madjik. Because you were wearing them, the Madjik protected you."

Henry opened his mouth to say something, then gave up. He could hardly take it in. On the night his parents died, four other children and their families were killed. He thought back to his conversation with the fire chief and the policemen - and how they didn't believe a word he said.

"I told them it wasn't an accident," he blurted out, thumping his bunched up quilt with his fist. "I told them. It was that man with the ponytail. I know it."

Santa Claus looked at him sharply.

"You saw someone?"

"He was standing on the street all day. He had a ponytail. And his ears..."

Henry jumped out of bed, rummaged around in the drawer and pulled out the camera. He set it on his table. Bright light flared into the room. Henry braced himself. The photograph appeared. Ponytail stared right at him.

Henry made it smaller.

"I hate it," he said. "But I couldn't get rid of it."

Santa took one look at the picture. His expression darkened. His face contorted into a snarl of anger. He turned away from it.

Henry grabbed the camera. The picture and the light vanished. He shoved the camera back in the drawer and dived back into bed with a shudder.

"His name is Bayne," Santa said. "He is a YotunMens - half elf, half human. He has scars on his ears because he cuts the tops off to look more human."

"And he killed my parents?"

"Trying to kill you."

"Why? Who is he?"

"He leads the Gaardreng, Omnitec's band of mercenaries and killers. They hide in the shadows, doing Omnitec's dirty work. They will not stop until they destroy me."

Henry felt his face pale. Omnitec was everywhere. Everyone had their stuff.

"Am I safe?" he asked quietly.

"For now."

Suddenly Henry remembered what he had read from Santa's memoirs.

"So your real name was Klasodin?" he said.

"It still is," Santa replied. "You can call me that from now on. But not to anyone else. And nobody can know I was here. You understand?"

Henry nodded.

Klasodin stood up and reached into his coat pocket.

"I have an early Christmas present for you." He produced a small parcel wrapped in gold paper and handed it to Henry.

"Thank you," was all Henry could manage. "Do I...?"

"Yes," Klasodin replied, his face suddenly lighting up, as if he was as excited as Henry. "Open it now."

Henry ripped apart the paper to reveal a navy blue box made from a heavy plastic, like the kind nice watches come in, only bigger. Inside was a large gold band - three inches wide - big enough to fit around Henry's leg.

"Put it on," Klasodin urged. "It goes around your wrist like a watch."

Henry put his hand through it. The band shrank to fit his wrist perfectly. Henry jumped. The band caught fire. Bright, gold flames burst from it. Henry opened his mouth to shout in pain, but there was no heat, no burning and no smoke. The thought of smoke made his spine tingle. He could see his old home as he floated backwards through it.

"I'm sorry," said Klasodin. "I should have warned you about the flames. I didn't think of the kind of memories they would bring."

"That's okay." Henry took a second to catch his breath. He listened to his pulse rate slow until it was no longer hammering a rhythm inside his head. The flames died down and vanished. A silver watch face with gold hands and numbers appeared on the gold band. "It's a watch?"

"It's called a Hafskod," Klasodin explained. "And it's a lot more than just a watch."

Two tiny gold flames danced around the rim of the watch face.

"I won't catch fire, will I?" Henry said in alarm.

"No. It is made from elven gold and is far more Madjikal than your camera." Klasodin's expression was serious. "The Hafskod will come off if you want it to, but you must never remove it. Whoever asks you, whatever their reason, never ever take it off unless I tell you to."

"I won't," Henry promised. "What happens now?"

"I need to go before someone realises where I am. When the time is right, I will send someone for you." Klasodin moved to the window, then turned back. "And Henry. Try to get some sleep. It isn't good for a boy to sleep as little as you do."

"I like to look at the stars."

"Me too," Klasodin smiled.

Henry felt a wide smile break out across his face. A laugh erupted in the pit of his stomach. Klasodin's features creased into a broad grin. He climbed nimbly through the window, slid it shut behind him and disappeared.

Henry ran to the window just in time to see a flash of white light shoot across the London skyline and out of sight. He looked down at the Hafskod on his wrist. One of the tiny dancing flames had vanished.

CHAPTER EIGHT

For the first time in nearly a year, Henry slept through the night. He woke up late the next morning and jumped out of bed. He could hear everyone laughing and playing downstairs. With less than a week until Christmas, the holiday had officially begun. He could feel the excitement. He couldn't help but feel excited as well.

Even with Klasodin's memoirs to read, he bounded downstairs and spent most of the day playing computer games and board games with the others. Someone decided there weren't enough decorations in the house, so Henry helped make paper chains and foil-covered cardboard stars to hang around the room like Mum used to do with him.

It was Archie's bedtime when Henry finally put on his pyjamas under his clothes and settled down on the rooftop to read, the purple blanket wrapped around him to protect him from the icy chill in the night air. The streetlamps provided just enough light.

"Klasodin, the elven overlord, had made his name during the Great Wars against the savage Nerivari from the deepest Underlands. Now he looked forward to a time of peace and prosperity as King of Alvahame. His Aesir gave Klasodin a title of his own, "Sin Ni Klas", taken from his own name, to mean "he who lacks nothing".

But the Aesir were not alone. A powerful enemy arose from its hidden dwelling, intent on keeping the northerly realm for itself. The Morivari, the dark elves of the underworld city of Svaravame, poured from their home and a brutal, bloody war was waged. When the snow-covered hills and plateaus were soaked in blood, a truce was agreed, but over the many years that followed, the Morivari broke the truce at will, always looking for the next opportunity to destroy the Aesir.

Klasodin had brought a large diamond from the city of the Vanir. He fused it with the gold among the roots of the fir tree at the basin of his new city, turning it into the Epicentre for Aesir Madjik. He fused a small ingot of the diamond-infused gold to his staff to connect himself to the Madjik wherever he was. The gold and the fir tree grew as Alvahame expanded up the mountains. The Aesir centred their Madjik on the gold and their power grew. They formed a Madjikal shield around Alvahame to keep out their enemies and life in Alvahame became more stable.

But Klasodin's spirit grew restless. A life of war and farming was not enough. The Aesir needed a purpose. They lived on the top of the world, at the edge of existence. Humans would dominate the world and tighten their grip around it as the centuries rolled on. They would not take kindly to another race looking to share domination. How could the Aesir make their mark? There was only one choice. Klasodin had to go out into the world and search for the Purpose.

The Aesir argued against it. Klasodin's oldest friend, Gronodin, wrangled with him for weeks, but his mind was set. Gronodin relented, dubbing him "Sin Te Klas" - to mean "he who walks alone". Klasodin bade farewell to his wife, Merrodine. He mounted Slepnir, his snow-white, eight-legged horse, and departed on his journey.

Klasodin wandered the Earth for decades, moving from place to place, exploring deserts, mountains and valleys, avoiding towns and cities. He spent every night under the stars, considering how many humans and how many elves were gazing up at the same stars at that exact moment.

As winter approached, Klasodin disguised himself. He drew his hair over his pointed ears, grew a long beard to hide his facial features and pulled his elven cloak around him. Now nobody would think of him as anything but a traveller. Being the greatest and most Madjikal of horses, Slepnir followed suit. His eight legs morphed into four and his white coat turned to a light brown, hiding him in plain sight like his master.

Klasodin joined some travellers journeying across the Asian wilderness and into Europe, introducing himself as Klas. He spent several months with them, then went his own way. Humans were the key, he decided, so he headed wherever they were to be found and stayed in towns, villages and cities. He joined farmers, fishermen and small rural communities. When he found no friends, he moved on to the next place, determined never to go where he was not wanted.

After many years, Klasodin knew the Earth and its people like the back of his hand and decided he yearned solitude once more. He headed south to Yotunhame on the opposite pole to the city of the Aesir. He spent days searching the desolate, snowy landscape until Slepnir soared over a mountain of ice and along a plain, under the shadow of a cliff. He came across a giant shard of ice, jutting out of the ground like a blade and carving into the cliff. Slepnir slowed, rounded the ice blade and ran into a small opening hidden behind it, under the foot of the cliff. The passage led deep into a large ice cave, which Klasodin made his home."

Henry's eyes were growing heavy. His head was fogged with tiredness. He closed Klasodin's memoirs. He climbed to his feet and wandered over the roof with the blanket wrapped around him. Holding it like that reminded him of Mum - in a good way - as long as he didn't dig into the memory too deeply.

His gaze fell on the large advertising placard nailed to the side of the building opposite and the excited little boy in the picture who was admiring his brand new Omnitec Streak mountain bike. His arms were wrapped around the Omnitec Quickfire, an Omnitec Neon tablet, toys and games. On top was a letter, which started:

"Dear Mum…"

There was a long list of items, each with a tick beside them. It finished:

"Just ask Omnitec."

Underneath, it read:

"Simply log on to our website and create your Christmas list. All Mum and Dad have to do is enter their credit card details and we'll deliver your presents."

While Mum smiled, her foot kicked the door shut on two tiny creatures with pointy ears and pointy hats carrying in a painted wooden tricycle.

The logline read:

"Who needs Santa when there's Omnitec?"

Henry's eyes shifted down to the street, where a lone figure leaned against the wall near a streetlamp.

His blood froze.

It was Bayne.

CHAPTER NINE

Henry dropped down to his stomach. He peered over the edge. Bayne leaned against the opposite wall. Four big men in thick, dark clothing converged on him and listened as he gave orders. Something moved above them. A shadowy figure crept over the rooftops ahead and in Henry's direction.

Henry shuffled backwards on his stomach, pushing himself over the rooftop on his elbows and toes, keeping his head low. The figure on the opposite rooftop stopped on the edge and waited. He pulled a flat, curved board from a bag on his back. Then he produced what looked like a gun.

The streetlights went out. Everything went black. Henry couldn't see a thing. He scrambled away on his knees. He fumbled his way over the ice cold roof with his hands. His heart hammered. He hated the dark. He always slept with his bedside light on. He couldn't climb down to the balcony without being able to see. He was trapped on the roof. He looked into the Hafskod. The face was clouding over, turning black.

"Help me," he breathed, not knowing why.

A tiny green flame burst through the black cloud covering the face of the Hafskod. It rose in front of Henry's eyes. It split into two. The green flames flew at Henry's eyes. There was a green flash. Henry blinked. Dark silhouettes materialised in front of him. It was like he had night vision. He could see enough to climb down. He scrambled over cold stone to the far edge.

He shot a glance over his shoulder. A figure rose in the night sky and hovered in the air over the opposite roof, his boots planted on what looked like a chrome snowboard. He wore goggles over a black mask and thick black clothes. He aimed his gaze in Henry's direction. He whipped a gun from his belt. He folded the barrel up and clicked it into place. A steel blade burst from the barrel to make a sword with a long hilt. He aimed the blade at Henry and flew at him.

Henry jumped to his feet and ran. He leapt over the edge and landed with a bang on the balcony. His ribs collided painfully with the rail. He scrambled through the window into his bedroom and landed on the carpet. He slammed the window shut.

His eyes darted through the window over the night sky, searching for the figure on the flying snowboard. No sign of him. Something heavy moved on the roof above him. Henry froze. He strained his ears for every sound. He backed away from the window.

A breeze brushed his hair. He wheeled around. The opposite window was open. A tall figure emerged from the bedroom door and stood between Henry and the open window. The balcony window scraped open behind him. Henry backed away. A second figure climbed in. They both wore dark clothing and goggles over a black mask. They closed in on Henry, towering over him.

The first figure removed the mask and goggles with gloved hands.

The blood drained from Henry's face.

Bayne grinned down at him. He had long, sharp teeth that were stained yellow. The tops of his ears were scarred. He pulled a strange-looking gun from his belt.

"They're all asleep." His voice was a harsh whisper. "It had better stay that way. Make a sound and we'll kill everyone here. I can't burn your house down this time. Too obvious. So after I fire one of these darts into your chest and knock you out, maybe I'll have you slip and fall in the shower. Maybe I'll just throw you off the roof."

Henry watched Bayne raise the gun and aim it at his chest.

The Hafskod suddenly felt warm.

A blue light flared from the gun nozzle.

Henry braced himself. He threw his left arm in front of him. He shut his eyes.

Bayne fired.

There was a clang.

He was still awake.

Henry opened his eyes. A gold shield covered his arm. A tranquiliser dart lay on the floor. Bayne stared at Henry in wide-eyed silence.

"Take that off," he growled.

Henry took a step back.

A lethal sharp blade rested on his shoulder. Henry looked around at the Gaard behind him, who had taken off his mask. He had dark eyes and a thick beard.

A figure climbed soundlessly through the window behind the Gaard. A hand reached around him, grabbed him by the throat and yanked him back through the window. The bearded man disappeared with a yelp. The window slammed shut. There was a scuffle. A punch. A kick. Another punch.

Bayne's eyes blazed with fury. The gun in his hand morphed into a sword with a deadly steel blade. He pointed it at Henry's throat. Henry backed away.

"No time for deception then," the YotunMens snarled.

A bright gold flash shot over Henry's shoulder and knocked Bayne off his feet. He scrambled up. A second flash blew him out of the window.

"Close the window, Henry," a deep voice instructed.

Henry ran over and heaved the window shut. He peered through it and watched Bayne pick himself up off the ground three floors down.

A tall, muscular figure swung himself in through the open balcony window and landed in a crouched position on the wooden floor.

"Elves and YotunMens don't die as easily as you humans. Unfortunately, Bayne will live to fight another day."

Long, golden-brown hair framed prominent cheekbones and an iron jaw. Pointed ears protruded through the hair. He wore a thick, hooded green cloak over a brown leather breastplate. A gold shield covered his left forearm and he gripped a stringless bow in his left hand. His sword was belted to his waist. Even in a crouched position, his head nearly touched the ceiling. He looked straight at Henry, his expression grim.

"If you want to live, come with me."

CHAPTER TEN

Henry still had Klasodin's memoirs gripped in his fist and the blanket over his shoulders. He stopped and looked around his room. His photos. He needed his photos. The camera. He didn't want to use it, but it was still his. What else did he have?

"Come on, boy," the elf urged.

Henry followed him to the balcony window. The elf stopped and peered through it.

"Who are you?" Henry whispered.

"My name is Rodin. Klasodin sent me." He turned to Henry and looked him right in the eye. "You must do exactly as I say - the second I say it."

Henry nodded.

Rodin opened the window with a flick of his right hand and leapt through it. He vanished in the darkness.

Then his face reappeared. Gold light beamed from his eyes, making Henry jump.

"What is it?" Rodin hissed.

"Your eyes."

"Yours do the same."

Henry looked in the mirror. His eyes flashed a green light.

"Come on," Rodin urged. "You can ask questions later."

Henry ran for the window. Rodin hauled him through and pushed him back against the wall. A dark figure on a chrome board flew across the sky in front of them.

Everything went black. Henry couldn't see a thing.

"I can't see," he whispered. "What happened?"

"The flames don't last long. Just keep an eye out for anything that moves."

Henry's night vision was gone. He stared into the darkness. His eyes strained to fix on a vague dark shape flying past, an armed man on a flying chrome board. Suddenly, the Gaard veered and flew right at them. He aimed the weapon in his hand. A hail of hard objects shot through the night and bombarded Rodin's shield. One deflected upwards, struck the wall and dropped to the balcony at Henry's feet. It was a steel dart, about fifteen centimetres long, with a very sharp point. Before Henry could reach down and grab it, the dart fizzed and dissolved in a blue cloud.

Rodin leapt up onto the balcony railing and balanced on the top without holding on to anything. He drew back his sword and hurled it into the night. There was a gasp and a distant thud. The figure on the board froze and fell out of the sky. Rodin's sword reappeared in his hand.

Swords clashed on the roof. There was a kick and a punch. Something heavy dropped off the roof past Henry's eyes.

Still balanced on the railing, Rodin leaned back, grabbed both ends of Henry's blanket in one hand and hauled Henry up by it towards the roof. A second pair of hands lifted him by his armpits, set him down on the roof and gave him a push in the right direction.

"Run for it," a young woman's voice ordered him.

Henry ran for the shape on the roof in front of him. He could hear fleeting footsteps right behind him. Objects zipped through the air around him.

A Gaard on a chrome snowboard emerged over the rooftop. He fired. Blue light flared. Deadly steel darts flew at Henry's head. A blade flashed in front of him and deflected the darts away. The Gaard veered and swerved to avoid the flying darts.

He aimed his chrome snowboard at Henry and shot straight at him. The figure behind Henry pushed him out of the way. There was a clash of swords. A punch. A kick sent the Gaard flailing through the air.

More Gaardreng circled them on their flying snowboards.

"Watch where you're going."

A hand shoved him back on course.

The shape in front of him was a sleigh drawn by four reindeer. A stocky, red-haired elf, still taller than any man Henry had met, leapt out of the sleigh. A Gaard flew at him, firing a volley of darts. The elf deflected them with deft lightning flicks of his sword. The Gaard veered to avoid them shooting back at him. Their swords collided. The elf drove his fist into the Gaard's armoured torso and sent him tumbling off the roof.

The red-haired elf leapt back in the sleigh and grabbed the reins.

There was no door into the sleigh. The sides were higher than Henry's head. He jumped, grabbed the top and tried to heave himself over. A hand grabbed the back of his blanket and dropped him in. He landed with a bump on a cold floor. He climbed to his feet. The inside was one empty space with the red-haired elf standing at the front. No seats. It reminded Henry of a Roman chariot more than a sleigh. Now he was in, he could see over the side. He stood against the side wall and peered over.

Something shot over his head.

"Keep your head down," came the female voice again, as she jumped into the sleigh behind him.

Her voice was light and silvery, but tough with it. She wore brown leather boots, black leather trousers and a dark green cloak with a silver fur lining. Lustrous, long, jet-black hair flowed in waves down her back and around her pointed ears.

She had ivory skin and was stunningly beautiful. She smiled gently down at him.

"My name is Amira. Well met, young Henry."

"Hi."

Suddenly her dark eyes hardened. Her jaw set. A silver dagger appeared in her hand. A sharp flick of her wrist sent the dagger shooting through the night air. There was a thud and a grunt of pain. Another dagger shot from her hand. And another. A body fell. A chrome board clattered.

Clashing swords rang out from somewhere close by.

A volley of darts collided with Amira's shield and clanged against the side of the sleigh. One spun over Henry's head and dropped onto the sleigh floor. It fizzled and vanished in a puff of blue smoke.

No more darts. Henry peered over the side. Rodin hammered his blade against two Gaardreng swords. A stream of Amira's flying daggers took down a third. Rodin ran one Gaard through. He sliced into the other and kicked him to the floor.

More armoured figures appeared on flying snowboards.

A hail of darts shot at the sleigh. They hammered into the side of the sleigh and struck Amira's shield, then flew in all directions, fizzing out in mid-air in tiny blue clouds. Amira shoved Henry's head down.

"In case you haven't worked it out, they're here to kill you. Look up again and I'll shoot you myself."

She looked up.

"Rodin," she hissed.

Rodin landed in the sleigh. The sleigh shot off. Henry tumbled back. Rodin caught him before he could slam into the back.

"Hold on there, young human," the red-haired elf called.

"Try not to kill our human for them, Appodin," Amira called in a sarcastic tone.

"He's fine," the red-haired elf called back. "It's how I learned. Ain't nothing wrong with me."

Appodin pretended to twitch. Henry laughed. Amira rolled her eyes.

The sleigh slid over the tops of the buildings. Two dark shapes flew at them. Four pairs of antlers glittered with bright gold light. The reindeer charged them down and sent them tumbling over the rooftops.

The sleigh took off and shot into the night sky. Henry's stomach lurched. He swallowed. He eased himself into a sitting position.

"You will get used to it," Amira said gently.

Henry opened his mouth to tell them he had never even flown in an aeroplane before, then thought better of it and clamped his mouth shut again. He glanced at his Hafskod. The dark clouds had cleared. The watch face glowed.

"Fly along the Thames to make sure we're not followed," Rodin instructed. "Then we'll turn and head north over England."

"The house," Henry uttered. "They're all in there."

"They're fine," Amira replied. "The Gaardreng just want you."

"I think we've lost them," Appodin called from the front of the sleigh.

Henry eased himself up onto his feet and peered over the side. The Thames and the river bank flashed past him. The sleigh descended until it slid over the water. The reindeer ran on the surface of the river, sending spray blowing back over Henry and the three elves.

"Stop showing off," Amira shouted at Appodin, who just laughed.

Henry watched the sleigh's runners carve through the water.

"How do they do that?" he asked.

"You're in a flying sleigh and that's your first question?" Appodin called.

"Everyone knows Santa's reindeer can fly. No one ever said they could water ski."

Appodin laughed.

"This sleigh can slide over anything."

Henry looked at the two elves standing next to him. Their faces were serious. Their eyes scanned their surroundings, darting from one piece of night sky to the next.

"It doesn't feel right." Amira said in a hushed tone.

"We should have left them behind by now," Rodin answered.

Henry looked down at his Hafskod. The edges of the watch face were clouding over. The Gaardreng weren't finished with them yet.

CHAPTER ELEVEN

The sleigh skimmed over the water. They had left London behind. Henry could only see vague dark silhouettes of buildings beyond the banks of the Thames.

A shadow flickered at the periphery of his vision. A dark shape flew through the air and out of sight. Another appeared. And another. Flying alongside the sleigh.

Rodin muttered something under his breath.

"Hold on," said Amira.

Henry planted his feet on the floor and gripped the side of the sleigh. It banked left and picked up speed. Henry clung on. The night sky shot past overhead.

The Hafskod was still clouding over.

The flying Gaardreng closed in around them.

Rodin gripped his stringless bow. He closed his right hand around where the string should have been. A gold string materialised. He pulled the string back until it tightened. An arrow of bright gold flame appeared.

He released. It burned through the night sky. It exploded on a shadowy flying shape, which dropped from the sky.

A hail of darts flew at them. Amira deflected them with her shield. She shoved Henry to the floor. She pulled out her own elven bow and sent a stream of gold arrows flashing into the night.

Henry sat back against the side of the sleigh. His blood froze.

Bayne was looking right back at him, flying above him on his snowboard. He discarded his dart gun and pulled out what looked like a small chrome bow.

With a flick of his wrist, it shot out into a large stringless bow. He held it the wrong way round, the bend of the bow facing his body. His fist clenched around it and aimed straight at Henry. The air blurred between the two ends of the bow. An orb of bright blue light pulsated between the two ends. Bayne fired.

There was a blue flash. A low boom. The sleigh was thrown to one side. Henry tumbled over and landed in the corner on his back. Another blue flash exploded. The sleigh jolted upwards. Appodin shouted something. The sleigh picked up speed.

Rodin wheeled around and attacked Bayne with a blitz of gold arrows. They exploded on his armour and threw him backwards.

Reindeer antlers glittered. An armoured body was punched into the air. There was a low boom. Another boom. Two blue flashes exploded around the sleigh. Henry flew up and bounced on the sleigh floor. Amira fired a stream of gold arrows. There was a scream of pain, then silence.

Henry felt the sleigh speed up, throwing his stomach back towards his spine. He watched the night sky fly past overhead, then thought better of it and shut his eyes.

Once he was more used to it, he opened his eyes and aimed them at the floor. The silver watch face on the Hafskod face was clear. No clouds. There were no dancing golden flames either.

The faces of the three elves were grim.

"Those boards took some leaving behind," said Appodin.

"Where did the weapons come from?" Rodin muttered, his eyes darting from his sword into the darkness.

Henry looked up too, half expecting to see more flying Gaardreng.

Amira glanced in Henry's direction and frowned. She took hold of Henry's wrist and looked at the Hafskod. She showed it to Rodin and Appodin.

"Klasodin gave you this?" she demanded.

"Yes. Why?"

"Surprised, that's all. If he says you are to have it, you have it."

"I don't know what it does yet."

"There is no instruction manual."

"You produced night vision and a shield without one," Rodin replied. "I would say that's a good start."

"And an early warning system," said Amira. "You saw it cloud over."

Henry nodded.

"So it sees enemies?" he asked.

"It detects the wrong kind of Madjik," she said.

"There's a wrong kind?"

"It would explain a lot," Rodin frowned.

"So you don't have flying snowboards?"

"As far as we knew, such a thing only existed in theory," said Rodin. "And those weapons are far beyond human technology."

"Where do your arrows come from?"

"These are Aesir weapons. They are made with Fyur, the purest form of Aesir Madjik. The arrows replace themselves, just as my blade does. It is complex Madjik and impossible for humans to replicate."

"Is that what they've done?" Henry asked. "Copied your Madjik? Bayne's gun had the same blue light as his weird crossbow. What is it?"

"We call it Azmar," Rodin replied. "It's a theoretical name for something we have never seen before. But Klasodin was certain it would happen if there really was a traitor in Alvahame."

"Why?"

"It's a fusion of our Madjik with human technology. And it had to have come from an elf in Alvahame."

"No arguments there," Appodin agreed from the front of the sleigh.

"They knew we were coming," Amira said. "They would never have sent so many for just one boy."

"No." Rodin sank down onto the floor of the sleigh. "There's a traitor in Alvahame."

"You think one of us is working with Omnitec - and doing all this?"

Amira's dark eyes looked hurt. Henry had seen the same look in some of his photographs of his parents. Suddenly he wanted to hug Amira, but he thought better of it. She was a warrior, after all.

"That's what Klasodin thinks." Rodin shrugged. "And if the traitor is willing to break one Foundation, why not all three?" He sat there, scowling at the floor.

"I don't understand," Henry said.

"There are three Foundations of Alvahame," Amira explained. "The Equality of all Elves. The Purity of Madjik. The Purpose. They are the core rules by which our society abides. There is no greater crime than breaking one of them."

Henry repeated them, trying to remember.

"Madjik is pure," Amira continued. "To combine it with any other form of magic or technology is to treat it with the utmost contempt."

"How do you know it's mixed with something else?"

"The darts aren't ours. They're human in manufacture. But the Gaardreng wielding them never had to reload. Just as we don't."

"The blue light," Rodin said irritably. "Orek always said if you mixed the two, the result would be blue."

Rodin and Amira exchanged glances. Amira's jaw set. She looked away.

Henry swallowed. They were going to argue about something.

Not again.

"And The Purpose is Santa Claus and giving presents?" he said hurriedly.

"Of course." Amira sounded subdued. She forced a smile. "And the traitor has broken this Foundation already."

"Is it easy for an elf to combine Madjik with our technology?"

"No. It would take skill and hard work. It is hard to imagine an Aesr wanting to betray us that badly. The idea of anyone betraying us is unheard of."

Waves lashed against rocks and cliffs. Henry peered over the side. He could just make out the splashing and foaming water against glistening rock. The sleigh left Britain behind, heading north over the sea.

"Time to pick up speed again," Appodin called. "Hold on, young human."

Henry sat down, his head and body slowly adjusting to the speed of the sleigh. He suddenly realised how tired he was.

"We won't see land again until we reach the Arctic," Amira said quietly. "Why don't you get some rest?"

"Is that where you really live? The North Pole? That's where Alvahame is?"

Amira nodded.

Henry leaned back against the side of the sleigh.

"Don't sleighs have seats?"

"Not the ones built for war," Appodin replied. "Makes it a lot harder to duck an arrow when you're sitting on a chair."

CHAPTER TWELVE

A gentle nudge in the ribs. Henry jerked awake. Cold air blew over his head and bright morning light touched his face. His entire left side ached because he was lying on a hard floor. Keeping his purple blanket wrapped around him, he eased himself into a sitting position, resting his head and back against the sleigh wall. He squeezed his eyes shut against the light, then tried opening them again. He looked up at Amira reclining next to him.

"We'll reach the Arctic soon," she said without opening her eyes. "I thought you might like to see it."

"Thanks," he mumbled.

Henry looked beyond Amira to the two elves at the front of the sleigh, his eyes still trying to focus, his head fogged with sleep.

For a second, Henry thought he saw Rodin watching Amira, but the elf warrior grabbed a flask, opened it and passed it to Henry. Steam wafted out of it. A strong, spicy smell drove up Henry's nostrils.

"This should wake you up."

Henry took a sip. It was sweet and warm. Hot, revitalising life spread through his insides like lava. He took a gulp. And another. His head cleared. He felt better already.

"What is it?"

"It's called Fyoreig," Rodin said. "Made from the sap of the Great Tree."

Henry gulped down some more.

"The Great Tree?"

"You'll see."

The sleigh tipped forward slightly. It started its descent. Henry scrambled to his feet to lean over the side of the sleigh. The sky was a pale blue. The golden sun rose over the distant clouds.

Islands of ice floated on a gleaming glass sea. Icebergs jutted out of the water. The rippling reflection of the sleigh and its four reindeer shot between two towering ice obelisks and flew over groups of sharp-edged ice blocks.

Then there was no water, just an undulating landscape of the whitest snow stretching ahead forever.

"How do you build on snow and ice?" Henry asked.

"There is solid ground in the elven realm," Rodin said. "No human will discover it."

"So Omnitec don't know about it?"

"They know about it, but they won't find it if they spend forever searching."

"I thought grown-ups didn't believe in Santa Claus. Most kids my age don't."

"Omnitec know all about him. They're trying to put him out of business, telling everyone how stupid it is to believe in him when you can order all the presents your children want and pay for them yourself."

"What if you can't pay for them?"

"Then Omnitec don't care about you anyway."

They flew just feet over the beautiful but bleak white landscape, rising steadily over mountains of snow. Suddenly the sleigh shot straight over a mountain peak and into a screen of cloud, which appeared out of nowhere.

The sleigh descended through wet, grey cloud. There was a bump, followed by the slither and crackle of runners sliding through frozen snow. The cloud dispersed. They slid over a vast, white plain. A large white shape bounded over the snow towards them. It charged right at them. It was a polar bear.

Appodin gave a whistle and the reindeer slowed to a gentle trot.

"It's going to attack us," Henry blurted in panic. "They hunt humans."

Appodin laughed.

The sleigh slid to a halt. The polar bear ambled on all fours and stopped in front of the reindeer. They sniffed each other and bumped noses.

The polar bear approached the sleigh. Its hard eyes like tiny gleaming pieces of coal scanned the occupants of the sleigh. It turned towards Rodin and grunted. Rodin responded with a low, guttural growl. They continued back and forth.

"What are they doing?" Henry whispered.

"Talking," Amira replied.

"They're friends?"

"Allies."

"So polar bears are friendly?"

"No. They are violent, abrasive and untrusting. They live by bartering and making oaths, and the breaking of an oath is punishable by the most gruesome death. Most would kill you for a lot less. But they are honest and reliable - if you can get them on your side. Grrhdrig here is the king of his tribe. Klasodin allows him within the elven realm and supplies him with fish when he needs them. In return, Grrhdrig gives us information and fights on our side in times of war."

Rodin and Grrhdrig finished their conversation. Grrhdrig gave a nod of recognition to Amira and aimed his piercing gaze at Henry. He uttered a low growl.

A green flame rose from the Hafskod in front of Henry's eyes. He could see Grrhdrig watching it too. The flame divided and formed words in flame green:

"Well met, young human."

Henry looked at the polar bear. Something told him he would have to try addressing him directly.

"Well met, Grrhdrig."

He bowed his head slightly as he said it. He blinked. His mouth had formed the words he knew, but he had uttered the same low growls.

Grrhdrig's mouth flattened into an emotionless smile. He gave a nod, then turned and bounded away on all fours, disappearing into the distance.

"I think he likes you," said Appodin.

"Didn't look like it," Henry replied.

"Were you expecting a hug and a kiss?"

"Appodin's right," Rodin agreed. "Grrhdrig has accepted you as an ally."

"What do I give him if I need something?" Henry asked, thinking how keen he was not to get on Grrhdrig's bad side.

"Fish."

"That's it?"

"Always fish, and lots of them. You don't have to drop them at his feet immediately, but he will expect you to honour the deal." Rodin frowned as the sleigh set off. "Grrhdrig said the earth groans."

"The Morivari are digging again?" said Amira. "Why?"

"I don't know. But I don't like it."

The sleigh shot over the snowy plain. An expanse of high, rocky cliffs rose on the horizon. The sleigh sped up and headed straight for them. The closer it slid, the higher the cliffs towered into the sky. Henry swallowed. They were really close now. They were flying straight at them.

At the last second, just when Henry thought they would crash and die right there and then, a narrow, snow-covered path appeared. It was very steep and just wide enough for the sleigh. The sleigh tilted violently as reindeer drove straight up the path between two sheer cliffs, heading in the same direction, but at a forty-five degree angle.

Henry realised his Hafskod was glowing.

The sleigh shot up the path and out onto a gentle incline. Snow-covered fir trees emerged from the distant snow, defined by the screen of silver cloud behind them.

"We call this the Levels," Amira explained. "The mountain, the clouds, the cliff and the Margullring ahead. Part of the South Passage into Alvahame. The Northern Route is the only other way in or out of the city."

The trees were further away than Henry had realised. The snowy expanse they travelled across was as big as the plain before the cliffs. As they came really close, he could see the trees were much bigger than any fir trees he had seen before. The screen of cloud looked more like a wall of thick ice, stretching as far to the left and right and as high into the sky as he could see. His Hafskod shone.

"This is the Margullring," said Amira.

The sleigh shot through the ice shield - the Margullring.

"Without your Hafskod, you couldn't get in," Rodin added. "You must possess Aesir Madjik to enter."

The reindeer pulled the sleigh along a snowy path through a dense mass of silvery fir trees. Wooden chalet houses with pointed roofs nestled among them.

"This is Hamedall," said Amira. "The village at Alvahame's southern rim. The Aesir Guard and their families live here."

They headed up the path through Hamedall, a bright light through the trees ahead showing the way.

An elf dressed like Rodin, his gold shield on his left arm, his stringless bow in one hand and his sword in the other, stepped in front of them. He saw who it was, gave a slight bow and stepped aside.

"Lord Rodin."

"Pellodin."

"An uneventful journey, I hope."

"The Gaardreng knew we were coming. We rescued the boy just in time. Be on your guard. They have weapons we have never seen before."

The sleigh slid off towards the gap in the trees ahead of them.

"Why did he call you Lord Rodin?" Henry asked.

"It is my official title. I do not care for it."

"Rodin is the Overlord of the Craft of War," said Amira.

"War is a Craft?"

"Everything we do here belongs to one of the Five Crafts. War is one of them."

"So every Guard answers to Rodin?"

"Every Guard, every warrior."

The trees gave way and the path opened out ahead.

Mountains jutted out of the snow and rose to meet the clouds to Henry's right. To his left, fields and plains met thick forest. Something moved out of the forest, then disappeared again through the trees.

"Caribou," Appodin called. "They roam all around here."

"Caribou are reindeer aren't they?" said Henry. "Do you go out and catch them?"

"Catch Caribou? No. They wouldn't have it. When they no longer want the wild life, they come down to us of their own volition and become reindeer."

"So they retire?"

"Hardly. They leave the wild behind, but there's nothing quiet about the life of an Alvahame reindeer. You saw what these four just had to fight their way through. Not that they didn't enjoy it."

An amused grunt came from one of the reindeer at the front.

The sleigh reached the peak and slid downward at speed into a giant basin surrounded by snow-covered mountains. It descended towards a terrace of large wooden chalet houses with pointed roofs, curving inwards, facing further down the mountain, circling the edge of the basin. Henry's eyes followed the line of houses around the entire basin until he could just make out the rooftops at the far end of the city, climbing up towards the mountain tops opposite.

Alvahame.

CHAPTER THIRTEEN

A wide, snow-covered avenue opened ahead of them, the one visible opening in a ring around the edge of the city. The sleigh surged down it, flying between sloping terraces of four-storey wooden chalet houses, which were lined with streetlamps and fir trees covered in bright lights.

"Our reindeer live on the lower floor," said Amira. "We keep our sleighs, snowboards, sledges and skis down there as well. Separately, of course."

"Why?"

"Have you any idea how angry reindeer can become when you treat them like nothing more than modes of transport?" Appodin called.

The avenue curved along Alvahame's outer circumference. The sleigh veered left, then took a series of turns through a maze of curved, snow-covered avenues.

"Alvahame is a perfect circle," said Amira. "There are no straight avenues and none lead directly from the circumference to the centre."

Eventually the sleigh turned left onto the widest avenue with the biggest, tallest houses. It curved gently left and right, then opened and straightened out, leading down into the very centre of Alvahame.

Ahead of them, rising up from the centre of Alvahame was a giant fir tree, taller than the Eiffel Tower, its trunk the depth of a tower or a skyscraper, but twisting and spiralling into the clouds.

"The Great Tree," Rodin announced. "Iddrassil. Over half a mile high."

Iddrassil glittered with thousands of tiny lights. A strand of gold tinsel wound its way from the bottom to the five-pointed star at the top. Gold baubles as big as houses were dotted over the tree. Wooden houses hid among its thick branches.

A lower branch the size of a street met the snow-covered avenue like a tributary. Its pine needles were taller than Henry. A house was built into the trunk at the end and the arch underneath it led inside the tree like a gaping mouth.

The sleigh slid past it and down into the basin, the size of several football pitches, with Iddrassil in the centre. Four other avenues led from Iddrassil - the steepest opposite headed towards the Northern Route. Two led left towards the fields and forests, and one right in the direction of the mountains. There was a large building on each corner - one for each of the Five Crafts.

The base of the trunk was as big as a castle. The sleigh skirted around it to the left, heading for a pair of enormous double doors in a giant atrium built out from the trunk. Appodin brought the sleigh to a halt in front of the doors and waited. The sound of a large bolt being thrust back echoed around them and the doors swung open.

A tall, thin elf with greying-brown hair emerged from behind the doors. He wore no cloak or armour, but was dressed instead in a brown leather jerkin over a couple of thick cotton shirts. He greeted them solemnly and began detaching the reindeer from the sleigh.

Rodin and Amira vaulted out of the sleigh. Henry clambered over, his trainers landing in the snow with a crunch. A cold, wet feeling seeped through them in seconds and crept up his legs. He gripped the blanket tight around him. The effects of the Fyoreig were wearing off. The icy cold bit at his face, stinging his ears and nose. He started to shudder and shiver.

All four elves were watching him.

"Equodin, this is Henry."

Equodin smiled warmly down at Henry and stooped to shake his hand, which disappeared in his long, giant fingers.

"Nice to meet you, Equodin."

"The pleasure is all mine, young Glondir."

Henry opened his mouth to ask what Glondir was. Equodin saw the quizzical look on his face.

"I am sorry. I saw the Hafskod and assumed it was the correct thing to call you."

"That's fine. I just don't know what it means."

"I will call you Henry until I hear otherwise. Now, come inside. You are really not dressed appropriately for a climate as cold as Alvahame's. Once you are fully clothed in Aesir-made attire, you will think nothing of it."

Equodin led the reindeer through the double doors into a giant barn, with straw-covered stable areas. The eyes of over thirty reindeer trained on Henry.

"They do not yet know you," said Equodin. "Come and help feed your travelling companions, then the others will trust you. I don't expect you've been formally introduced either." There was a hint of a reprimand in his tone.

"Too busy fighting off the Gaardreng," Appodin muttered.

"It was that serious?"

"It was."

"And you fought with them all the way to Alvahame?"

Appodin shrugged.

Equodin tutted.

"So, Henry Frey, meet Blaze, Vega, Bardag and Gratall."

All four inclined their heads on cue. Equodin provided Henry with four giant carrots, which he handed out, followed by a bowl of oats the size of a barrel.

"They are four of our bravest reindeer and very experienced in battle. None of them would ever refuse a fight with Alvahame's enemies. If only it stopped there."

Vega looked a little sheepish.

"You will, of course, have heard of eight of our residents, but we do not entertain such a concept as celebrity here."

Henry finished feeding the four. The other reindeer had turned away.

"Come on," said Amira. "You need clothes and food. It looks like we beat the morning rush."

The Hafskod read five-thirty. Two tiny flames danced over the face.

Henry bade farewell to Equodin, Appodin and the four reindeer, then followed Rodin and Amira through the stable.

"So, do I call you Lord Rodin?"

"No. You call me Rodin."

They entered a large circular space the size of the sports hall at Henry's old school. It was surrounded by wooden walls. Seams of gold coursed along the grain of the wood. Light gleamed from irregular-shaped windows dotted over the walls. But when Henry looked closer, he saw they were diamonds. A railed wooden staircase rose from the middle of the floor and curved parallel to the walls as they spiralled upwards and out of sight through Iddrassil's hollowed trunk. Walkways stretched from the staircase and connected with arched doorways scattered at regular intervals in the walls. Henry looked up to take it in and a breeze of fresh pine wafted into his face.

"The Hollow," said Rodin. "The inside of Iddrassil and the centre of Alvahame. It goes all the way to the star at the top."

Henry walked past a couple of flights of curving wooden stairs leading downwards under the floor. They reminded him of the stairs inside a castle.

"Where do we go now?" he asked.

"The star," Rodin said.

"The star at the top? How?"

"We're going to fly."

"There's no sleigh."

"We don't need one."

CHAPTER FOURTEEN

Henry's eyes followed the curve of the Hollow as far as he could and imagined himself soaring up there, weaving in and out of the stairs and walkways. The Hafskod glowed on his wrist, as if it anticipated what was coming next.

"It's the Hafskod, isn't it?" he said.

"You just need the Madjik," Amira replied. "Keep the Hafskod on and you will fly all the way up. It's like running or jumping." She spread her arms and lifted into the air. She circled around him. "Treat it as second nature and just rise into the air."

Henry took a breath and relaxed. He willed himself to lift into the air. He could feel unseen forces pushing him up from beneath and lifting him up from above. His feet left the floor. He rose into the air, watching the walls sink downwards past him. Amira was right. It felt as natural as running or walking, as if he'd been doing it all his life. He floated up after Amira. He looked down at Rodin, then at the floor.

He stopped. He was already several floors above the ground. It was a long way down. If he fell.

He wobbled. He dropped. The ground shot up at him. His stomach threatened to leap through his throat.

The Hafskod glowed.

The Madjik.

He steadied himself and hung in the air.

Rodin nodded approvingly.

"You didn't panic. As long as you're inside Iddrassil and you have the Hafskod, the Madjik will keep you in the air."

Henry flew upwards with ease. He experimented - flying up, then letting himself drop and catching himself just in time. He laughed. Something resembling a grin crossed Rodin's face. Henry dropped and caught himself just above the floor. Rodin grabbed him and threw him upwards. Henry shot up after Amira who picked up her pace. He followed her, looping and twisting around the staircase, weaving through the wooden walkways, following the Hollow's curved walls as they wound upwards.

At the point Henry guessed they must be about halfway up, Rodin pointed to an arched opening on their right.

"My home is through there."

They flew upwards, getting faster and faster as Henry became used to the speed and started to enjoy himself. The Hollow narrowed at the very top. Amira landed on a wooden platform under an archway and led them towards some spiral stairs leading upwards. To their right, a circular tunnel led downwards around The Hollow. It was lined with hard, glistening ice.

"The inside of the tinsel," said Amira. "It winds around Iddrassil and all the way to the ground. Some of us fly up and down the Hollow. Some of us use the tinsel."

"Up or down?" Henry asked.

"Up or down."

"Don't you crash into each other all the time?"

"We never crash. Our reactions are lightning fast."

Henry looked down at his watch. One dancing flame burned brighter.

Footsteps hurried down the stairs towards them. A boy appeared. He was a couple of years older than Henry. He had short, blond hair and human ears. There was a thin gold band around his wrist. The boy landed on the floor in front of Henry and scowled. His eyes went straight to Henry's Hafskod. His scowl darkened. He marched forward and barged into Henry's shoulder, then jumped off the platform and flew down the Hollow, out of sight.

"That was Yohann." Rodin scowled. "Looks like Klasodin told him you're here."

Amira led the way upstairs to a large, open space with windows in every direction at different angles.

"You're in the centre of the star," she said.

A large kitchen lay at the far end. In the middle was a seating area where two elves were waiting for them. One was a familiar figure who looked a lot leaner without his thick red coat. They were both dressed in green and brown.

"Welcome Henry," Klasodin beamed. "This is my wife, Merrodine."

"Come in Henry." Merrodine smiled warmly and pointed him in the direction of a staircase over her left shoulder. "Your room is up there."

"I'm staying here?"

"Of course. Now why don't you go up and take a hot shower. I've left you some clothes up there as well. Then we'll have a nice big breakfast."

Henry's stomach rumbled. He took the wooden stairs and entered a large room with a floor-to-ceiling window at the far end jutting outwards. He could hear voices below. The elves were already deep in discussion. He crept back out of the door and leaned towards the stairs.

"Oh, Klasodin," Merrodine reprimanded her husband. "You gave Henry the Hafskod - with Yohann still here? How did you think he would react?"

"We need help," Klasodin said shortly. "Yohann should understand that."

"He's a boy. He's bound to be upset."

"He will be fine. Henry is the one we need."

"It's worse than we thought," Rodin reported. "The Gaardreng wielded weapons, the like of which we have never seen before. They were fused with Madjik."

"The boy's watch clouded over until it was as black as night," said Amira. "The weapons reloaded themselves automatically and they gave out a blue flash."

"Azmar." Rodin's tone was bleak. "It is as you suspected. We have a traitor."

"I will convene the Council," Klasodin decided.

"For all we know the traitor is a member of the Council," Rodin replied. "How many Aesir could have done this?"

"Why?" Klasodin sighed. "We have everything we need. What more could any elf possibly want?"

"Unquenchable thirsts and insatiable wants are human qualities," Rodin said.

"You think Yohann could have done this?"

"Not alone. There has to be an elf involved."

"How is that possible?" Merrodine demanded.

"We have an entire department dedicated to studying the humans and their ways," Amira suggested. "Who knows what effect that could have on one of us?"

"I don't believe it - any of it," Merrodine insisted.

"We have no choice," Rodin said simply.

Klasodin muttered something.

"We are talking about one among thousands," Amira added. "There's no need to lose all hope."

"If only that was all," Klasodin uttered. "In years gone by, the ValdFyurring would have met its quota with time to spare. Not anymore. Those letters look more like shopping lists every year."

Henry crept back into his room. His hollow stomach growled. Did the Aesir really think so little of him and his kind?

He took a hot shower and changed into his Aesir clothing. There were brown trousers made from very soft leather, which fitted over sturdy, yet extremely comfortable, fur-lined brown boots. His long-sleeved t-shirt and shirt were made of the same thick, soft material as his pyjamas, which he wore under a brown leather jerkin. There was a fur-lined brown coat, which he would save for later.

He made his way downstairs and Merrodine beckoned him to the window. He could see over all one side of Alvahame. They were about level with the top of the basin. He could just see the trees of Hamedall that he had passed on the way in.

A gold glow on the periphery of Henry's vision closed over the windows and he found his view zooming in so he could see more clearly. Down below, Alvahame was coming to life. Elves of all ages poured out of the houses lining the city's snow-covered avenues. Sleighs, skis, toboggans, snowboards and reindeer shot down the slopes into one of the five Craft buildings, along Iddrassil's branches or into the stable at the base.

Henry checked his watch. Just before six o'clock.

"We start early here," said Merrodine. "We don't need as much sleep as you."

"Does school go on all day?"

Merrodine laughed.

"No. They finish at one o'clock."

The coffee table in the seating area was covered in bowls of steaming porridge and plates piled with toast as well as pots of tea and Fyoreig.

"So what happens now?" Henry asked, after a breakfast of porridge and more Fyoreig. "How long am I staying?"

"Are you in a hurry to go home?"

"No." He remembered where he lived. "I don't have a home anyway."

Klasodin opened his mouth to say something, then thought better of it.

"It's too dangerous to take you back," he said finally. "I think you should stay here - until Christmas morning at the very least."

"What about Yohann?"

"I'm sure you will get along fine."

"He doesn't want me here."

"He will understand."

Henry opened his mouth to protest, but the expression on Amira's face told him to drop it. He gave up.

"So what do I do now?" he said, suddenly feeling very out of place and wondering why he was there at all.

"How would you like to go to school today, maybe meet a few Aesir your own age?" Klasodin suggested.

Henry didn't like socialising, but he wanted to meet more elves. In his mind's eye, he could see an assembly hall full of elves, all watching him. He could feel himself squirm at the thought.

"Where is school?"

"You remember the baubles on the tree?" said Merrodine. "Each bauble is a classroom. They are very small classes compared to what you're used to. You won't find it too overwhelming."

Henry followed Rodin out of the star and watched him step off the platform. He hung back, then took a run up and jumped off the end. He dropped. The walls shot past him. A walkway flashed past him, just missing him. He slowed his descent and touched down where the wall jutted out, before curving the other way. He peered over the edge. Below, the Hollow thrived with life. Elves shot and flew in every direction, up and down the Hollow, in and out of the arched walkways. Aesir children flew in chattering groups at top speed for their classrooms.

Henry swallowed. The reality of where he was going hit him. He hadn't been to school in a year.

CHAPTER FIFTEEN

A group of young Aesir children flew past him and just missed him as he dropped. A few adults gave him a wider berth. Elves sailed past him in every direction. Henry stopped trying to dive out of their way. He dropped faster, letting the flying Aesir avoid him and got in line right behind Rodin.

Rodin veered and landed on a platform a couple of levels below his home. Henry followed him over the wooden walkway and stopped where the tubular tunnel of shining ice crossed over it. A group of Aesir children shot past on their snowboards. Henry jumped back.

Amira shepherded him onto the ice.

"Your boots won't slide unless you want them to."

Henry took short, careful steps over the ice, looking left and right for more speeding elves. He placed his foot on the wooden walkway opposite and breathed a sigh of relief as three young elves shot through on their snowboards, spiralled up and around the tunnel and sped out of sight.

The wooden walkway led outside and along a branch the size of a country lane. Its green needles were taller than Henry. He followed Rodin down some stairs carved into the branch, down a sloping tunnel and through the glass door at the end, which opened out into a dome-shaped classroom of gold-tinted glass giving views over Alvahame.

The second Rodin entered, the fifteen elves Henry's age stood up as one. Their teacher stopped talking. She had a slight build and shoulder-length, mousy-brown hair.

"Lord Rodin," she said, her eyes as wide as the children's. "This is a rare honour."

"Thank you," Rodin replied. "Please ask the children to sit down."

The children sat down in unison.

"May I briefly interrupt your class, Monira?"

"Of course. Of course."

Rodin stood aside so they could all see Henry.

Henry swallowed as all eyes trained on him. Amira gave him a gentle push forward.

"This is Henry Frey from London," Rodin announced. "Some of you will know him from your Human Studies classes."

Henry froze. He didn't like the sound of that. What had they seen?

"He will be staying in Alvahame for a while and your class will be the ideal place for him to experience our city at first hand. Would you take him as a student?"

"Of course."

"I know you will all make him feel welcome."

"We would be honoured. Wouldn't we class?"

"Thank you, Monira. I'm sure Henry will be at home here."

Monira smiled and blushed like a love-struck schoolgirl. Henry could imagine Rodin posters plastered over her bedroom wall.

"It has already been agreed that Ellodine will look after Henry once classes are finished," Rodin added.

Amira waved Henry goodbye. Rodin gave him a manly slap on the back, throwing him two steps forward. The door shut behind them. Henry was on his own.

"Welcome Henry," Monira smiled. "Take your seat next to Ellodine."

Sixteen pairs of eyes watched him take his seat next to an Aesrine with long blonde hair, who shot him a bright smile.

Henry sat down next to her, doing his best to keep his mouth shut and not stare. Ellodine was as pretty as Amira. He fixed his eyes on the front, painfully aware that most of the Aesir children in his class were still watching him.

"Hello," Ellodine whispered.

"Hi," Henry breathed back.

"Well Henry, we are focusing on careers at the moment," Monira said. "So you have picked the ideal time to join us. This is the age when all Aesir children think about their futures and you might learn a lot about Alvahame as well. I wonder. Can you think what important role our children might play even now?"

The hairs stood up on the back of Henry's neck. He realised Monira had aimed the question at him. Fifteen hands shot up. Henry could feel Monira watching him expectantly. One answer lingered quietly at the back of his mind. Could it be that easy?

"Test the presents?" he said in a small voice.

"Correct," Monira beamed. "Now, let's review some of the basics and give Henry a chance to learn them as well. Do you know what we call the core rules of our city?"

"The Three Foundations?" he answered immediately.

"Wonderful! Can you name one?"

Henry thought back to his conversation with Amira and Rodin in the sleigh. One answer came pretty quickly. He was more relaxed already after two correct answers.

"The Purpose."

"Excellent. Let's have someone else give us the other two. Rimida."

"The Equality of Elves and the Purity of Madjik."

"Excellent. And what else does Henry need to know? Zadira?"

"The Five Crafts."

"Who can name all Five? Balnir."

"Care, Creation, Education, Giving and War."

"That's right. Now who here has thought about which area of Alvahame they would like to work in? Forodin?"

"Testing gifts in the Craft of Creation. I want to ride every bike and every board there. I have some ideas of my own as well."

"Rimida?"

"Gift wrapping in Giving."

"Zadira?"

"Gift design. Creation."

"Raiodin?"

"I want to be a warrior in the Craft of War - like Lord Rodin."

"Yes, unfortunately, we will always need brave Aesir to protect Alvahame. Balnir?"

"I want to be in charge of the Black List. I suppose that counts as the Craft of Giving - funny really."

"Balnir, I'm not sure that position even exists."

"It will."

"No it won't," Ellodine shot back.

"Yes it will," Balnir insisted. "Most of these humans don't deserve what we give them. The good ones should receive presents and the bad ones should get nothing."

"That's awful," Ellodine protested. "You can't earn a gift. That isn't why Klasodin does it."

"It will be. My dad works for Gronodin. The ValdFyurring can't handle that many gifts. Why should the good ones pay?"

"Nobody should pay."

"They will. It's the Black List this year. They'll bring in the Gold List next year. They have to earn their place on that.

Just as well too. The ValdFyurring is failing." Balnir sniggered. "Bit like Klasodin himself. They reckon he's going senile. Doesn't know what he's doing anymore."

Ellodine jumped to her feet, fists clenched. Henry reached out instinctively and grabbed her arm. Fights were never good.

"THAT'S ENOUGH." Monira roared so loudly the glass bauble they were in shook violently. Henry clutched the side of his chair. He was sure the classroom would shake free from its branch and drop to the ground, killing them all in an instant.

The class sat down in silence.

"Ellodine. You will not shout or fight in my classroom."

"Yes, Monira."

"And Balnir. I will not have anyone speak about their elders like that, especially the founder of our city and everything it stands for. I want you to apologise to the entire class right now."

"Sorry."

"And to Henry for speaking so disrespectfully about his race."

"Sorry."

"I don't care what you've heard, Balnir. If I ever hear that kind of nastiness expelled from your mouth again, you will serve detention for a month."

Monira assumed her previously pleasant demeanour.

"Now. I hear footsteps. I think our guest has arrived."

The door opened slowly. A blonde Aesrine peered in. She had a pleasant, friendly face, and wore more green than any other elf Henry had seen. She looked to be about Rodin's age.

"Welcome, Visrine," Monira said, inclining her head slightly.

"Please. It's Larodine." She had a very soft voice.

"Children, our special guest has come to talk about her career," Monira announced.

"I work in the Craft of Care," Larodine explained. "I tend to the trees of Hamedall and help take care of Iddrassil itself. It is very rewarding work."

"What's Visrine?" Henry whispered to Ellodine.

"It's the equivalent to "Your Royal Highness" in your culture. Visrine is what you say to an Aesrine."

"That's a female elf, right?"

"A female Alvahame elf. Aesr and Visir are the male versions."

"Strange work for a princess."

"She's not interested in royalty. She does what she loves. Her husband is in the Hamedall Guard. They're happy and they work hard. What more could they want?"

CHAPTER SIXTEEN

Break time came. Most of Henry's class piled out without giving him a second look. Ellodine lingered, as did Zadira and Rimida. Rimida was taller than the two other girls. She had long, curly hair. Zadira had straight light-brown hair and sharp green eyes.

"They've all seen humans before," said Rimida, a sympathetic smile on her face. "You're nothing new."

"Some Aesir like humans a lot," Zadira added, a wicked gleam in her eye.

"I like Human Studies," Ellodine scowled.

"You love Human Studies," Rimida laughed.

"We've all seen you watching…"

Ellodine elbowed Zadira in the ribs, but Zadira laughed and lifted a trapdoor in the floor.

"Come and see how we all spy on you," she grinned, disappearing down a steep flight of stairs.

Henry followed, then wished he hadn't. Between him and a big drop to the ground was nothing but curved, gold-stained glass - the bottom of the glass bauble.

Zadira jumped up and down. The floor wobbled. Henry's heart skipped a beat.

"Come on. It's fine."

Henry stepped gingerly over the curved floor. Rimida joined them and a red-faced Ellodine followed.

"We're only teasing, Elle," Rimida said. "Why don't you show him?"

Three gold spheres, each three feet in diameter, hovered in mid-air.

"These are LagFyurrings," said Ellodine. "They connect us to the wider world. Every Christmas we watch you open your gifts. We use them for our Human Studies lessons. We see the letters you write and we can look in on you if we choose."

Zadira smirked. Ellodine scowled at her.

"Now Gronodin has brought in the Black List," Zadira rolled her eyes, "we can look at case studies to see how they decided who would be on the Black List and who wouldn't be." She shot Henry a sideways glance. "We all know you quite well."

"Me?" Henry could feel the skin on his face and neck getting hotter.

"You're one of the Valdiri."

"And the only one in living memory who wouldn't want a Madjik camera," came a voice from above. Balnir peered in. "Then you deservedly get put on the Black List. Klasodin handpicks you some gifts anyway and you're still not happy."

"Leave him alone," Ellodine snapped.

"Well, it's not just you," Balnir continued. "It's what you humans are like. You all want whatever you can grab and there's always one more big, shiny object to get your hands on. You're like magpies."

"Some of your things are cool," Forodin said, shoving Balnir out of the way and poking his head down through the trapdoor. "Like cars. Have you ever been in a Ferrari or an Aston Martin?"

"No," Henry replied. "My parents didn't have a car."

"What about an aeroplane?"

"No."

"Oh." Forodin looked mildly disappointed. "What about the London Underground?"

"Yeah, I've been on that."

"If I were a human, I'd be an F1 driver or a pilot."

Henry realised he could see himself in a LagFyurring. He was in his old classroom, stealing the money for the class trip. Now he was in his old flat, shoving Klasodin's memoirs in the drawer and the purple blanket into his wardrobe.

"We never knew he even had memoirs," said Zadira.

Henry couldn't watch it.

"Make it stop," he shouted, turning away so he couldn't see it.

His image disappeared.

"And you're supposed to be Glondir." Balnir shook his head.

"He is Glondir," Ellodine insisted.

"How would we know? The other Valdiri are dead. But it doesn't matter now anyway. The ValdFyurring is beyond help. No Madjikal human can help us."

Ellodine opened her mouth to shout at him, when Raiodin peered down, his mop of thick fair hair hanging around his face.

"We've been challenged," he grinned. "Avrodin's class."

They all looked at Henry.

"He suggested a game of "Nail the Human", but Yohann wasn't too keen. He'll probably hide somewhere."

"It's a snowball fight," Balnir explained. "You might want to hide as well."

"I'll be fine," Henry scowled.

He climbed up the steps and left the classroom with the others. Nerves bubbled in his stomach, but he wasn't going to show them. They all thought they were so much better than him.

He watched them shoot down The Hollow and out of sight. Ellodine lingered and led Henry outside onto the snow and found the rest of the class by the trunk under one of the giant lower branches.

"They're playing Ambush," said Raiodin with an evil grin. "We have to get the whole class once around Iddrassil. They'll target our weakest link. They picked a good day for it."

All eyes were on Henry.

"I can throw a snowball," he scowled.

"Not like us you can't."

"I bet I can."

"Yeah right," Forodin sniggered.

"You're the target," said Raiodin. "Why do you think they challenged us today?"

Henry swallowed.

"We'll go anti-clockwise," said Balnir. "We need two scouts."

Forodin produced a wooden snowboard and jumped on it. Raiodin did the same. They slid forward without even pushing off, gathering up snow and placing their snowballs between their feet.

Henry gathered some snow in his gloved hands and made a snowball. He zipped up his elven coat. His classmates had gathered around him - Balnir at the front, Ellodine to one side and Rimida behind him. Why she got to hide, Henry didn't know.

Alvahame buzzed with activity, but there was no attack. They passed under the next lower branch.

Shouts and screams came from around the tree. Snowballs thudded against their targets. Henry strained to get a better view.

A volley of snowballs hit his group like machine gun fire. Henry took one, two, three snowballs in the face and landed on his back in the snow with a crunch. Stars fizzed in his eyes. His face burned ice cold.

"Their human's down," came a shout.

Raucous laughter echoed over the snow. Elves in Henry's group sniggered.

"Everyone, stop and defend your positions," Balnir commanded - a note of irritation in his voice.

The snowballs flew.

"Are you okay?" Ellodine said gently.

Henry nodded. His face stung like he had been hit by three frozen-solid rocks that had been fired out of a cannon.

"You can sit it out if you like," she offered.

Henry eased himself up onto his elbows. His head swam. He gave it a couple of seconds to clear and climbed to his feet. He still couldn't move his face.

"Keep your head down this time," Balnir ordered him. "Like I told you, you humans don't throw like we do."

A laugh sounded from above. Henry shot a glance up. Yohann smirked down at him from between a bunch of pine needles. A snowball caught him in the face and he disappeared. Henry's class laughed.

Forodin and Raiodin circled them, gathering piles of snowballs between their feet, then set off again.

"Remember," Ellodine whispered. "For you this is like bringing a snowball to a gunfight. Be careful."

The ambush came. They were ready. Henry ducked a volley of snowballs. His classmates hurled them back.

"Run for it," Balnir ordered.

Henry ran behind his group. The elves in front of him left him behind. He couldn't bring his feet out of the snow fast enough.

Suddenly they all stopped and turned.

"Keep running, human," said Balnir.

Henry ran, lifting his knees high to kick his feet out of the snow. His class pelted the other elves with snowballs.

"Now," said Balnir,

Rimida burst out from hiding behind Balnir and Zadira with an armful of snowballs and bombarded the elves in the other class, taking down four with sniper-like precision. Henry could tell she threw much harder than anyone else. Avrodin's class all dived for cover.

"Run," Balnir ordered.

They all ran for the branch where they had started. Henry struggled after them. He reached the finish line, puffing and panting. His class cheered. He rested his hands on his knees and gasped for breath. The cold air stung his lungs. His face sang.

A bell sounded. They all hurried away until just he and Ellodine remained. She took him by the arm and stood him against the trunk. She looked around her to make sure nobody could see them. She removed her gloves and placed her hands on Henry's face.

The stinging cold and throbbing pain leached from his skin. His face felt warm again. He breathed out a deep sigh.

"Thanks," he sighed. "That's better. How did you do that?"

Ellodine shrugged.

"I don't know. But don't tell anyone I did it." Her jaw clenched. She pointed a finger in his face. "Nobody."

"Why?"

"No one knows I can do it. And there would be a huge fuss if they did."

"Why? Isn't it just something Madjikal you elves can do?"

"No," she said seriously. "I am the only one. Come on. We'll be late for class."

CHAPTER SEVENTEEN

That afternoon, Henry trudged through the snow after the other elves in the smaller group Monira had assigned.

"Hurry up, human," Forodin called in his usual laconic, languid style.

"Unlike you, I don't have to walk through it every day," Henry snapped.

"Don't you have snow?"

"In London, we have slush. Anything more gets cleared away before I go to school."

"Cleared away?" said Balnir. "What a waste of good snow."

"Shut up, you idiots," Ellodine scowled.

"It's not like he can use his lack of height as an excuse," said Forodin, who like Balnir and Raiodin, was a lot taller than Henry. Forodin was slightly taller and leaner than his two friends and had darker hair. "Ellodine's his height and she manages alright."

"That's because I'm an Aesrine. I'm used to it."

"All those films of yours we watched in Human Studies," said Balnir. "Elves are these tiny little things with squeaky voices. Must have given you a real shock to see what we're like for real. Not so superior anymore, are you?"

"Here we go," Zadira rolled her eyes and sounded very bored, like she had heard it all a hundred times before. "Balnir hates humans."

"I just think they need knocking down a peg or two," Balnir insisted.

"Give it a rest, Balnir," Rimida added. "You just want to send large lumps of coal to every human child in the world. That would make you happy."

"I bet Henry never thought he'd meet the real-life Grinch here in Alvahame," Raiodin grinned. "We should paint him green in the middle of the night and see if anyone notices." Everyone apart from Balnir laughed. Raiodin gave him a friendly shove. "What do you want to be in Giving for anyway? You're an army general. War's the one for you."

"He wants to teach all humans a lesson first," Rimida said primly.

"Why is everyone turning on me all of a sudden?" Balnir protested.

"To give Henry a rest."

"Yeah, he took one for the team earlier," said Raiodin. "And he got back up. I've never seen a helper do that before."

Balnir shrugged.

"What annoys me the most, and it's not just me, is how Klasodin shows them more kindness and generosity than anyone ever has before. He brings these human helpers to the greatest place on Earth, and what do they do in return? They take. He can talk about their Madjik all day long, but do any of them really care about anything apart from all the cool presents he gives them? No."

"What's your point, Balnir?" Forodin looked bored.

"Alvahame comes first. When I see a human treat this great city the way they should, when they put it first and contribute like we all do, then I'll think differently about them. Madjik or not - we don't need them."

Raiodin threw his head back, shut his eyes and pretended to snore.

"I am so BORED. I hear this every week."

"It's true every week."

"But I stopped caring many months ago."

"How can you not care?"

"We need them, Balnir. It's not Henry's fault you're jealous," Ellodine retorted.

"Jealous of what?"

"You want a Hafskod for yourself."

"If you got to wield Klasodin's staff, we'd actually be telling you to talk more," Zadira said.

"I can do what?" said Henry.

"Here we go," Balnir muttered.

"I just want to know. What can I do?"

"Klasodin's staff," said Ellodine.

"Big, long stick," Forodin added with a grin.

"I know what a staff is," Henry snapped.

"Haven't you seen it?" Ellodine asked, aiming a kick at Forodin, who darted out of the way quicker than Henry had ever seen anyone move.

"Not quick enough," Forodin grinned.

A snowball from Rimida hit him in the face.

"That's not fair," he protested.

"What staff," Henry demanded irritably.

"Klasodin has a staff," Ellodine explained. "He takes it everywhere. He uses it to deliver presents. Apart from him, only his human helpers can use it."

Henry opened his mouth to tell them he didn't see it when Klasodin visited him in his attic room, then thought better of it. He wasn't supposed to tell anyone Klasodin had ever been there.

Raiodin stopped outside the giant corner building dedicated to the Craft of Care.

"Well, at least we get one of the boring ones out of the way first."

"Care is not boring," Ellodine retorted. "How is looking after all of this boring."

"It's boring. War is interesting. Weapons are cool and exciting."

"The stuff in Creation is awesome," Forodin added. "This is really boring."

"Every time I hear about pruning trees, I want to collapse and die."

Ellodine scowled at a grinning Raiodin.

"Try any of this in there and you will collapse and die."

"I am so sorry. I forgot Mummy worked in there, Visrine." Raiodin grinned, standing in front of Ellodine and giving a florid, exaggerated bow, his left hand behind his back, his right gesturing grandly in front of him.

"I am going to punch you."

"He's only joking," Rimida insisted, grabbing hold of Ellodine's arm just in case. "And if he isn't, we can teach him a lesson outside afterwards. I have a snowball with his name on it."

Raiodin held up his hands in surrender.

"Yeah, you don't want to get in the way of one of those," Balnir said enthusiastically. "The way you took down Avrodin and his class. That was brilliant."

Rimida smiled shyly.

"Yeah, Rimida. Why do you want to be in Giving? Wrapping presents? Is that the best you can do?" said Raiodin.

"My family's been in that Craft for generations."

"But Giving?"

"What could be better than Giving, showing people generosity and love, especially those who don't have anything else? Not that you boys understand that."

Raiodin rolled his eyes.

"Yeah, I know, piety, generosity, blah blah blah. Look what you could do in War."

"You'd be brilliant," Balnir agreed.

"I want to give, not maim or injure or kill," said Rimida, and stomped into the Craft of Care.

The others followed her. Henry tramped in after them and stepped gratefully onto a hardwood floor.

"Which one's your Mum?" he whispered to Ellodine.

They moved through the various hospitals, clinics and surgeries for elves, reindeer, trees and plants. There was even a walk-in clinic for injured animals from the forests, who all seemed to know where it was and how to find it without any directions. Henry passed a couple of caribou, an arctic fox and a polar bear and could feel them watching him with interest. He thought about saying hello to the polar bear, but seeing as it didn't greet him first, he decided against it.

Ellodine pointed to the softly-spoken Larodine, who had addressed the class earlier and was now showing their group around. Larodine waved back.

"Larodine's your mum?" he breathed.

Ellodine nodded.

"So you're a Visrine as well?"

Ellodine scowled.

"No I'm not. Mum and Dad don't want it and neither do I."

Larodine shook Henry's hand on the way out. She smiled and told him he was free to come to her and ask for anything he needed at any time. Henry left the Craft of Care and trudged after the others in the direction of the Craft of Education, certain that Ellodine's mother was the nicest person in the world, elf or human.

"We're getting the other boring one out of the way," Raiodin called back to him.

"We're leaving Creation for last," Forodin said.

Henry caught up to Ellodine.

"So if you're royalty, what does that mean?" he said between breaths. "Who are you related to? And what are you? Daughter? Niece? Third cousin? Third child of the fourth daughter of the seventh nephew, which means you have royal blood, but don't really matter in any way?"

Ellodine shot him a dark scowl. She marched away and into Education before Henry could catch up.

"Just asking," he muttered. "Why's it all such a big secret?"

CHAPTER EIGHTEEN

Leglodin, the head of the Craft of Education, looked like a professor in his crimson velvet coat and grey hair, Henry thought, as he followed the Aesr through lecture halls, classrooms and laboratories. They stopped in a high-ceilinged room filled with more floating gold globes.

"This is where we conduct most of our Human Studies lessons. Nothing quite competes with a real-life, practical example. And we can see everything through the LagFyurrings. Even you." Leglodin peered down his nose at Henry.

Henry swallowed. Everyone apart from Ellodine grinned.

"And of course, as we refine the way we give gifts and decide upon whom to bestow them, it will be the Human Studies department who will gather, analyse and collate the vast amounts of data."

Henry caught up with a furious Ellodine as they left.

"He's a pompous idiot," she muttered. "So smug at the thought of becoming more important. He has no idea what he's doing or the damage he'll cause."

"Because he'll say some kids aren't good enough?"

"That's right."

"Belief's important, you know," she said seriously. "If nobody believes in Father Christmas or Santa Claus, then he won't come. The Valdfyurring's Madjik thrives on belief. Without it, there would be no connection between us and the human world. Santa Claus wouldn't exist anymore. Just think of all the children who wouldn't get anything."

The Craft of Giving was next. Merrodine awaited them at the entrance.

"Come in children," she welcomed them.

"Thank you, Visrine," Balnir said dutifully.

"Now, now, Balnir. You can't say my husband is a crazy old fool, then bow and scrape in front of me. That isn't how we work."

Balnir's face turned crimson.

"I didn't mean to insult you, Visrine. I just think when something doesn't work anymore, changes should be made."

"How very pragmatic of you, Balnir. Not to mention cold, unfeeling and not at all what I would expect from an Aesr."

"The ValdFyurring can't cope. You see it in Human Studies all the time."

"It works fine," Ellodine snapped.

"What's wrong with it then?" Balnir demanded.

"Someone's sabotaging it."

"A traitor? In Alvahame? Never."

"Now children," Merrodine said gently. "Let's get on with our tour, shall we? As I understand it, you Balnir, of all young Aesir, want to work here."

"On the Black List," Ellodine grated.

"The Aesir who work in the Craft of Giving want to give, not take away," Merrodine reprimanded him.

"But that is what's happening, isn't it?" Henry blurted.

"Saved your life last year," Balnir retorted.

"Because someone tried to kill him," Ellodine snapped.

"Out there. Not in here."

"There's no traitor here," Raiodin insisted.

"Rodin thinks so," Henry muttered.

Raiodin blinked.

Balnir opened his mouth, took a glance at Merrodine and thought better of it. She led them upstairs. Raiodin held back and waited for Henry.

"Really?" He whispered, his eyes wide.

Henry nodded.

"The Gaardreng's weapons had a tainted form of Madjik in them. I think they called it Azmar or something."

He watched Raiodin's face pale.

They entered a large, open room at the top. It was carpeted with a soft, red wine-coloured carpet, which ran around the room and up a couple of steps to a raised dais in the centre. In the middle of the dais were two leather armchairs and matching footstools. The gold coffee table between them was covered with a stack of papers and a row of gold pens. Beside each chair was a floating LagFyurring.

"The biggest part of what we do is in Iddrassil itself," Merrodine said. "But my favourite part is right here. That's my chair. The one on the left as you sit down."

Henry looked at her blankly. He watched the young elves step onto the dais and look at the chairs, the coffee table, the papers and the LagFyurrings with sheer wonder painted on their faces - even Forodin, who looked casual about pretty much everything.

"I've never been in here before," Ellodine whispered.

"It's even more wonderful than I imagined," Rimida breathed.

"What do you do here?" said Henry.

All the young elves apart from Ellodine rolled their eyes.

"This is where Klasodin and I read the letters," Merrodine replied.

"Every letter from every child?"

"That's right."

"You read them all yourselves?"

"Of course? What could be better?" She pointed to a gold hatch in the ceiling. "They come from up there. We read them. We show each other the ones we like. We look at what they have asked for and decide what to give them. This room is where I truly feel at one with the world and with every child on it. Well, not just children of course. There are plenty of adults out there who believe in Klasodin too."

Eight mugs of hot chocolate materialised on top of the gold coffee table. It was the best hot chocolate Henry had ever tasted - thick, chocolatey and creamy. Merrodine ushered them out once they were finished.

"I'll take you inside Iddrassil later." Merrodine took hold of Ellodine and hugged her. "I hope you are taking good care of our human guest."

"I am. The boys are rubbish."

Merrodine laughed.

"Did you enjoy your visit to your mother? I know she was looking forward to showing you around."

Ellodine nodded.

Something dawned on Henry.

"You're Ellodine's grandmother?"

"Not exactly. There are a few generations and a few "greats" in-between, but yes, I am. Ellodine doesn't like to admit it. She's embarrassed by us, aren't you?"

"No. I just don't like being called Visrine, that's all."

"I know. I'll see you later."

They trudged towards the Craft of War. The rest had already disappeared inside.

"You could have told me," Henry said irritably.

"What for?" she replied, her jaw set. "I wanted you to know me for me."

"Difficult not to."

Ellodine smiled.

"Around here, it matters," she said quietly.

"I know. It's the same where I come from. But it makes no difference to me."

Her smile brightened.

"Good."

The Craft of War had a huge armoury on the ground floor, so Aesir warriors could reach their bows, swords, shields, sleighs and snowboards with the greatest of ease.

"They all have their own," said Amira, taking the role of guide. "But you always need more." She led them upstairs to where more Aesir were engaging in combat training - with and without weapons.

"Any of you younglings care to take me on?" Appodin grinned, swinging his sword with abandon.

Raiodin's hand shot up first.

"Which Craft do you want to be in?" Henry whispered to Ellodine, watching an armoured Raiodin trying to take on Appodin with his own sword.

"I don't know."

Henry's eye shot towards the crashing swords. Appodin was better, but he could see Raiodin was pretty handy with a sword already.

"I thought you all did."

Ellodine shrugged.

"I think I'm the only one. I'm just not sure."

Henry soon found himself in Aesir armour, grasping an elven sword, taking on Appodin, who towered over him.

"We'll try a few easy strokes," Appodin suggested.

Appodin taught him a few moves, then Henry went for it and hit Appodin with everything he could think of.

He left the Craft of War an hour later with a grin on his face. He'd loved the duel with Appodin and the archery practice afterwards - even if he didn't manage to hit the target with either weapon.

"War's the best, isn't it?" Raiodin grinned, his broad face flushed with perspiration and excitement.

Henry nodded.

"You didn't do too bad in there - for a human."

"Boys." Zadira rolled her eyes.

CHAPTER NINETEEN

The Craft of Creation was like the biggest toy shop Henry had ever seen. He entered through the giant double doors to an atrium several storeys high, overlooked by mezzanine floors, balconies and tall shelves stacked with every toy and game Henry could imagine and many he had never seen before.

"Welcome." Salvodin greeted Henry with a wide, friendly smile. He had long light-blond hair and pale skin. "I'm a toy designer here - everything from dolls and cars to dart guns, bikes and snowboards. Good to meet you, Henry Frey." They shook hands. "I haven't met a human yet who didn't love it in here and I'm sure you will too."

He took them through to another room that was just as big, with young elves playing board games and computer games. Upstairs, more young elves were riding bikes of all styles and sizes.

"What better excuse than to come in here and play with everything you can see?" Salvodin said grandly, gesturing around the room.

"They test toys?"

"They test everything, which means they have to play with everything - for hours at a time - really push every toy and game to its limits. And now you are a citizen of Alvahame, it's all yours too."

Henry realised his mouth was wide open. He snapped it shut.

"Do you own many of the things you see here?" Salvodin asked.

"No. Not many."

"Well, some you won't have even heard of. There are games and toys here so advanced, they won't be on general release in London for years to come."

"Wow."

Forodin had made a beeline for the far corner. Others stood aside for him and he jumped on a snowboard arcade game.

"Forodin is something of a star here," said Salvodin. "They say special talents emerge every few generations. And he is very good."

"At what?"

"Speed. He'll find the limits of anything and push it further. Doesn't matter how fast, he'll drive it faster and drive it perfectly. Even for an elf, his reactions are quick."

Raiodin and Balnir stood at another game. A holographic image appeared in front of them. Balnir pointed at it. Swords appeared in their hands. A forest materialised around them. Large, ugly creatures with faces the colour of coal with streaks of iodine and sapphire charged towards them carrying clubs, swords and chains. The two young elves battled them together.

"The real Nerivari were much more dangerous," said Salvodin. "But that's only the beginner's level."

Henry watched Forodin stand in his languid style on the board, a slightly bored look on his face, as the countdown to the beginning flashed on the screen in front of a steep slope down a snowy mountain. Suddenly he zipped down it, veering to one side and the other, shooting through every gate.

"New course record again," he said casually, a few seconds later.

He beckoned to Henry.

"Come on, human. You need to learn to snowboard."

He met Ellodine's glance.

"Don't worry. I'll teach him properly."

"Since when are you and the human friends," Balnir sneered.

"Just teaching him to snowboard."

"Why you?"

"Who better?" Forodin shrugged. "Which foot you want to lead with?"

Henry thought.

"Left."

"Good. You're right-handed, right? It's always better to lead with your shield arm. Climb on that way. Feet apart. Knees bent. Weight low. It's all about balance and how you move your weight."

"It's the same as when you ascended The Hollow," said Ellodine. "Use your will."

"I'm doing the teaching," Forodin insisted. "Aesir snowboards are made with Madjik. They move when you want them to. They're like a foot or a hand - an extension of your own body. You move it just the same."

Forodin set the game to the easiest level. The ground on the screen in front of Henry was almost flat.

"The board moves like you're actually on snow. It just hurts less when you fall off at high speed."

Five minutes later, Henry fell off for the third time. Salvodin hauled him to his feet.

"Just making sure you're being looked after," he said. "And you couldn't have found a better instructor. Don't worry if it takes some time. Humans aren't as well equipped for snow sports as elves."

"Tell me about it," Henry grumbled.

"What did you request for Christmas?" Salvodin asked. "Have you seen it here already? Maybe you could try it out."

Henry said nothing.

"Oh, of course." Salvodin gave himself a light slap on the forehead. "The Black List."

Henry felt about ten centimetres tall.

"Sorry," Salvodin murmured. "I won't mention it again. What would you have asked for otherwise?"

Henry thought back to last year.

"A new camera," he said.

"I suppose the other one wouldn't work around other people," Salvodin said sympathetically. He shot Henry a look. "Well, I was looking forward to giving you your first Christmas present. Something every resident of Alvahame should have."

Salvodin handed Henry a wooden snowboard with gold streaks through the grain of the wood, the size of a small skateboard. It was smooth with curved edges and a slightly curved base.

"For you, Henry Frey. Our latest model. It's everything. Snowboard. Sledge. Luge. Skeleton. But slicker and quicker. It will become what you want it to be. And it will mould itself to your build and your needs. Try it outside on real snow, maybe flat ground where you can start as slowly as you like."

"Thank you."

Henry couldn't wait to try it out. He rushed outside and found some deep, soft snow. He placed it on the ground and stepped carefully onto it.

"Don't these normally come with straps?" he said.

"Ours don't," Forodin replied, jumping onto his own board next to Henry's without it moving. "They don't need them. Bend your knees, correct your posture and balance. Then move off."

Henry set off slowly, his arms out either side of him to keep his balance, Ellodine beside him, the others around him.

"You can slow down or speed up whenever you like," she said, returning Forodin's glare. "Doesn't matter if you're going up or down."

He slid slowly around the base of Iddrassil, keeping within arm's length of the trunk, waving to Equodin as he passed the open stable doors. He circled Iddrassil again and again, picking up speed, his circles getting wider and further away from the trunk, until he was sliding up the avenue heading towards the South Passage. Ten minutes after that he was zipping around with the others and had nearly crashed three times into various Aesir coming the other way.

"You ready for the big one?" said Ellodine, once the others had slid off for lunch. She pointed to the star. "We're going to snowboard all the way up there."

"Through the tinsel?"

"It's usually pretty quiet about now. You'll be fine."

CHAPTER TWENTY

Henry's snowboard picked up speed, sliding up and around the ice tunnel. Ellodine looped-the-loop and corkscrewed ahead, then slowed until she was just in front of him.

"Come on. Can't you catch me?"

She laughed and shot over the ice. Henry sped up and chased after her. He zipped over the ice, faster and faster. He jumped over the exits and doorways, travelling so fast his momentum took him up the walls, shooting round and round, the circles decreasing, his turns getting tighter as they headed towards the top of Iddrassil.

Suddenly, a wooden railing appeared to his left. A doorway shot towards him. Ellodine slid through it. Henry flew through it, slipped over wooden floorboards and ground to a halt before he smacked into the opposite wall.

"Wow. You were really quick." Ellodine's eyes were wide and bright with excitement. She scampered up the stairs and Henry chased after her.

Merrodine greeted them with open arms. Klasodin sat at the far side of the room, staring into his LagFyurring.

"I still can't believe you live in the star," said Henry.

"It's the best spot in all of Alvahame," Merrodine beamed. "Not our idea, of course, but the Aesir wanted to honour Klasodin."

Klasodin slumped in his leather chair, his face expressionless.

"I'm glad to see you two are getting along so well," Merrodine continued, pouring some tea. "I know how much Ellodine was looking forward to meeting you."

Ellodine's face turned crimson. Merrodine gestured to the sandwiches.

"Help yourself, Glondir."

"Why do people keep calling me that?" Henry asked.

"It's your official title. It belongs to the wearer of the Hafskod."

"But what does it mean?"

"It means you are the chosen Valdir. Santa Claus's official human helper."

"Isn't that Yohann?"

"Yohann is a helper, but he was never Glondir. I don't think that was ever made clear to him, unfortunately."

Merrodine shot an irritable glance at her husband.

"What's wrong with him?" Ellodine whispered.

"Gronodin called for a Council meeting tonight. We are so far behind there is talk of bringing in the Gold list - where children have to earn their gifts. It's going to be a disaster. Not what we wanted at all."

After tea, Henry whizzed down the ice tunnel after Ellodine, reacting like lightning to exits and the occasional elf appearing from nowhere. He slid onto the wooden floor of The Hollow where Merrodine waited for them.

"How did you do that?" Henry marvelled, skidding to a stop and stepping off his snowboard. "We were really fast."

"This is my city, young Henry. Nothing leaves me behind. Now put your board away."

"Where?"

Merrodine held out her hand and Henry's board flew into it. She took hold of Henry's shoulder, turned him round and pressed his snowboard into his back just below his shoulder blades. She stepped away. It stayed where it was. Henry stretched around, searching for it with his flailing fingers.

"I can't reach it."

"You don't need to," Merrodine replied. "It will come to your hand as easily as it did to mine. Now follow me."

Merrodine headed for the nearest staircase and led them down it as it curved around the sides of the trunk, heading underground.

The stairs opened out into a chamber the size of a massive theatre. It was spherical shaped with a flat, circular floor and walls lined with rows of elves sitting at tables stretching around the circumference of the room with gaps for stairs and walkways. Their hands moved faster than the human eye could follow, wrapping presents. Toys and games appeared on their gold table surfaces. They wrapped them, pressed them into the table top and they vanished. Then a fresh toy appeared. Rolls of wrapping paper and ribbon materialised in the same way, each specific to the present. Henry's eye roved around the room over thousands of elves all wrapping gifts.

He followed Ellodine down the stairs to the circular floor. In the middle stood a giant gold fir tree, nearly the height of the room. The presents around the base of the trunk were each the size of a car. The elves working on the tables around the tree were making presents. Henry watched Salvodin finish the last details on a mountain bike, then take the bike in both hands and press it into the trunk until it disappeared. Madjik surged up the tree. The columns around the room, a fusion of gold and diamond, burst into flames of pure Madjik.

"This is the Hall of Ecromir," Merrodine announced. "We make and wrap every single present here."

"Where does everything come from?" said Henry, watching a tricycle appear on a desk nearby.

"From the ValdFyurring."

"That was the gold in the roots, right? Where is it?"

"You're inside it. This entire spherical chamber is the ValdFyurring. The walls, the tree, the desks, the floor."

Henry shook hands with Ullnir, a gadget specialist in the Craft of Creation. He wore a brown cloak and his dark hair was tied back in a ponytail, but he reminded Henry of a robot. His face was impassive. The tone of his voice was plain and emotionless. He spoke mainly in facts.

Ullnir took an electric red Ferrari big enough for two small children with Edward written on the side - and pressed it into the trunk. Madjik flames flared around the room.

"Each individual, unique gift is placed into the ValdFyurring," he explained to Henry.

He pointed up and behind them to where the same car appeared on a desk in front of an Aesrine who looked like an older version of Rimida. In just a matter of seconds, the car and a mass of bubble wrap were tightly packed inside a large box and wrapped in red and gold paper.

"The ValdFyurring keeps every gift and reproduces it as many times as we need," Salvodin added.

"It stores every single thing you make?" Henry said, watching Ullnir turn his attention to a miniaturized version of an Aston Martin DB9.

"Every item we make," Ullnir replied. "Every raw material and every part. Or at least it did."

"Certain gifts have gone missing," Salvodin explained. "They simply disappeared from the ValdFyurring like they were never there."

"Which ones?"

"The newest, most popular ones," Ullnir said in his matter-of-fact way. "Our latest computers, tablets and games, consoles and televisions. Some toys too."

"Could they be lost?" Henry asked.

"No," Ellodine snorted in disgust.

"We had never lost anything before," Merrodine added.

"It's the best explanation we can come up with," Salvodin shrugged. "This has been happening for over a year now."

Ullnir sat at a workstation and started working on circuit boards and what looked like components for a games console.

"We are having to rebuild some of our best designs from scratch," the gadget specialist explained. "And from memory. But it will not be enough in the time we have."

"Could someone have stolen them?" Henry suggested.

"Only Klasodin can remove anything from the ValdFyurring using his staff," Salvodin said. "There's no other way. But somehow, they've disappeared."

"Someone found a way," Ellodine insisted.

"We can't prove that," Merrodine cut in.

"I bet I could."

"That's enough, Ellodine," Merrodine said firmly. "Now I need to get to work. You can show Henry around. And don't forget his appointment."

Merrodine headed off to her station. Henry watched her hands blur as she wrapped three dolls, a teddy bear, two train sets, one toy robot, a remote control car, a little girl's bakery oven, some chocolate and a board game in no time at all.

"They just appear from the ValdFyurring?" Henry asked.

"That's right," Ellodine said. "At each station you can see what you need next and call it from the ValdFyurring."

"So it's full of presents?"

"There's more than just presents. It keeps anything as long as it's not alive. Santa Claus never delivers pets. But it holds food, raw materials and weapons. There are designs in there so advanced that they won't reach the human world for decades."

"But could you get one out for yourself if you wanted?"

Ellodine shook her head.

"Each desk recognises whoever sits at it. You can't even extract presents unless you're authorised. You have to be

Klasodin or Rodin or just a couple of others to access weapons. And you can't do it without Klasodin knowing."

"What if someone learned how?"

"The ValdFyurring is flawless. How could they?"

"But it's either that or the ValdFyurring has failed."

"No Aesr would betray us." Ellodine scowled. "I know just how it happened."

"How?"

"Klasodin's staff. He can use it to access anything in the ValdFyurring and summon it to him. But there is someone else who can use it."

"You mean the human helper. Yohann." Henry felt a surge of annoyance. "Because he's human, so it must be him?"

"None of the Aesir would betray us," Ellodine insisted.

"What? Because you're all so perfect?"

"He doesn't like it here. Nobody likes him. Do you?"

"No." Henry thought. "Do you have flying snowboards in there?"

"Of course we do" Ellodine said. "But none of us use them."

"Could Yohann get a flying snowboard out on his own?"

"No. I don't think so."

"Then the traitor must be an elf."

Ellodine scowled.

"Anyway," Henry continued. "Looks like you have loads of presents left. Not exactly a disaster, is it?"

"They've stolen our best technology," Ellodine argued. "If human children don't get it from us, they will go to Omnitec for it and they will stop believing in Santa because he didn't give them the presents they wanted. You know, like you did."

Henry scowled.

"Then more Aesir will say we shouldn't be giving gifts at all," Ellodine continued, her face reddening, her tone angry. "Alvahame will collapse. Christmas will never be the same again. The children with nobody to buy them presents will get nothing." She gave Henry a sad smile. "And you know what happens to children who get nothing and start to believe no one loves them or cares about them anymore."

"All kids should have presents," Henry said with feeling.

"I think so. I would have given you all the things you asked for – and the pyjamas, the blanket and the memoirs." Suddenly there was a wicked gleam in her eye. "Come on. I want to show you something."

CHAPTER TWENTY-ONE

Ellodine stepped up to the nearest present, a couple of feet higher than the top of her head, and held out her hand to Henry.

"Stand here and hold on to me."

Henry held her hand. His face burned with embarrassment. He could see Merrodine wrapping a small pink bike with stabilisers. Her eyes were fixed on the task in hand, but a faint smile spread over her face. Henry was sure she was watching them.

He shot a glance at Ellodine, who looked right back at him. He felt a rush of excitement. He swallowed.

"Don't let go until I tell you," she told him. "I don't want you crashing into anything or going splat on the floor."

Ellodine stepped forward. Henry did the same. He stepped right up to the gold gift. They exchanged glances. They stepped forward together. Everything disappeared.

He could feel his legs and feet hanging with nothing holding him up. He was floating, suspended in the air. He opened his eyes. His stomach lurched. The floor was a very long way down. He was in a tall, cylindrical chamber as wide as the Hall of Ecromir.

Suspended in the air were columns and columns of wrapped presents. Each gift had its own slot and hung independently from the ones above and beneath. There were gaps in every column. Every gift was lit up by the seams of gold and diamonds embedded in the wooden walls, glittering like bright sunlight through windows.

Each column was a combination of five vertical stacks of single presents, making every column pentagonal and each individual gift in easy reach. Henry jumped as a wrapped present the shape of a small bike materialised in its place next to him.

Still holding hands, he and Ellodine floated gently down towards the floor.

"This is the Sleigh Room," Ellodine said excitedly. "I think this is the most amazing place in the world."

"It's incredible," Henry agreed.

"This is where every gift goes after it has been wrapped."

"How does Klasodin deliver them?"

"He goes out in his sleigh with his staff. When he is in the child's house, he uses the staff to call the gift to him."

"It's like a giant game of Tetris," said Henry, looking all about him in every possible direction. "But why do they all hang in weird places?"

"Each gift has its own position. We don't just pile them up from the bottom."

"Do you come here whenever you like?" Henry whispered, his eyes dancing from one column to the next, then flitting around the chamber.

"No. You have to be granted permission." She grinned at him. "I've been down here more than most. More than I should."

"So how does Klasodin know what gift is for which child?"

"He says the ValdFyurring and the staff do it for him," Ellodine replied. "But he knows. He could do all of it without them."

"In just one night?"

"You'll have to ask him about that."

They were sinking slowly, but the floor was still a long way down.

"Does Madjik always make you float like this?" Henry asked.

"Only inside Iddrassil." Ellodine shot him a sideways glance. There was a dangerous glint in her eye. "But we don't have to do it this slowly."

"What does that mean?"

"Hold on."

"Why. . . ?"

Henry swallowed the rest of his words. They dropped. They plummeted down towards the ground. The floor shot up at them. They were going to crash. Suddenly Ellodine tilted forward. They curved away from the floor and swooped around the circumference of the Sleigh Room. Ellodine stretched out both arms. Henry held onto her hand and stretched his out too.

They flew around the Sleigh Room, then lifted off and soared upwards. Ellodine weaved them in and out of the columns of gifts. She shot up towards the ceiling, then peeled back. They flew upside down and looped the loop. They spiralled down towards the floor and circled up.

Henry realised he was laughing out loud. The Sleigh Room span around him. Columns of gifts in their coloured paper shot towards him, then swung away as Ellodine veered in the other direction. She slowed down and circled one column after the other so they could look more closely at all the gifts.

"Look at them all," she said dreamily, thrusting upwards towards a new column, then floating down next to it.

Henry took a good look at each gift. One was a teddy bear, on top of an upright flat rectangular shape taller than Henry. It was a snooker table. It looked like it was balanced on a smaller box.

"It's a doll," said Ellodine.

"How do you know?"

"I've seen every toy, every box often enough. I know what they all are without feeling them or seeing who it's for."

"Go on then," Henry challenged her with a grin.

"Fine. So, that's a doll. That big box is a doll's house. That's a mountain bike - still in the box - needs putting together. MP3 player. Toy robot. Cricket bat. Train set. Computer game. Tablet. Headphones. Book. Board game. Snowboard. Sledge. Hat. Watch. I could do this all day."

"You can't prove any of it."

"Merrodine will tell you - I know them all."

She dropped suddenly. Henry's stomach leapt to his throat. He let out a laugh. They circled the Sleigh Room and floated gently to the floor, which looked and felt to Henry like solid gold. Ellodine checked her watch.

"It's time for us to go."

Henry knew where they were going next.

"Have you been to one of these before?" he asked.

"No. I'm only allowed in this time because I'm looking after you."

"Does Glondir usually get in?"

"I don't know."

"How do we get there?"

"There's only one way in and out of the Sleigh Room."

Ellodine placed her feet deliberately on the floor. Henry did the same. They sank through the floor and landed in a hallway with a door in front of them. Henry realised they were still holding hands. He suppressed the urge to smile. They both let go at the same time.

Ellodine swung the door open into a giant chamber with a long table in the middle. Every elf belonging to the Council of the Aesir was already there, including Merrodine, who took up her place as Head of Giving. Klasodin sat at the head of the table in his high-backed chair. Rodin beckoned Henry and

Ellodine in and gestured them to sit on chairs set against the wall next to Amira.

Henry felt every pair of eyes follow him as he sat down.

Klasodin gave him a subtle smile. Blond-haired Salvodin from the Craft of Creation was a friendly face. But Henry did not find many others. Most members of the Council of the Aesir did not look pleased to see him.

CHAPTER TWENTY-TWO

"Now the human is here, the Council can get down to why it has been convened," said an elf with greying red hair, his face riddled with lines and creases.

"That's Gronodin," Ellodine whispered, "one of the original travellers from Vanahame. He's Klasodin's oldest friend and his second-in-command."

Gronodin looked straight at Henry. His eyes narrowed.

"For a start, I will not call him Glondir. I still take exception to you handing out Hafskods without any forewarning, Klasodin. Not to mention giving gifts to a child on the Black List."

"It needed to be done," Klasodin said plainly. "The five children are the Valdiri. Henry is Glondir."

"Not in my eyes he's not. And why you gave him anything is beyond me."

"It saved his life."

"You still shouldn't have done it."

"THERE SHOULDN'T BE A BLACK LIST IN THE FIRST PLACE," Klasodin roared, his face reddening. He thumped the table with his fist, making a couple of elves jump. "All children should receive presents. If you want to cut back, try not giving everything to the ones with the longest lists."

"If they deserve it, they should have everything." Gronodin insisted.

"You still don't understand, do you?" Klasodin shook his head. "The damage you do by spoiling children, or by not showing love to those who need it most. We are not here to reward them, we show them love by giving them gifts."

"We can't do it anymore. The ValdFyurring is failing."

"There is nothing wrong with it," Klasodin snapped.

Gronodin grimaced. He leaned back in his chair and folded his arms. The lines and wrinkles on his face made Klasodin's second-in-command look tired and thin.

"Orek," he sighed. "You talk some sense into him."

Orek leaned forward, his long, unkempt grey hair hanging around his face, his spectacles resting on the top of his head.

"We've lost some of our most modern designs. Our equivalent to the Omnitec Quickfire is gone. Televisions, mobile phones and tablets are gone. Is it a coincidence that these specific items have vanished? I don't know. The ValdFyurring is functioning at a slower rate and it is taking us longer to produce the gifts we do have."

"The Margullring is weaker," Rodin added. "We're vulnerable."

"Which supports what I am trying to say here," said Gronodin. "Our Madjik simply cannot cope with the excessive demands placed upon it by modern day human children. We have to cut back."

"We haven't had a Glondir," Klasodin interjected. "And there is a very good reason why the ValdFyurring is not performing."

"How likely is it that an Aesr or Aesrine, one of our own, could have betrayed us?" Gronodin demanded, glaring at Klasodin, then looking round the table.

"There are so few of us who could even attempt such an act," Orek said. "But to delete entire designs. I mean, we're building again from scratch. Even the prototypes are gone. It's taking time. Who could even do that? Apart from Klasodin?"

Rodin jumped to his feet.

"How dare you?" he snapped.

"I'm just saying." Orek held up his hands in defence. "I think it's impossible. I mean who here would know where to start? How many of us could even access them?"

"A select few in this room," Klasodin replied.

"You're not suggesting it's one of us?" Gronodin said incredulously.

Henry looked around the room. Every elf was silent.

"We have tried to fathom the causes." Ullnir the gadget specialist spoke up - in the same plain, robotic tone Henry had heard in the Hall of Ecromir. "We have worked together across the Crafts."

"It does seem as if the ValdFyurring is on the wane," Salvodin agreed. "There are no signs of failure, other than it appears to have reached its capacity."

Klasodin snorted in disgust.

"What are the chances of the ValdFyurring functioning at full capacity before Christmas Eve?" Gronodin asked.

"Next to none," said Ullnir stated. "And even if it does, it will be too late to produce everything we need."

"Not to mention time to wrap and prepare every gift," Salvodin added.

"I think it is safe to say that we will not be delivering every present we initially planned," Gronodin sighed. "I say we vote. All those in agreement that we instate the Gold List as of now."

"Now hang on," said Rodin. "There are other solutions."

"None of which can be reached in time," said Orek.

Rodin glared at him.

Gronodin raised his hand. Orek raised his. Every other council member followed suit - except Klasodin, Merrodine and Rodin. Even blonde Larodine from the Craft of Care reluctantly raised her hand.

"MUM," Ellodine gasped.

"I'm sorry, dear," Larodine said quietly. "We have no choice."

"It isn't your place to shout out," Gronodin reprimanded her.

"Don't speak to her like that," Klasodin snapped. "You've just ruined thousands of children's lives. Don't add her to the list."

He got up, hauled open a door behind him, marched out and slammed it shut.

Silence.

"Well done," Rodin said dryly. "You have just ruined Christmas."

"Next you'll be accusing me," Gronodin answered him.

"Not a bad place to start," Rodin shot back.

"Now hold on," Gronodin protested.

"There is a saboteur," Rodin insisted.

"I find that unlikely," said Orek. "Who would have the know-how?"

"You would be another," Rodin accused him.

"Unbelievable," Amira blurted.

Rodin turned around, his expression suggesting he had forgotten she was there. He cleared his throat.

"We have proof there is a traitor working with Omnitec," he said quietly. "It is why we brought Henry here." He aimed a scowl at Gronodin. "Shame you had to drive Klasodin out before he could be heard."

"Nobody drove him out," Gronodin insisted. "He left of his own accord."

"We both know that isn't true," Merrodine said coldly.

"Fine." Gronodin sat back in his chair and folded his arms. "Present this evidence."

"We went to rescue Henry," Rodin reported. "The Gaardreng were lying in wait. They had no way of knowing when we would arrive or which route we would take."

"Hardly proof, but continue."

"Their weapons," Rodin grated, "were only human technology in part. There was Madjik. Just sharing it with them breaks one of the three Foundations."

"We know Alvahame law," Gronodin shrugged. "Where is the proof?"

"Are you suggesting I am a liar? A second ago you couldn't even consider the possibility of a traitor."

"I find it hard to believe."

"Their technology could be further ahead than we thought," Orek suggested.

"Flying snowboards," Rodin said, his voice louder. "Crossbows that replenished their rounds automatically with no magazine or quiver. A crossbow that fires Azmar out of the air and almost blew us out of the sky."

"There's no need to shout," said Amira.

"There is every need." Rodin's voice was gentle. He glared at Gronodin and Orek. "And the more you protest, the more convinced I am. There is a traitor. Someone is sabotaging us from the inside. And it is someone here in this room."

"No prizes for guessing who you think it is." Amira jumped to her feet and strode out, slamming the door behind her.

Rodin watched her leave. He looked like he had been slapped in the face. He turned and scowled at Orek.

"No wonder you wanted her here - to have your daughter fight your battles for you. A low blow indeed. The kind of behaviour I would expect of a traitor."

After that, the meeting of the Council of the Aesir descended into a shouting match. Merrodine rose swiftly from her seat and ushered Henry and Ellodine from the room, ordering them to go home at once.

Ellodine led Henry to the base of The Hollow, then headed for her home in Hamedall muttering about traitors and stupid grown-ups.

Henry was soon on the roof of his bedroom, one middle point jutting out of the star, leaning back against the wall that formed the top point. He was cocooned in his purple blanket, his pyjamas on under his clothes. He gazed up at the clear night sky lit up with innumerable gleaming stars and let out a contented sigh. He would never get bored of such a sight.

The glow from the gold star gave Henry enough light to read. He pulled out Klasodin's memoirs, determined to find out what else Klasodin wanted him to know.

CHAPTER TWENTY-THREE

Klasodin wandered the earth as a cloaked horseman, resting every night to allow Slepnir to race through the darkest skies in his true form, hunting animals and birds for sport. He shared the spoils with Klasodin and watched with disgust as Klasodin cooked his portion over an open fire.

One night, Slepnir was chasing a particularly shifty owl, soaring over the houses of a village in the hills near the Black Forest in Germany, when something caught Klasodin's eye. With the greatest reluctance in the world, Slepnir pulled up whilst firing an angry, murderous glare after the escaping owl, and descended towards the open window of a small wooden house on the edge of the village.

On the sill of the open window was a plate of oats, raw carrots and a cooked chicken leg next to a bowl of water and a glass of milk. On the window frame was a child's chalk drawing of a man in a long beard and a thick coat riding an eight-legged flying horse. Neither Klasodin nor Slepnir were hungry - they had eaten particularly well that day - but it seemed impolite not to eat the food laid out for them, so they finished everything on the sill.

Inside, the room was sparse. On the worn wooden floor, against the bare far wall, lay a small bed. A tiny shape was curled up on the bed under a blanket. Klasodin closed the window before they left.

"A child," he whispered to Slepnir, as they flew away. "A child left it for us with no desire for anything in return and no concern for their own safety. It appears we were not as careful as we thought. Perhaps we should leave the mountains of Europe for a while."

But after such an experience, Klasodin did not want to leave. Wary of trying the same village again so soon, the next night he landed Slepnir in the middle of a muddy street running through a small town of wooden houses and chalets nestled in the Alps. Pulling his cloak around him, hiding his features and ears with his hair, Klasodin rode slowly through the town and saw a light ahead. Slepnir morphed into his four-legged form and they kept riding.

The house with the light was more like a shack. The door was hanging off its hinges and the wood was rotting. As Klasodin gazed at it, the door creaked open slowly and a young man emerged carrying a lantern. He put the door back carefully, then stepped off the veranda and made his way down the street towards Klasodin, his head down and his shoulders hunched. Suddenly he looked up with raw, tearstained eyes and saw Klasodin.

"What troubles you, young man?" Klasodin asked him gently. He did not want to frighten him.

"I have just experienced the worst night of my life, good sir. At least, it is the worst so far, as my life promises to slide into a constant state of decline."

"And why is that?"

"I have just lost my true love." The young man sobbed and wiped his nose on a dirty handkerchief.

"Does she not return your love?"

"On the contrary, she loves me more than ever."

"Why is your love lost?"

"Because she cannot marry me," the young man wept.

"Will her father not allow it?"

The man took a couple of shuddering sobs, then a deep breath.

"Her father is as a father to me as well. Nothing would please him more than our marriage. But he is a poor man. A widower with three daughters. He cannot afford a dowry and without a marriage settlement, we cannot wed. Worse still, my Gwendolin is the oldest daughter. If she cannot be married, then she must be sold into slavery." The young man's face disappeared behind his handkerchief. "This was the last time I shall ever see her." He collapsed onto his knees and wept.

Klasodin's heart melted.

The young man climbed to his feet and hurried away, apologising for burdening a stranger with his troubles. Slepnir trotted towards the house without Klasodin having to ask. Slepnir stopped at the rickety wooden steps and turned to look at Klasodin, a meaningful look in his eyes.

He dismounted Slepnir and crept up to the window. The sound of a young woman sobbing desperately attacked his ears before he could see inside the shack. By the light of one lantern on a rickety old table, an old man sat in his rocking chair, rocking slightly, as his daughter knelt beside him on the floor, her face hidden by her hands and resting on his knee. Klasodin watched as Gwendolin's father stroked her head with his hand, doing all he could to comfort her. He had nothing else to offer.

So consumed was Klasodin by the picture before him, that he did not notice someone else come into the room, whose eyes were immediately drawn to the bearded stranger at the window. She jumped and caught her breath. Gwendolin and her father looked up from their sorrow. Then a third young woman appeared and gaped at him as well.

"I beg your pardon," Klasodin began. "I did not mean to intrude. I was simply drawn to the only light in the town."

"Please, come in, stranger," said the old man, getting carefully to his feet and opening the front door. He ushered

Klasodin inside without giving him a chance to refuse. "How can we help you?"

"I am travelling into the mountains and I have lost my way."

"You must be tired and hungry," said the old man, ushering Klasodin into his rocking chair. Klasodin sat down carefully. It didn't look like it would take much weight. "My name is Ullrich. These are my daughters - Gwendolin, Beatrice and Persephone."

Klasodin didn't have a chance to greet the three young ladies, who were already rushing around preparing food for the stranger. He watched Persephone hurry out with carrots and water for Slepnir.

They all sat around the table as Klasodin ate. Again, he wasn't particularly hungry, but he knew it would be wrong to refuse. It was a sparse meal: the bread was stale, the chicken was no longer fresh and water was all they had to drink. But after seeing the effort his hosts had gone to, Klasodin enjoyed his meal.

"I cannot thank you enough," he began, ashamed at taking what little they had.

"Oh no, I won't hear of it," Ullrich replied. "We must thank you." The daughters all nodded their agreement. "Tonight has been a night of great sorrow for us and we are very grateful for the distraction."

"Please, tell me your troubles," said Klasodin, anxious to do something for them in return, but the family all shook their heads.

"That would be no way to treat a guest," Ullrich laughed.

With that, they all left the table, ushered Klasodin into the only bedroom in the house and shut the door behind him. Klasodin did as his hosts asked. He lay on the bed and rested. Despite groaning under his weight, it was comfortable, but he was in no mood to sleep. He opened the window and gazed out *at the stars. They were just as beautiful when viewed from Ullrich's tiny house as they would be from any other. He peered through the door at the family of four, sleeping on makeshift straw mattresses on the floor in the living quarters. He looked towards the fireplace, knowing that with one wave of his staff, he could have a great fire roaring. But he did not want to give himself away. He glanced over at Slepnir peering in through the window and knew they were of one mind.*

Early in the morning, while the family still slept, Klasodin took his staff and filled the fireplace with chopped wood. With one more flick of the wrist, the fire roared.

Slepnir appeared at the window and dropped a boar and a pig at the door. They were soon roasting on a spit above the fire.

Ullrich's family awoke to the great feast and Klasodin enjoyed one last meal with them. When they had eaten, he waited until Ullrich's attention was elsewhere, then produced a stack of gold with a flick of his staff and left it by the fireplace.

"What is your name, stranger?" Gwendolin was watching him.

"My name is Sin Ni Klas," he replied.

"Saint Nicklas," she said.

Klasodin nodded. It sounded like a good human name.

"I knew there was something different about you."

Klasodin gestured towards the gold.

"A gift for you and your family."

"We didn't ask for anything in return," said Gwendolin.

"I know," Klasodin replied, a smile on his face. "I gave it to you anyway, because I wanted to. I don't ask for anything in return either."

With that, he left, as any traveller would.

CHAPTER TWENTY-FOUR

To leave the gold wasn't enough. Klasodin arrived in town the next evening to hear a loud shout of delight. The door to Ullrich's home flew open. The same young man tore down the muddy street, jumping in the air and shouting at the top of his voice.

Ullrich was a sensible man, not given to extravagance or overblown demonstrations of wealth. He repaired the rickety front door and there was a roaring fire every night. He bought the land next door and started building a house for Gwendolin and her betrothed, who both joined him early each morning to start the work.

Klasodin returned every night for several months. Gwendolin's new home took shape. Excitement built in the town. Lights stayed on later. Visitors chatted excitedly around Ullrich's table. More people turned up to work on the house and only reluctantly put down their tools at night.

One night Klasodin tore himself away. Slepnir soared through the night sky, before swooping down and landing next to a familiar open window. Just like last time, it was dark inside, but there was a plate with carrots, oats and chicken beside a bowl of water and a glass of milk.

Slepnir helped himself to the oats. Klasodin tucked into the chicken. Suddenly he stopped. Someone was watching him. A pair of beady eyes gazed up at him. The little girl stood up straight and climbed onto a chair to get a better look at him.

"I knew you would come back," she whispered. "I saw you flying in the sky."

"Thank you for this wonderful food," Klasodin smiled. "What is your name?"

"Eva," the little girl replied, feeding a carrot to Slepnir. "What's his name?"

"He's called Slepnir."

"Hello Slepnir," she whispered. She stroked his nose and he lowered his head so she could stroke his mane. "You've only got four legs today." She looked up at Klasodin. "What's your name?"

"My name is Sin Te Klas," he said quietly.

"Santa Claus," she said.

It seemed as good a name as any.

When Klasodin next returned to visit Ullrich, the winter festival was approaching. Slepnir's hooves trudged through the snow. Something caught Klasodin's eye. A window was open. He steered Slepnir to the right to investigate. On the window sill was a plate of carrots, a bowl of steaming hot vegetable soup, a bowl of water and a cup of hot tea. Klasodin peered inside and saw one big bed with two small shapes wrapped in blankets.

After finishing what was on the sill, Klasodin and Slepnir took a detour around the little snow-covered town and found five more open windows, each with food and drink for man and horse. One had a blanket and a brush for Slepnir's coat. Another had a flagon of whisky which Slepnir seemed to think was for him. Klasodin tucked it away in his cloak and promised to share it when there was no more flying to be done. Ullrich's window was open, with two glasses of hot wine standing on the sill.

Klasodin finished the hot wine and surveyed the building work next door. The foundations and floor were laid with a veranda and steps leading down to the street, but it was all covered in snow. Klasodin glanced around him to make sure nobody was watching. With a wave of his staff, the snow disappeared from the floor. Twenty seconds later, there were walls, a first floor and a roof.

"Ride Slepnir through the village," Eva whispered on his next visit, after he had finished his food. Her eyes were sparkling and she was so excited, she could barely keep still. "Come back when you've seen it," she breathed.

Six tiny houses had open windows with food waiting for Klasodin and Slepnir, all with sleeping children inside.

"I kept your secret," Eva whispered upon his return. "I told them you were shy, that you only ever visit when they are asleep, so they didn't stay up to wait for you."

A month later and word of the kind-hearted travelling stranger had spread to nearby villages. Thirty more children had left an open window offering food and drink.

As the day of Gwendolin's wedding approached, Ullrich's street was draped in flags, flowers and bunting. A fir tree had appeared in the middle of the street and wreaths were hung on the houses. The winter festival was only two days away.

Ullrich awoke the next morning to find the new house had mysteriously been finished during the night and there was enough wood piled up outside to burn roaring fires all winter. Klasodin did not appear for the wedding, but chose to watch from the hills as the entire town joined to celebrate in the snow.

Henry struggled to keep his eyes open. His head lolled. His arms, his hands and the pages were heavy. He let them fall. He fell asleep.

Everything moved. The star shook. Alvahame shook. It was an earthquake - swallowing the city whole. No. Only he was moving. Someone was pushing him with their hands. Shaking him. Trying to wake him up.

He jerked awake. He blinked. The sun was bright. The sky was a deep blue. A hand shook him by the shoulder.

Ellodine was kneeling next to him. Her eyes were red. Tears streamed down her face and dripped onto Henry's blanket.

"I thought you'd gone as well." Her voice was broken.

"No. I . . . What?"

"It took me ages to find you? Why are you out here?"

"I was reading. I . . . What?"

Ellodine slumped down next to him.

"It's Klasodin. He's gone. And nobody knows where he is."

CHAPTER TWENTY-FIVE

A bowl of warm porridge was waiting for Henry on the coffee table, but there was no sign of Merrodine. He shovelled it down, then followed Ellodine down the Hollow. It was as busy as the previous day, with elves hurrying to work and school, but the Hollow was deathly quiet. There was a sombre mood in class. Monira came in, her face grave.

"Gronodin is to address the city from the Hall of Ecromir."

The classroom darkened. An image of the Hall of Ecromir appeared in front of them on the classroom wall, curving around them.

Gronodin stood in front of the gold fir tree with the Council of the Aesir gathered behind him. His face looked more wrinkled and tired than it did in the Council Chamber.

The seats around the walls of the Hall of Ecromir were filled. It looked like an Amphitheatre and Gronodin was the performer. Henry noticed Rodin in the background - his face was like thunder.

"Some time in the night, Klasodin disappeared from Alvahame, his staff with him," Gronodin announced. "And yet more designs have vanished from the ValdFyurring. Delivering any gifts at all this year has just become a hundred times more difficult. We now have to take drastic action. As of right now, the Gold List comes into effect."

Rumbles and murmurs swept around the Hall of Ecromir. Rodin looked like he wanted to tear Gronodin's head off.

"School is suspended until further notice. Children are to help in any way they can. Their teachers can advise further. And nobody is to leave Alvahame. Anyone attempting to leave will be sent back by the Guards."

Klasodin's second-in-command took a breath.

"I am sorry it has come to this, but we are left with very little choice. If we all pull together, perhaps this Christmas can still be a success. Thank you."

The rumbles and murmurs rose in volume around Gronodin. They turned to shouts. Angry tirades bellowed. Questions were fired at him. Gronodin held up his hands to stem the tide. The image vanished.

Silence.

"I want you all to report to Merrodine at once." Monira's voice trembled. Her face was pale. "She will assign you your duties."

They all filed out. A thought struck Henry. He had the memoirs. They wouldn't need him in Alvahame. Maybe he could find Klasodin for them.

"Wait here," he murmured to Ellodine. "I forgot something."

He leapt off the platform and flew up The Hollow as fast as he could. He landed on the Star's platform, raced up the stairs to his room and found what he needed. He grabbed his coat and threw his snowboard on his back. He turned to leave, but stopped.

In the corner of his room was a small Christmas tree with a single present underneath, wrapped in gold paper. The tag read "To Henry, from Santa Claus."

He hadn't seen it earlier. A parting gift from Klasodin? A rush of excitement surged through him. His heart pounded. He tore through the paper and opened the box.

A sleek Omnitec Shoot camera. Eighteen mega pixels. Big screen. Chrome finish. Small and slim enough to fit in his trouser pocket. The long life internal battery was charged and ready to go.

But Klasodin never gave Omnitec gifts. The Aesir made their own equivalents. What would one even be doing in Alvahame?

It was just what Henry wanted. He didn't have his old camera with him. He didn't have anything anymore. Why shouldn't he keep it?

Henry shoved the new camera in his pocket, tore down the stairs and leapt down The Hollow. He landed next to Ellodine, who was arguing with Balnir.

"Happy?" Ellodine grated.

"No," Balnir retorted. "Who wanted this? And don't say there's a traitor."

"If the ValdFyurring lost those designs because it couldn't cope, why didn't it lose more?" Ellodine demanded. "Why has it worked fine since? And why does this only happen at night when nobody's using it?"

They dropped down The Hollow after hundreds of Aesir school children, all discussing the same thing. They landed. Everyone surged towards the stairs. Ellodine nudged Henry and pointed.

Amira beckoned and gestured to them to follow her. They pushed their way through the crowds out into the quiet stables where Rodin and Equodin waited.

"I meant just you two," Rodin objected.

Henry turned around and realised Balnir, Forodin, Raiodin, Zadira and Rimida had followed them.

"Sorry," Rimida muttered, and turned to leave.

"If something's going on," said Forodin, holding her back, "then why have two, when there are seven of us?"

"What do you need, Lord Rodin?" said Raiodin.

"I can't get out of Alvahame, but we have to find Klasodin and we need his staff," Rodin said. "I don't know if something happened to him or if he left of his own accord."

"He wouldn't ever leave," Ellodine insisted.

"You think one of our own is a traitor?" said Balnir.

"I have no doubt," Rodin replied.

"The Gaardreng have Madjik in their weapons," Henry added.

"Omnitec has Madjik?" Balnir said in a small voice. "But that means one of us gave it to them."

Rodin bent down to Henry's level.

"I cannot leave Alvahame, but you can. Klasodin has disappeared with his staff. Yohann is gone as well. Start with him. For all we know he has the staff."

Henry nodded.

"We'll go," said Ellodine, her board already in her hand.

Henry held out his hand. His snowboard flew off his back and slapped into it.

"Nice," Forodin grinned.

"Appodin guards the South Passage," Rodin continued. "Perrodin will let you through at Hamedall. Then you're on your own."

"We could go with them," Raiodin offered.

Rodin shook his head.

"One elf youngling and one human won't be cause for concern. If seven are seen leaving, the entire Aesir Guard will come after you."

"We'll get them out," said Balnir. "They won't suspect us."

Rodin patted Balnir on the shoulder.

"Are you sure depriving children of presents is really your calling?"

"You don't think it is?"

"No."

Balnir looked like he had been slapped in the face.

Amira gave Ellodine a squeeze. She threw her arms around Henry, then followed Rodin back into The Hollow.

"Will you need the reindeer?" Equodin asked.

"No. We'll stick to snowboards," Ellodine answered.

Vega stamped and snorted irritably.

"Next time," Henry called to him.

The six young Aesir and Henry slid out of the stable and up the avenue to the South Passage. Henry and Forodin brought up the rear, following the rest as the avenue grew steeper and headed away from the centre of the city. Forodin weaved left and right next to Henry, his eyes darting in every direction.

Suddenly Forodin shot straight at Henry. He collided with him. Henry flew through the air and landed in deeper snow four metres away. Forodin landed next to him. An arrow crunched into the snow where Henry had been. A second zipped through the air and landed next to it. The others dived for cover. A scattering of arrows dotted around the snow. Then they stopped. Henry lay in the snow. The others stood stock still, looking around them.

Henry saw it coming from the direction of Iddrassil. An arrow shot into the snow in front of him. Another just missed his foot.

Everyone scrambled for safety. Another arrow whistled past Rimida's head. Henry propelled himself away and slammed against the wall of the nearest wooden house. He watched more arrows rain down on the snow in front of him.

Balnir peeked out. An arrow shot past his face.

Raiodin hauled him back.

"Someone's actually trying to kill us," Balnir said indignantly.

With Raiodin leading, they slid single file, hugging the side of the line of terraced houses, edging their way up the avenue. Forodin shoved Henry ahead of him, constantly looking back as they slid up the mountainside.

Arrows spattered in the snow just a metre away.

"He's changed his position," Forodin called.

Henry heard more arrows thud against the rooftop above. Something heavy slid. A load of snow fell off the roof and dumped on his head. Everyone else muttered and shouted as the snow covered them.

Henry brushed the freezing snow off his face and looked back over Forodin's shoulder. Some of Iddrassil's branches hung out past the end of the avenue where he could see them, but there was no sign of anyone.

They edged their way up the avenue.

More arrows bulleted into the snow in front of them.

Henry shot a glance back over Forodin's shoulder.

A hooded figure emerged on a branch. He aimed a gold bow at them.

"He can see us," Henry shouted.

An arrow shot straight at him. Henry ducked. It darted into the wooden wall behind him. Forodin gave him a shove up the avenue.

They all peeled from the wall and slid carefully up the mountainside.

An arrow shot past Henry's ear.

Another arrow grazed Forodin's shoulder.

Henry remembered his Hafskod.

An arrow flew past his face.

The shield shot from his Hafskod over his forearm. He let Forodin overtake him. He saw an arrow coming. It clanged against the shield.

"Just watch the arrows," came Forodin's voice.

A hand grabbed his right wrist and hauled him up the hill. Henry fixed his eyes on the next arrows, beating them away with his shield, flying backwards up the hill. The archer on the branch was getting smaller. His next arrow shot into the snow just behind Henry's snowboard. They veered suddenly with the curve of the avenue and the archer was gone. Henry spun himself around.

"Nice move," Forodin murmured. "The thing with the shield wasn't bad either."

They sped away on their snowboards and weaved their way through the maze of curved avenues. As they reached the turn onto the avenue that would take them out of Alvahame, Forodin flew ahead, then banked and waved to the rest to slow down.

They skidded to a halt in a flurry of snow. Zadira stopped sharply in front of Forodin and sent a blast of snow into his face.

"There are four guards as you leave the basin," Forodin grinned, hurling snow at Zadira. "Appodin's one of them."

"There are four of them?" Rimida gasped. "What are we going to do? They'll catch us. We'll all get in trouble. Ellodine and Henry will never get out."

"We'll have to fight our way out," said Raiodin with wild eyes.

Forodin met Henry's glance and rolled his eyes.

"No," said Balnir. "They just need a distraction. If we can avert the attention of the other three guards, Ellodine and Henry can leave safely. Appodin and Perrodin can take care of the rest." He looked down appraisingly at Henry. "You're pretty good on your snowboard already. Can you make a dash for it at the right moment?"

Henry nodded.

"Of course we can," Ellodine insisted.

"Good," Balnir replied. "I have a plan."

CHAPTER TWENTY-SIX

A snowball shot out of nowhere and struck Alrodin in the face. He hit the snow with a grunt. Appodin and the other two guards drew their weapons in a flash and looked about them. Were they under attack?

"Rimida," a young female voice shouted. "You missed."

Five young Aesir spilled onto the avenue, laughing and joking, hurling snowballs at each other. Appodin recognised them straightaway. Something dawned on him.

"What are they doing up here?" he snapped, faking as much anger as he could. "Send them to Iddrassil."

Alrodin jumped to his feet, muttering and cursing, and followed the other two after the children. An argument ensued. A shouting match echoed over the snow. The guards and the younglings disappeared.

Two shapes emerged from under the snow, just where the avenue started to curve out of sight. Henry and Ellodine shot up on their snowboards.

"Thank you, Appodin."

"You're welcome young Ellodine, Glondir. Now get going before they come back."

The two younglings shot up the incline, crested the peak and headed out of sight, towards Hamedall.

Perrodin stood aside as they slid through Hamedall.

They shot through the Margullring. Henry sped behind Ellodine over the expansive snowy plain he had crossed in the sleigh. It stretched on and on as Henry flew over the snow. He felt light and weightless, like he could take off and fly away. A numb, giddy euphoria breezed through his brain.

The snow plain came to a sudden stop ahead. Henry snapped out of his reverie and slowed down. Ellodine flew at the edge.

The steep path appeared, carving downwards through the cliff. Henry's snowboard tipped down onto the path. His stomach lurched. He shot down. It was so steep. The cliff walls flying past him made it seem even quicker. Ellodine crouched on her snowboard to go faster. Henry let out a laugh and crouched low on his board.

He tore out of the path and over the expanse of snow ahead. He flew over the vast snowy plain, the first he had crossed in Rodin's sleigh.

He slid after Ellodine up the mountain. The screen of cloud appeared suddenly at the peak and Henry shot through it. He was flying through the air. He had no idea where the ground was.

He heard Ellodine's snowboard crunch down onto the snow. He bent his knees slightly, ready to take the impact, and landed with ease. The cloud disappeared. The bright sunlight gleamed off the white landscape. Henry shielded his eyes until they got used to it.

"We're leaving the elven realm?" he said, pulling up alongside Ellodine. "Where are we going?"

"Mannhame," she said. "Technically, it's in the elven realm, but you have to cross a small part of the Arctic to get to it."

"It's like an island?"

"That's right. Keeps everything safer that way."

"What is Mannhame?"

"It's a separate settlement. Yohann lives there. If he does have something to hide, it'll be there."

Henry checked his Hafskod. There were no dancing flames. He followed Ellodine as she angled left and headed what Henry assumed must be east. Her trajectory straightened out. She slowed down so he was just a metre behind her, then sped up again, leaving a trail of flying snow in her wake, which blew straight at Henry.

Henry sped up. He caught up to her and shot past. She chased after him. They flew over the snow, aiming for the distant mountains, chasing each other, weaving in and out, leaving interwoven patterns in the snow behind them.

Hills and mountains rose up on either side. They followed a valley cutting through them, pursuing and racing up one side then the other, their paths meandering and entwining, until the mountains on either side began to sink back into the snow. The peak to their right shrank down to the size of a hill, then to nothing more than a gentle rising slope. Ellodine gestured to Henry. She banked right, the side of her snowboard carving a groove in the deep snow, and headed over the slope.

It stretched ahead of them, bordered by hills on its left, and mountains, which rose once more out of the snow on their right. The slope plateaued suddenly and they shot into a screen of cloud which appeared from nowhere.

Henry couldn't see a thing but grey cloud in his face. He fixed his trajectory, concentrating on the two sounds of his and Ellodine's snowboards sliding through the snow, hoping he would still see her to his left when they emerged from the cloud.

The cloud disappeared suddenly. She was still beside him. He looked back at the grey screen behind them, then kept going. They slid up another gentle climb. A screen of cloud appeared in the distance. The closer they slid, Henry could see it wasn't cloud, but a wall of ice, stretching as far as he could see in every direction. The Hafskod beamed in recognition of where they were. Henry flew through the ice screen.

The snowboards started downhill. There was a scattering of fir trees ahead.

"Who else lives here?" he asked.

"Anyone who needs to be near Alvahame but wants to live outside of it," Ellodine called back to him. "I think Klasodin found it. They started building here when Alvahame was finished."

"But who would live here and not in Alvahame?" Henry questioned.

"A lot of human helpers end up living here. Or when an elf and a human fall in love and have children - they live here."

"But the Aesir themselves never just up and leave?"

"It doesn't happen much."

"So they don't like humans living in Alvahame?"

"Of course they do. They just seem to like it better here." Ellodine caught Henry's look. "Very few humans even know about our city. The ones who live and work here will always be outnumbered."

"So is this where I'll end up?"

Ellodine scowled.

"Live where you like."

The silver fir trees grew in number, springing up all around them the further down the slope they ventured. Ellodine moved in front of him.

"Follow me and stay in my path," she said. "It's like thick forest down the bottom."

She slowed down to a relaxed speed and weaved casually in and out of the trees. Henry followed her, doing exactly as she did. The forest thickened around them, forcing Ellodine and Henry into a lot of tight turns, their snowboards thrown upwards by thick roots jutting out of the ground. Henry stretched out his arms, pushing himself away from the tree trunks when he veered too close. He shoved one too hard. His shoulder collided with the next and spun him around. He slowed down and let Ellodine take a couple more metres on him.

Eventually the slope eased off and the trees thinned out. Ellodine slid gently down the rest and came to a stop in a curved bay protected by trees, before the snow met the water's edge. Henry skidded to a halt next to her.

They stood on the shore of a still lake, which glistened in the sunlight like a silver sheet. It was surrounded on all sides by tall fir trees sweeping down to it on the side of the surrounding hills. Large stone houses with pointed roofs were hidden among the trees. The more Henry looked, the more he could see. Some were right on the water's edge with their own wooden jetties. Others sat further back with tracks leading through the forest to the water's edge.

Henry wandered closer. The lake had frozen to thick ice. Some patches shone brighter than others. Ice stars sent jagged fingers through the frozen silver surface. He stepped closer, his eyes following the patterns.

Suddenly Ellodine grabbed his arm and yanked him back.

"I wasn't going to fall in," he protested.

"I know," she hissed. "Stay out of sight. And keep your voice down." She crept forward and pointed around a tree trunk to a large, four-storey stone house set back from the lake, looking out over its own garden. "That's where Yohann lives."

"He lives there?" Henry said in amazement. "How? It's huge."

"He asked for a big house here. Klasodin gave it to him. No human helper has ever moved out here so quickly."

"That's weird, right?" Henry frowned.

"Very." Ellodine picked up her board. It shrank and she threw it onto her back. Henry did the same. She picked a path through the trees, heading around the lake towards Yohann's abode. "I don't trust him and I want to look around before he sees us."

Henry followed her through the trees, picking a path up and away from the lake so they circled around the back of the house, then headed down to it from above. A track through the hills led down to the empty paved driveway at the back of Yohann's home. Ellodine crept up the driveway and peered in through the window.

"The television's on. Someone's in there. Doesn't look like he has visitors."

She strode up to the door and banged her fists on it.

Henry swallowed. For some reason, he had a feeling the visit wasn't going to go as smoothly as he hoped.

CHAPTER TWENTY-SEVEN

A heavy duty bolt scraped back. A lock clicked. The door swung open. Yohann peered around it. He grinned.

"Oh look. The boy with my watch. Come in."

Yohann still wore the thin gold band around his wrist.

"Where's the Klasodin's staff, Yohann?" Ellodine demanded, marching in.

Henry followed. Yohann shut and locked the door behind them. The hairs stood up on the back of Henry's neck. His stomach hollowed with nerves. His eyes darted everywhere as he followed Ellodine past a winding staircase and a couple of closed doors into a large open plan area with double-doors opening out onto the garden and the frozen lake beyond. There was a kitchen area to his right. To his left, there were two giant flat screen TVs fixed to the wall. Below, shelves were piled with toys and games, games consoles and toy guns.

Yohann stood in front of the TVs. Sensors on the wall flashed as they detected him. The holographic forest Henry had seen in the Craft of Creation burst into life around him. Yohann turned around.

"You two want to play? You can get as many as four players on this. We can take down the Nerivari. I don't know what the Aesir are so afraid of."

"I've heard some terrifying stories," Ellodine said coldly. "Pray to Odin you never meet one."

"Guess I'll play by myself then."

"Where's Klasodin's staff?" Ellodine demanded.

"I don't have it," Yohann said. "Haven't seen it for ages."

"When did you last see it?"

"Dunno." Yohann shrugged. "Week ago maybe. Klasodin had it last. Not me."

Ellodine muttered under her breath. She turned and ran upstairs. There was a crash, then more thudding as she ran from room to room.

"She won't find it," Yohann said casually. "I told her."

Yohann closed his fingers around a holographic sword. He crouched as a band of Nerivari charged. He swung and stabbed. Soon the Nerivari lay dead around him. Yohann waved a hand. A menu came up.

Ellodine's feet pounded up another flight of stairs.

"I'm bored of this one." Yohann waved a hand. A menu appeared on one screen. "You should see this new game." The words "NINJA WARRIOR" flashed up in front of him. He chose his weapon - a ninja sword. Henry jumped. A group of ninja warriors in all black, an array of deadly weapons in their hands, circled Yohann. He grinned. "It's not out anywhere yet. But I got a copy."

Yohann spun, punched and kicked, then slashed at one ninja and ran a second through.

Ellodine pounded back down the stairs.

"There's nothing in this house - just a bed and clothes on the floor in one room. Does anyone else live here? Do you just come here to play games?" She saw the screens. Her eyes widened. "Nobody gets to take this out of the Craft of Creation."

"I did." Yohann looked at them both. "Still not impressed? Alright, try this."

He grabbed a chrome snowboard from the corner and placed it where he had been standing. He chose "NINJA

WARRIOR 2100" from the menu. A modern city flashed up around him. He jumped on his snowboard. It rose into the air. His sword became a light sabre. More warriors on flying snowboards flew at him. Yohann flew, twisting one way, then the other.

Ellodine marched forward and shoved Yohann off his board. Yohann crashed to the floor. The game stopped. Ellodine grabbed the board and hit him with it.

"Ow!" he yelled, throwing his arms in the way to protect himself.

"Where did you get this from?" she shouted.

"Gerroff."

She beat him with his snowboard as he cowered on the floor.

"Where did you get it from?" she shouted. "Where?"

Yohann curled up into a ball and didn't answer.

Henry checked his Hafskod. There were no dancing flames. The watch face was clouding over. The black clouds grew in front of his eyes, closing in on the centre.

"That's why you're not surprised to see us," he said. "You're in with Omnitec. Omnitec gave you this stuff. You stole the rest."

"You're the traitor," Ellodine screamed.

"No I'm not," he shouted back. "I'm just helping. He gave me this stuff for helping."

"You're still a traitor. No wonder nobody likes you."

Yohann's expression darkened. His face contorted into a grin. He had his hands behind his back, like he was feeling for something.

"Of course I betrayed you," he sneered. "I hate you. You all think you're so much better than me. Well you're not. You hide up in the North Pole because everyone out there would hate you if they met you. I hope Omnitec do it. I hope they destroy it all. The city, that stupid big tree and Christmas. All of it."

His eyes blazed with anger. Henry's watch face had clouded over until just a tiny speck in the centre was visible.

"They know we're here, don't they?" he said.

"That's right," Yohann grinned. "They'll be here any minute. I wonder what they'll give me for this."

Henry saw it coming. He grabbed Ellodine and shoved her out of the way. The shield shot over his left arm. Yohann pulled the mini crossbow from behind his back, which he had hidden in his trousers the whole time. He fired.

The arrow clanged against Henry's shield. Yohann fired again and again. Arrows deflected off Henry's shield. Yohann scrambled to his feet, ran and dived over the kitchen counter. He reached over and fired. Henry and Ellodine ran for safety behind a pillar. More arrows whistled past Henry's head.

Ellodine pulled an elven bow from under her coat. She fired a blaze of gold arrows, which flashed through the air and exploded around Yohann. More gold arrows flashed into the cupboards on the wall. Pots, pans, plate and cutlery rained down on Yohann's head or crashed to the floor around him.

A moving black shape caught Henry's eye. A black figure ran across the garden, followed by two others.

"It's too late," came Yohann's taunting voice. "You can't get away."

Ellodine pointed to the double doors leading to the garden and the lake. She handed Henry her gold bow, then grabbed both their snowboards.

"Fine," called Henry. "Did he approach you or did you work it out?"

"He approached me. Of course, I knew already."

Henry gripped the elven bow with his left hand.

"Why did he need you?" he asked.

"For Klasodin's staff," Yohann replied.

"And Omnitec are in on it too?"

"Of course. They're all in on it."

With his right hand, Henry grasped for the gold bow string as he had seen Rodin do back in London. The gold string materialised in his hand.

"And you really don't know where the staff is?"

"No idea. Who cares? We don't need it anyway."

"Why not?" Ellodine called.

"Elves." Yohann laughed. "Think you're so clever. None of you have any idea."

Ellodine nudged Henry. More black figures ran over the front garden. She pointed at the doors. Henry carefully pulled back the string. A gold arrow materialised.

"One more thing, before you die," Yohann sneered. "It's annoying me - the way you say "him" - as if there's only one traitor in Alvahame."

' Ellodine paled visibly.

Henry pointed the arrow at the floor. He pulled back the string.

"There's two of them?" he called.

"As far as I know!" Yohann laughed.

Ellodine nodded to Henry. He turned, aimed at the kitchen counter and released the arrow. It shot like lightning at the counter and exploded in a gold flash. Yohann ducked for cover.

Henry grasped for another string. It appeared in his hand. He pulled back the string. An arrow materialised. Henry fired again. Yohann cowered as the arrow exploded into a cupboard over his head.

The string stayed in his hand. Another gold arrow appeared. He aimed for the double doors. He fired. They blasted outwards. Ellodine ran at them. Henry fired another arrow. The doors smashed and shattered. Ellodine leapt out. Henry ran.

The front door he'd come through earlier opened behind him. Henry turned and fired an arrow. The gold flash exploded on the front door and blew the Gaardreng back out of the house.

He ran for the window. He fired at the dark figure on the lawn. He leapt out and ran. Ellodine sat on a large sledge. Henry climbed on behind her. A back and side rails locked into place either side of him and behind him.

"Hold on," she said.

He threw his arms around her waist and clung on. He could hear the shouts of the Gaardreng clambering through the wreckage of the house behind them, chasing after them to capture or kill them.

CHAPTER TWENTY-EIGHT

The sledge shot off down the snow-covered garden. Henry's stomach lurched back into his spine. The sleigh skimmed the icy lake. They veered right and sped over the ice, back in the direction they had come, heading for the forest. Arrows zipped past them, thudding into the tree trunks and clattering into the ice. There was a loud crack behind them. A fissure tore through the ice, rending it in two, chasing after the sledge. Ice stars shattered. Henry fired a glance over his shoulder. Figures in black were shooting over the ice after them.

The sledge whooshed over the frozen lake. It shot up the snow bank, then zigzagged in and out of the trees so fast they were flashing past before Henry saw them. He held onto Ellodine, his head and torso thrown left and right.

The forest thinned. The trees dispersed. The sledge flew up the hill and burst through the Margullring. It slid down the next hill at breakneck speed and up again to shoot through the screen of cloud. It flew down the gentle hill and veered left at the end to follow the line of mountains to their right. Mountains to their left rose out of the snow and thrust into the cold arctic air.

Henry looked back. Five men in black gear on chrome snowboards crested the mountain behind them and chased after them.

"I thought we'd lost them," he said in Ellodine's ear. "And how did they get into Mannhame? How did they even find it?"

"They had help," she replied.

"Does that mean they can get into Alvahame?"

"Probably."

A volley of arrows shot into the snow around them.

"Shoot back at them," Ellodine told him.

Henry manoeuvred himself. He gripped the bow in his left hand and aimed up the mountainside behind him. He clenched his right fist. The string of Madjik appeared. He stretched it back. The gold arrow materialised. He fired. It exploded into the snow and sent one Gaard tumbling down the mountainside.

"Come on. You need to fire quicker," Ellodine urged.

"It's not easy working this and twisting around at the same time. I need one of their crossbows. I could use that with one hand."

"You don't need them," Ellodine insisted. "Our Madjik is pure. It should never be mixed with anything else."

"A better weapon would make our lives a lot easier," Henry grumbled.

"Madjik is different. You don't understand."

More arrows shot past them and collided with the snow in front. Ellodine swerved violently and skirted around them.

"Start firing," she said. "They're catching up."

"Drive faster."

"Stop distracting me and start firing. You don't need to hit them. Aim at their feet or the snow in front of them."

Henry reeled off as many arrows as he could, some striking the snow in front of the pursuing Gaardreng, some hitting the ground too early, some flying off in the wrong direction. A couple flew right at them or exploded in the snow, forcing them off course.

"That's it," Ellodine said. "You've got them worried."

Henry kept firing, holding the bow up in his left hand so the shield on his arm protected them from flying arrows.

They neared the mouth of the valley. It opened out into a white expanse beyond.

"Are we going back to Alvahame?" Henry asked.

"We can't," Ellodine replied. "They'll chase us all the way. Fire at the snow. Fire every arrow at the snow. Now."

Henry aimed at the ground. He fired as quickly as he could. Clouds of snow plumed everywhere. He couldn't see the Gaardreng or the mountain behind. The sledge veered left to go back to Alvahame.

"Keep firing. Fire as many as you can." Ellodine leaned over the left side and brushed the surface of the snow with her fingers. Tracks carved through the snow in front of them and curved further left, as if they were already a mile further ahead. "That should send them round in circles for a while."

She dragged the sledge right. Henry lurched left. He clung on for dear life and heaved his body back upright. Ellodine reached over the right side and touched the snow with her fingertips. The tracks behind them, which they had just made, disappeared. Henry watched more snow-covered ground stretch behind them, between the sledge and where they had turned. Smooth snow. No tracks.

Ellodine took the sleigh into the cover of the mountains.

"I don't know where else to look," she said. "I thought we'd get more from Yohann. We'll just have to take the long way home."

"Is there nowhere else?"

"Mannhame is south-west of Alvahame. There's nothing else in that direction."

Henry looked down at the Hafskod. No flames were dancing. The watch face was clear. Their enemies were gone.

A gold flame rose up from the centre.

"Why does everything on this Hafskod look like fire?" Henry muttered. "There's a gold flame. I think there'll be something inside it for me to see."

The flame parted. Henry leaned forward, resting his chin on Ellodine's shoulder and stretching out his arm in front of her so she could see. What looked like a map appeared in the air, hanging over the Hafskod, drawn in gold light, translucent so they could see it and see through it.

The map showed the Arctic, the elven realm with Alvahame at its centre and the second elven realm just off it to the south-west. A tiny gold dot moving east showed the sleigh heading away from Mannhame, away from Alvahame, towards another destination marked on the map.

"The ice palace," Ellodine gasped.

"What? Is that Klasodin's as well?"

"No. It belongs to Omnitec."

Henry felt a shiver up his spine.

"Omnitec has a place in the Arctic?" he said.

"They say it's for research into geothermal fuels and other environmentally-friendly methods of production," Ellodine replied. "The whole place is supposed to be carbon neutral. So they say. Anyway, it's all rubbish. They want a base in the Arctic so they can hunt down the Aesir and destroy Alvahame. That's why they're there."

Henry thought for a second. Alvahame was in trouble. If there was anything he could do to save it, he had to do it. Look what Klasodin and his elves had done for him. He had friends there now. The best one was sitting in front of him, steering the sledge. There was only one course of action and there was no one else to take it. Henry felt his heart pound. Fear and excitement coursed through his body.

"We have to go there," he said.

"Are you sure?"

"Very."

"But it's dangerous. If they see us, they'll kill us. I'm supposed to look after you."

"If we want to save Alvahame and save Christmas, we have to do it. There's nowhere else we can try."

Ellodine took a deep breath.

"You're right. We have to, don't we?"

"I want to go."

"Me too."

The sledge picked up speed. Henry relaxed and held onto Ellodine. Her long, blonde hair flowed in the wind, blowing around his face. It was annoying at first, but then Henry decided he liked it. Her hair smelled really nice. Humans did love elves. Ellodine had said so. But they all lived in Mannhame and Ellodine was Aesir royalty, so she couldn't live there. Could a human live in Alvahame forever?

Henry blinked.

Stupid. He didn't even like girls.

He thought of his foster home back in London. Only it wasn't his home and they weren't his family. But could the city of the elves be where he belonged? Could he live in Alvahame forever? He'd never see Mrs Mcready and the children in her foster home again. Suddenly that didn't sound very nice either.

But that didn't matter now. He was on an adventure of his own. He watched the snowy landscape fly past and felt himself relax. Ellodine's hair smelled really nice. The sledge was quite comfortable - for a sledge.

"We're nearly there." Ellodine's voice sliced through Henry's consciousness and made him jump. "Were you asleep? Your head was resting on my shoulder."

"Was it?" he mumbled. "I guess I was asleep. Sorry."

"It's okay. I didn't mind."

The sleigh slid to a stop. Henry swept Ellodine's blonde hair aside and peered over her shoulder. They sat on the edge of a v-shaped plateau, which came to a rough point nearby as two high cliffs of ice and snow met, then headed off at an acute angle, creating a flat snowy plain below.

In the centre of the plain, a giant ice palace rose out of the ice and towered over the cliffs. It had two long towers, one at each end. Each tower was crowned with points stretching to the sky like giant icicles, as if two kings of the ice giants had placed their crowns there.

It made the hairs stand up on the back of Henry's neck. It looked impossible to break into. The walls were so high. He couldn't see any doors or windows. He couldn't think of a worse place to be lost or captured.

A tiny figure emerged on the roof. Henry and Ellodine rolled off the sleigh onto their stomachs. Henry trained his eyes on the figure. He was an armed Gaard, dressed in black, brandishing a weapon, which Henry couldn't make out from such a distance. The Gaard looked around him and disappeared.

Henry and Ellodine lay pressed to the snow, keeping still, breathing with as little movement as possible. After a while, the Gaard returned, looked around him and moved on again.

"Great," Ellodine breathed. "Breaking in there just got even harder."

CHAPTER TWENTY-NINE

The Gaard appeared and disappeared at regular intervals. Henry lay on his stomach in the snow, gripping the elven bow he'd pulled from his rucksack. His eyes scanned the ice palace and the icy terrain around it, but he couldn't see a way in. He scowled down at the Hafskod on his wrist.

"This would be where you do something," he muttered.

"You talk to it?" Ellodine giggled.

"This is the second time." Henry stared at it, almost expecting something to happen. "Help me," he said finally. He looked up at Ellodine, who seemed more curious than amused. "It worked last time."

A gold flame rose from the Hafskod and hovered in front of Henry's face.

"Wow," Ellodine breathed.

The flame turned to ice and became a gleaming icicle hanging in the air.

"The power of ice and fire," Ellodine said, her eyes wide.

"What?"

"Madjik is the power of ice and fire. We don't see much of the ice part, except for being able to snowboard up hills and never feeling the cold. Klasodin always said there would be a special few who could do more. I never thought it would be a Glondir."

"That makes two of us."

160

The icicle glittered as if the sun were shining on it. The sound of a breeze arose around them, like the wind blowing through sand. The snow started to move. The top layer blew towards them. Henry and Ellodine huddled together, threw their coat hoods up to protect their faces and put their heads down. Henry could feel a sheet of snow cover him. Then everything was still.

Henry lifted his head. Ellodine was covered in snow. It looked like he was too. They both shook the snow away and looked each other up and down. Their clothes, their snowboards and their bows were the colour of ice. They were camouflaged. The icicle from the Hafskod was gone.

They pulled the sledge apart and lay on their stomachs on the snowboards. Henry set off slowly, sliding along the top of the cliff, Ellodine behind him.

"Could we just slide down this cliff and up the walls of the ice palace?" he suggested.

"Can't do verticals. Forodin tried. It wasn't pretty."

The tiny, distant figure of the Gaard appeared.

A breeze sounded in front of Henry, but he couldn't feel any wind. The snowboard sank deeper into the snow and ploughed a path through it. The snow parted and built up into a white wall either side of him to hide him from the Gaard.

The path sloped downwards. Henry felt his snowboard tilt and dig into the cliff. The walls of snow rose higher until they were all he could see. After about twenty metres, the path turned sharply to go back on itself. Henry eased his snowboard around the hairpin bend, then took tight bend after tight bend, zigzagging down the cliff face.

After what felt like hours, he slid out at the bottom and hid with Ellodine behind a mound of ice. Ellodine slapped his snowboard on his back and did the same with hers.

A chill surged up Henry's spine. Omnitec's ice palace looked even bigger from the bottom - a looming monster with spiked towers thrusting up to the sky.

The Gaard emerged. He wore a thick coat over black combat gear. He had thick stubble and a fur hat. He brandished a crossbow. He looked around, then moved away.

Henry's wide eyes fixed on the ice palace. He counted off the seconds in his head. The Gaard resurfaced. Henry was waiting for him, but he still jumped.

"Three hundred seconds," he whispered.

The Gaard looked around him and disappeared.

"Let's see if it's the same again," Ellodine breathed.

Three hundred seconds later, the Gaard appeared, looked around and moved out of sight.

Ellodine jumped to her feet and brandished her bow.

"Let's see what happens," she said.

She grasped the silver string as it appeared and pulled it back. An arrow of ice materialised. She fired. It sailed up through the air and stabbed into the side of the ice palace at the very top of the wall.

Henry opened his mouth to say how little that helped, when he saw the strain of silvery rope in her hands. His eyes followed it across the icy ground and up to the arrow embedded in the ice palace wall. Ellodine wrapped the rope around her waist then passed it to Henry. There was enough for him to do the same.

The rope tightened. Henry held on. The rope contracted. It yanked Henry and Ellodine off their feet. Henry's stomach lurched. They flew up in the air and sailed high over the icy plain. The rope shot into the arrow. Henry and Ellodine hurtled after it and tumbled over the top of the wall.

The roof was a sheet of ice. Henry slid over it. The rope snapped tight. It jerked around his waist and dug in hard as it tightened. Henry gasped. The rope hauled him back over the ice. He slid into the wall with a thud. Ellodine landed with a bump beside him. The rope whipped out from around their waists and disappeared.

Henry gasped for breath, leaning back against the wall. His heart hammered. He felt a grin stretch across his face. A quiet laugh erupted from his stomach. He shot a glance at Ellodine next to him, who smiled back at him, her eyes alive with exhilaration.

Heavy feet in big boots with spiked soles crunched over the ice.

"He's coming back," Ellodine whispered.

They looked around them for somewhere to hide. The roof was a long, flat silvery surface with a tall tower at each end. Dotted in-between were several smaller structures that looked like giant periscopes of rectangular, icy tubes.

They ran for the nearest one. There was a gridded door a metre off the ground. Ellodine eased the door open, heaved herself up and swung herself in. She crawled along a short horizontal ledge, then dropped out of sight and landed with a dull, metallic thud. Henry climbed up onto the steel platform and shut the door quietly behind him.

Heavy spiked boots crunched closer.

He slid away from the door and peered over the edge. Ellodine looked up at him through the darkness, her face a couple of feet below where he was sitting. He eased himself over and let himself down until he was hanging by his fingertips, then dropped and landed lightly with bent knees.

He ducked down onto his hands and knees and started crawling along a steel, square-shaped tunnel. Ellodine was already sliding along it, pushing herself forward with her hands.

The Hafskod burst into life. A torch beam shone from it, lighting up Ellodine and the tunnel ahead.

"Stop looking at my bum," Ellodine mouthed with a smirk on her face.

"Better than your face," Henry mouthed back.

Ellodine let out a little snort of laughter.

Spiked boots crunched in the ice above - very close by.

Henry crawled after Ellodine, trying to keep quiet.

The spiked boots moved quicker.

Henry could imagine the Gaard looking around frantically, certain he had heard something.

He crawled faster. He passed openings to identical tunnels, heading off at right angles to his left and right, each too dark and too long to see the other end.

The gridded door to the vent they had just climbed in swung open. A heavy body hauled itself inside.

Ellodine reached the end of the tunnel. Henry scrambled after her.

A narrow shaft with metal walls led down into the darkness – further than he could see. A ladder ran down it on their side. Ellodine started climbing.

Heavy, spiked boots landed with a bang on the tunnel floor behind them.

Henry gripped the top rung and swung himself onto the ladder.

Knees thudded down on the tunnel floor.

Henry ducked down, hanging off the rungs, arms stretching as far as possible.

A beam of light flashed down the tunnel and grazed the top hairs of his head.

He held his breath. He froze on the ladder.

There was an irritated grunt. The boots collided with the sides of the vertical tunnel as the Gaard hauled himself out. The light vanished. The door slammed shut.

Henry breathed a sigh of relief.

Ellodine's eyes blazed. Her jaw clenched with fury.

"Ice palace?" she hissed angrily. "It's just a disguise. It's all metal inside. What are they doing here?"

"Keep going," Henry whispered. "Let's find out."

Henry and Ellodine climbed down the ladder, passing more dark tunnels leading off the shaft on both sides.

A low humming sound made them both stop dead. Cold air blew through the tunnels. Henry and Ellodine clung to the ladder as it swept over them.

"What are all these tunnels?" Ellodine whispered. "Where's the wind coming from?"

"They must be air vents," Henry replied.

"What do they do?"

"They blow cold air in to stop computers and machines overheating."

Ellodine muttered something under her breath.

Henry stopped and twisted himself around. Set in the opposite wall between the vents were computer consoles with flashing buttons and touchscreens. They were lined with gold that pulsated with a blue light.

Ellodine frowned. Gripping a rung with one hand, she stretched as far behind her as she could. Her fingers glowed.

"I knew it," she hissed. "Aesir gold. Or it was before they ruined it."

They were about halfway down. Ellodine swung herself into a tunnel. Henry climbed in after her. They crawled along it and reached a grid of faint light glowing through the floor at the end where the tunnel went straight up.

Henry and Ellodine knelt over the grate that was letting out the light.

A cacophony of noises burst through it. Rumbling, grating, scraping.

Ellodine pulled up the grate and rested it on the floor. The hole was big enough to climb through. She dropped down. She gave a yelp and disappeared.

Henry's heart pounded. He jumped in after her. He landed on a metal floor, lost his balance and staggered back.

The floor moved under his feet. He reeled and fell backwards. He crashed into something hard behind him, which toppled over and crashed into something else.

There was a whir.

Something shot at his face.

CHAPTER THIRTY

Three robotic arms wielding a hammer, a screwdriver and a blowtorch jabbed at him.

He rolled to one side.

Ellodine grabbed his arm and hauled him out of the way. They retreated and pressed their backs against the wall, keeping their feet on the stationary steel platform. They watched open-mouthed, their eyes scanning the vast metal chamber filled with a long row of conveyor belts and automated assembly lines.

To the left, steel jaws spat out hunks of steel, graphite, fibre glass, carbon fibre and hard plastics. Robotic arms shot out, pistoning, hammering, twisting, turning, screwing and scissoring. Sparks flew.

Freshly honed bike frames sailed across on the conveyor belt that Henry had crashed on. The conveyor belt veered left and merged with two others. Handlebars, wheels and chains were melded and screwed on. Brakes were bolted on. More robotic arms spray-painted the finished mountain bikes a bright red, then added the name "Speed Demon" on the bar. More bikes were finished in blue, green, purple and black. Behind them were smaller bikes, tricycles and pink bikes with stabilisers and baskets on the front. There were lightweight racer bikes with curved handlebars, scooters, skateboards and cars that toddlers could climb into and pedal. There were little rechargeable electric cars. Every freshly-made toy reached the end of the conveyor belt and was sucked up a giant vent at the end.

Henry shot a glance at Ellodine who gazed at it all with wide-eyed horror. Suddenly, she leapt and skipped over a couple of assembly lines to a ladder just beyond the air vent they had come from. She jumped onto it and beckoned to Henry.

He leapt over the first conveyor belt. A passing bike frame caught his trailing foot. He tried to jump again, but landed on the second conveyor belt which took his foot from under him. He fell over and landed on the bike behind him with a crash. He winced in pain. The frame rammed right into his ribs. A robotic arm jabbed at him. He rolled out of the way. He scrambled to his feet, tiptoed between the belts and jumped over to where Ellodine waited for him on the ladder. She rolled her eyes in irritation. He scowled at her.

"Someone's going to find the mess you made," she said in an accusing tone.

"Well, we can't all be perfect like elves, can we?"

"Just follow me."

She climbed down and jumped off at the floor below. Henry followed. They climbed down the ladder through floor after floor, watching thousands of robotic arms perform every task, from the minutest detail of a circuit board, mother board or memory card to fusing together laptops, tablets, mobile phones and televisions. There were remote control cars, toy robots, video games, cameras, train sets and toy dart guns.

Ellodine climbed down first again. Henry saw her jaw drop and her face pale. Her eyes filled with tears. Henry jumped down beside her. He gasped. He felt his spine tingle with fear. The assembly lines and robots weren't making toys anymore.

Blackened steel jaws spat out two hunks of metal at a time. One was steel. The other was a fragment of gold. Three needles shot down and stabbed into the gold. It turned murky green and blue. More robotic arms fused it with the steel. They moulded it into shape and covered it in chrome until it looked like the flying snowboards Henry had seen the Gaardreng use. Across the floor he could see similar methods used to make the guns and steel darts he had already seen the Gaardreng use. Some were the guns with steel blades almost impossibly concealed within. There were the little chrome bows that could become the larger ones firing bolts of Azmar, which Bayne had used to attack the sleigh leaving London. Smaller weapons were welded to the sides of one line of flying snowboards. Every new weapon was sucked up into the vent at the end.

Henry checked his Hafskod. It was clouded over. Only the tiniest speck in the centre of the watch face was still visible.

Ellodine wiped her face with her hand.

"It's horrible," she choked. "Who could treat Madjik like this? And they're making so many of them? How many armies do they need?"

"Maybe it's not just for them." Henry looked to the end lines, where guns and blasters he had never seen before were being put together. "I've seen this in films. When people make that many weapons, it's usually to sell them. I mean, if you're the only one with Madjik in your weapons, you'll have a product nobody else has and everyone else wants. You can charge as much as you like. It'll sell anyway."

Ellodine leapt up onto the ladder.

"I can't look at it anymore," she uttered. "I have to know who's behind this."

Henry watched all the weapons flow by. Why shouldn't he have one? Ellodine could keep her bow. He picked a dart gun. There was a little chrome bow, which would snap into a larger shape and fire bolts of Azmar. They were both very light. Each came with a safety button so he knew there would be no accident if he tucked them into his trousers. Each had a replenish button and the option for a laser sight. Just what the stupid elven bow needed. He tucked them in his trousers and climbed down.

The ladder stopped at a floor where bullet proof vests and body armour were being made by the thousand. Ellodine pulled up a grate from the floor and jumped in. She ducked down and crawled into the vent. Henry climbed down after her and replaced the grate over his head.

Strands of light radiated through the grates ahead of him. Babbling voices came from below. He crawled as quietly as he could, not daring to make a sound, placing every knee and hand with the utmost care. He breathed gently, silently through his open mouth. One wrong move and everyone would hear. One wrong move and they would never escape.

CHAPTER THIRTY-ONE

Henry stopped over a grate. Ellodine knelt opposite him, a grid of light imprinted over her face. They peered down.

Professional video cameras on heavy duty tripods were lined up on either side of a fifty-inch flat screen showing a pretty brunette reporter in a low-cut, cherry-coloured top.

In front of it, assistants in suits, a makeup artist and a hairstylist bustled around a man with dyed, yellow-blond, short-cropped hair. His face was smooth and without a single line, but heavily tanned to an orangey-brown colour. His bright white teeth dazzled as he gave a fake smile. He wore a silver suit and matching tie. His lips pursed. His small, dark eyes stared at the TV screen like an assassin about to execute his prey. He seemed oblivious to the hustle and bustle around him.

Three large screens behind him showed men in lab coats working. There were graphs, diagrams and blueprints of the ice palace and pictures of Arctic scenery, all worked by laptops at the sides of the long room.

The silver-suited man waved everyone away irritably. He had chunky hands, the same orangey-brown colour as his face, with a gold signet ring on his little finger.

A harried-looking female assistant standing at the side of the cameras and clutching a clipboard to her chest gave him a countdown.

"Five. Four. Three. Two. . ."

"Mister Drock," the reporter said in honeyed tones, smiling with perfect white teeth.

"Please," the man in the silver suit replied, flashing whiter teeth back at her. "Call me Zandor."

It was more a rasp than a voice. Years of chain smoking clung to his throat. He didn't speak loudly, as if he thought he was so important he didn't need to, because people would always listen. From his accent, Henry was sure he had grown up in London.

"Zandor, you are the Chief Executive of Omnitec International. While most CEOs enjoy luxurious offices in some of the greatest cities in the world - London, New York, Paris maybe - here you are in the Arctic. Please, tell us more about your Arctic factory."

"My dear," Drock replied. "I would hardly refer to our Arctic Ice Palace as a factory. You see, in our everlasting quest as a force for good, Omnitec's ongoing research into geothermal fuels has led us here to the Arctic, giving us a unique opportunity to be at one with nature."

"But you do make toys there."

"We create here, as a way of testing this new, clean fuel, given to us by Mother Nature herself. And the results are second to none."

Drock gestured to the screens behind him. Diagrams showed pipes reaching miles down to the Earth's core and fuel pumping back in to power machinery. Scientists in lab coats tested the results.

"Everything we do here is powered by the Earth itself. Omnitec's scientists are the first to develop geothermal fuels as a genuine power source for large-scale production, which will ensure Omnitec's position as the market leader in technology as well as carbon-neutral manufacturing."

After more back and forth, the interview eventually came to an end. The broad smile vanished from Drock's face.

"Cameras all off?"

"Yes sir."

"Where'd they find that dumb bimbo?" he muttered.

The videos and images on the screens behind him were shut down and stored in a file marked "Media".

"Bring up the more accurate version."

A diagram flashed up on the screen. Pipes pumped waste down into the depths. A gas pipeline led from a distant country in the east. A core of energy sat in the heart of the building and a seam of gold led up the shaft Henry and Ellodine had climbed down.

Ellodine held her hand over her mouth.

"Have our gas suppliers called to renegotiate yet?"

"Yes sir. They want our weapons to be part of any future deal."

"Is that it?"

"Three European countries and five private security firms."

"Where do they want to meet?"

"They want to come to us."

"Of course they do. Tell them a negotiation team of no more than three. They come here in our transport. We search them before they board and again when they disembark. Serious consequences will follow any betrayal of trust."

"Of course."

Two assistants hurried away through a pair of double doors to Zander Drock's right. A male assistant burst through a door at the top of the room and whispered in Drock's ear.

The Omnitec CEO's tanned skin paled visibly. He tugged at the collar of his shirt, as if it were suddenly too tight. He muttered something under his breath and marched through the double doors at the top of the room, his assistant in tow.

Ellodine turned and slid silently up the tunnel. Henry crawled after her. She sped ahead without a sound and stopped at the far end. Henry could just see her face in the darkness lit up by the grate she kneeled over. Henry joined her and peered down.

Drock paced in front of a sleek glass desk with nothing on it but a brand new Omnitec Ice desktop computer. He stopped and patted himself down, then searched his pockets frantically for something he couldn't find.

"Who the hell let him in?" he grated angrily, rolling up his sleeve, revealing a forearm the same colour as his face.

His assistant appeared and stuck a fresh nicotine patch on his arm.

"Nobody let him in. He just appeared - as always."

The assistant turned and disappeared. A door opened somewhere below Henry and Ellodine where they couldn't see.

A tall, male figure with long, black hair, a thick, thigh-length black coat and black trousers and boots ambled into Drock's office as if he owned it. He slouched on a sofa opposite Drock's desk, leaving just his sprawling legs visible.

Henry could feel the tension swell in his stomach. There was no greeting or hello, just an uneasy silence. Zander Drock eased himself into the transparent chair at his desk, not taking his eyes off his visitor.

"To what do I owe this pleasure?" His steady rasp sliced through the silence.

"Curiosity really," came the reply. It was a younger voice, the tone casual, indifferent even. "I couldn't help but notice the fuss in your . . . palace."

"I was merely presenting our environmental credentials," Drock grinned.

"Curious," the voice said. "Hardly something that sets you apart from your rival."

"They don't know that," the Omnitec CEO replied smugly. "And who's going to tell them?"

"Let us hope they never find your waste pipes - or the weapons."

"Our new clients are as dedicated to discretion as we are."

"I assume your weapons will be ready on time."

"We're well ahead of schedule," Drock said confidently. "We'll be there."

"Performing your most important function."

"The state it's in, we'll walk through it like there's nothing there." Drock paused, his eyes analysing his companion. "We could supply you with the best weaponry available to elf or human - for the right price."

A laugh came from the sofa.

"I don't think that will be necessary," the voice sneered. "Something did arouse my attention though."

"What?" Drock said.

"Our human mole received a surprise visit."

"The Gaardreng were ready."

"And yet they got away." The voice had a dangerous edge to it.

"They were prepared for an escape," Drock said hurriedly, shifting in his seat.

"They were younglings."

Henry swallowed. He glanced up at Ellodine, who looked back at him with wide eyes.

"They mean us," she mouthed.

Henry nodded.

"No harm done," Drock said as calmly as he could, his voice unsteady.

"Clearly Grimnir has softened. I never took him as one who welcomed failure and gave his enemies a free head start."

Zander Drock swallowed.

"Klasodin has disappeared, his staff with him," he croaked.

"Do you know where they are?"

"No." Drock cleared his throat. "I don't need to. Gronodin runs Alvahame now. We've won already."

"But you have not located Klasodin or his staff. You have no control over this latest human stain. You have not won. You have no idea what the enemy is doing."

A faint grin of triumph crept over Drock's face. He flashed his bright white teeth.

"I have an ace up my sleeve."

He tapped a few keys on his computer, then turned the screen for the visitor to see.

"Another triumph for human technology?" the visitor in black sneered.

"I am reliably informed that the new human helper is as mesmerised by shiny objects as the old one," Drock grinned. "And this morning, the bait was taken."

Fear turned Henry's stomach. He shrugged innocently at Ellodine, who looked up at him in alarm.

"I know where Glondir is right now."

Drock tapped a computer key.

Henry felt the colour drain from his face.

Drock's jaw dropped. He stared at the screen with wide, unblinking eyes. He tapped the key again. Nothing changed.

"That's not possible," he gasped.

"Something wrong, Drock?" the voice laughed.

"He's . . . here." Zander Drock's eyes flashed wildly around his office. "Glondir is here, in the ice palace."

"You had better sound the alarm then," the voice said mockingly.

The Omnitec CEO grabbed his office phone and punched a button with a stubby finger.

"GAARDRENG," he yelled into the receiver. "GLONDIR IS IN THE ICE PALACE. SHUT IT DOWN NOW. HE MUST NOT ESCAPE."

CHAPTER THIRTY-TWO

The alarm rang out through Omnitec's ice palace. It echoed and resonated through the air vents, piercing Henry's skull until he felt like his ears were about to bleed. Ellodine shoved him back the way they'd come. He crawled as quickly as he could, hands on the floor of the tunnel, pushing himself along on his toes.

"Left now," Ellodine whispered, as they passed a tributary tunnel.

"What? Why?"

"Just do it."

Henry took the left turning. He could see the faint gold light shining through a grate in the ceiling ahead. He pushed open the grate and clambered out into the base of the tall, laddered shaft they had taken on their way down. Ellodine jumped up next to him, replaced the grate and pushed him aside. She looked straight up to the top.

"I want to try something," she whispered. "If Aesir gold runs all the way up, it should work. Even if it isn't quite what it should be."

She stopped for a second and took a deep breath.

"Hurry up," Henry hissed. "They'll find us."

"Shut up," she snapped.

Henry scowled.

She took a breath, bent her knees and jumped. She flew straight up the shaft. Henry let out a laugh. He looked at his Hafskod, which was shining in reaction to the gold. He jumped and flew up in the air. He shot after Ellodine, keeping his arms in so he didn't collide with the wall or the ladder on the way up.

Ellodine landed on the third rung from the top and sprang up into the tunnel. Henry planted his feet on the fifth rung. He opened his mouth to order her to get out of his way, but the expression on her face stopped him. She frowned, looking down the tunnel.

"I think there's . . ."

A beam of bright light shone into her face from down the tunnel.

"Got you," a deep, accented voice said smugly. "Move and I will shoot you in your pretty little elf head."

Henry gripped the ladder rung with his left fist and dug into his trousers with his right. He pulled out the mini chrome Azmar bow.

"Now where's the boy?"

"I came alone."

Henry scowled. Trust her to do the brave thing.

The Gaard shifted his heavy frame along the tunnel.

"If you're lying to me. . ." he growled.

Henry readied himself to fly up into the tunnel. He sprang. Nothing. He dropped. He grabbed the ladder with one hand. His body and legs slammed into the steel rungs. Sharp pain streaked through his ribs. His left knee throbbed. He found his footing. He leaned into the ladder, his heart pounding, trying to catch his breath. He didn't dare look down.

The Hafskod was clouded over. The watch face was hidden.

"What was that?" the voice snapped.

"Nothing," Ellodine replied quietly, her voice trembling slightly, her eyes fixed on the Gaard in front of her.

Henry was stuck, rooted to the ladder. He couldn't get his arms or legs to move.

The Gaard inched forward, struggling to move his heavy frame through the tunnel and aim his weapon.

The Azmar bow snapped silently into place. It was bigger than Henry remembered. He had to move now. He took one rung at a time, winding his left arm around the rung before moving his feet, holding the bow out to stop it tangling with the ladder, keeping his head out of sight. He wound his arm around the top rung and heaved himself up.

"I saw you," came the Gaard's voice. "Stay where you are."

Henry sprang up into the tunnel and landed on his side. He aimed and fired. A blue flash erupted from the bow and blew down the tunnel. It exploded on a heavy dark shape halfway down, which slumped to the floor.

"You've killed him," Ellodine hissed.

Henry scrambled forward and checked the Gaard's pulse.

"He's just unconscious," he said, breathing a sigh of relief. "Come on."

Henry slid to the end, stood up, jumped and caught hold of the ledge with his fingers. He pulled himself up, grunting with the strain, until he could see out over the roof of the ice palace. He heaved himself up onto his elbows, then felt Ellodine pushing his feet up. He climbed up onto the small ledge and looked out through the gridded door. He could hear more heavy feet crunching over the ice. He looked to his Hafskod. Still clouded over. He tried to make the shield appear. Nothing. He tried again. Why didn't it work?

Ellodine pulled herself up. Henry hauled her onto the cramped surface next to him. Her knee landed on his thigh. He winced. She moved. It shoved into his stomach instead, which was better.

"We're going to have to shoot our way out," he whispered.

She scowled at him, then at the mini chrome bow in his hand.

"Not with that you won't," she hissed.

"I'm not using that stupid bow and arrow."

"The bow and arrow's not the problem. You are."

"Well I'm not a perfect elf, am I?"

"Put them down. Now."

"No."

"How can you even touch those awful things?"

"They're weapons."

"They're corrupted Madjik. They're Azmar. You remember our Foundations?"

"So?"

"It's like spitting in the face of Klasodin and the Aesir. Those weapons are twisted."

"They're weapons. You have them too."

"Ours are pure Madjik. Made to defend our city and what it stands for."

"Oh yeah? Well I can defend Alvahame better using these. So I will."

Henry produced the dart gun in his other hand just to annoy her. She glared at him. He thought and tried to make his snowboard leave his back. Nothing. He used the chrome bow to scrape the board off his coat. Ellodine caught it. Henry planted his feet on it. He pulled the ice bow from his rucksack and hooked it over his shoulder, just in case. The string appeared, gripping it to his body.

Henry looked at Ellodine. They listened for voices or boots crunching on ice. Nothing.

"You ready?" he breathed.

She nodded. He took a breath. Time to make a run for it.

CHAPTER THIRTY-THREE

Henry eased the door open and jumped out. He landed on his snowboard and slid away. Ellodine leapt out after him and slid for the wall where they had landed before.

Shouts sounded behind them.

"Stop where you are."

Leading with his left foot, Henry swerved over the ice. He could see a small group of Gaardreng running towards him, either side of the vent he had emerged from. Dart gun in one hand, chrome Azmar bow in the other, he fired. His index fingers squeezed the triggers again and again in one constant motion. Steel arrows and blue blasts shot from his weapons. The Gaards dived for cover.

Ellodine fired an ice arrow, which shot into the air and sailed over the snow-covered escarpment they had come from, burying itself in the snow thirty metres beyond the cliff edge. She fired a second arrow into the wall near her. A rope appeared, connecting the two arrows like a very long zip wire.

"You first," she shouted. "And leave those behind."

"No."

"Your Hafskod won't work if you don't."

He stared at her, then at his weapons. She was right.

He slid for the edge, firing a volley of shots at the advancing Gaards, then flung both weapons over the side of the ice palace. He grabbed his ice bow in his left hand and leapt off the roof. He flew through the air, whipped his bow over the tight line of rope and grabbed the other end with his right hand. He shot down the zip line at breakneck speed. His stomach lurched up towards his throat. The rope trembled with a fresh impact and friction. Ellodine was sliding down behind him.

His bow whooshed over the rope. He flew over the ice cliff. The snow shot up at him. He let go of his bow with his right hand, gripping it with his left. He sailed through the air and landed on his snowboard on the snow with a thud and a soft crunch, sliding left foot first away from Omnitec's ice palace.

Ellodine landed behind him.

"Keep going," she ordered. "Don't stop."

Henry bent his knees. His snowboard flew over the snow, travelling faster than he ever had before. He glanced down at the Hafskod. The cloud had vanished. The watch face was silver and clear.

The undulating Arctic landscape whizzed past him. Henry fixed his eyes on the path ahead, aiming straight, then veering left, heading in the direction of the elven realm. He slid up a gentle rise at lightning speed. A silvery cloud screen appeared from nowhere. The ground dropped away and he flew through the air.

He landed and the cloud cleared. He found himself flying through a wide valley, which rose up and closed around him the further he slid.

Black shapes crested the mountain tops to his right and chased after him. He could see more out of the corner of his left eye. His heart pounded. He thought he'd lost them.

"Faster," Ellodine shouted from behind him.

The valley bottlenecked at the end, then opened out into a path winding its way through the snow-covered hills. A scattering of fir trees appeared ahead of him around the first hill.

The black-clad Gaardreng slid into view from his right, flying over the hills after him. Henry veered left and aimed for a gathering of silvery fir trees.

Ellodine shouted something to him but he couldn't hear.

He sped along a path winding gently through the trees, then burst out the other end and slid up the side of a hill, before taking off, flying through the air and landing on the other side, watching an expansive silver forest lurch towards him.

He descended straight into the forest. The trees were more densely packed. It was darker and harder to see. Henry wove a path of tight turns, aiming for bright light ahead.

Ellodine shouted at him again. He ignored her. He knew what he was doing.

He shot a look over his shoulder. Ellodine waved frantically at him. But there was no sign of the Gaardreng.

A figure emerged in front of him. Henry drew a sharp intake of breath. The hairs stood up on the back of his neck. It was Bayne.

Henry veered left. His snowboard hit a root and threw him into the air. He landed off balance and smashed his shoulder into a tree trunk. He bumbled ahead, bumping up and down, then found a route of smoother snow. The trees thinned and he shot out of the forest, through more white hills. Ellodine shouted at him again.

The path carved left and right around the hills, heading downwards. The hills either side gave way to a wall of ice. The path widened into a road. The walls of ice rose on either side. Henry looked up - to see Bayne peering down at him. Henry gazed back at him in defiance. The snow beneath his board hardened to ice. He picked up speed down the hill and veered around a corner. He headed for two giant fir trees which leaned over to cover the path and obscure the way ahead.

He flew underneath them. It became dark very quickly. The ice walls turned to stone. They rose on either side and arched above him. They disappeared in the darkness. It became pitch black.

He looked to his Hafskod for light but there wasn't any. He fixed his eyes ahead, but couldn't see anything. He slowed his snowboard, but he was still sliding into pitch black. He thrust his arms out in front of him, groping ahead of him.

Ellodine had stopped screaming. He looked back and could just make out her silhouetted figure behind him. She looked like she was waving at him. She was speeding up, trying to catch him. He couldn't see any sign of Bayne or the Gaardreng behind her. Were they safe? He looked forward. Where was he going?

Something moved in front of him. A figure sped towards him. Something struck his legs. It sent him flying through the air. He tumbled to the ice and bounced. He landed on his back with a grunt of pain. Hands grabbed him roughly and yanked him to his feet. A sack was thrown over his head. Arms hauled him away. Ellodine screamed. There was a scuffle. Her scream was stifled suddenly.

"Welcome to Svaravame," said a callous male voice. "The home of the Morivari. You will like it here."

CHAPTER THIRTY-FOUR

Henry sat alone on a stone seat in a dark cell, staring miserably at the silhouetted bars opposite him. He leaned back against a damp stone wall and a drop of ice cold water trickled down his neck. The floor and walls were made of the same black rock and they all glistened with water. Seams of emerald and gold ran through the rock, providing the only faint light.

"Our human visitor," came a familiar voice. Henry jumped. He knew the voice, but couldn't work out where from. "Welcome Henry. Or is that Glondir?"

A pale face appeared through the bars. Raven black hair. Pointed ears and prominent cheekbones. Long black coat. Black trousers and boots. He looked around the same age as Amira. He was tall and had the features of an elf, but unlike the Aesir, he belonged in the darkness. Henry knew where he had seen him before - in Zandor Drock's office.

"You recognise me. But it's not my face you recognise." A knowing smile crossed the elf's face. "You were a little closer than we thought when Drock found you with his silly little device."

Silence. Henry stared at him, pulse throbbing.

"I'll take that as a yes. Anyway, you're in my home now. This is the city of Svaravame and I am Morikend, king of the Morivari."

Morikend touched a long, ivory-coloured finger to the bars. They vanished in an instant. Henry's entire being clenched. Morikend was going to kill him.

"But you can hardly appreciate the beauty of our great city from the basement. You must be hungry. Come."

Henry levered himself carefully from his stone seat.

"Where's Ellodine?"

"I'm afraid she's gone," Morikend replied with an apologetic tone. "She ran off."

"Someone attacked us."

"We have guards protecting our city, just like the Aesir. When two strangers charge headlong into our territory, what choice does any soldier have? Unfortunately your friend was gone before we could clear up our little misunderstanding." Morikend looked down at Henry, a slight look of amusement on his face. "Did you think I was going to kill you? Follow me, young Henry."

Henry followed the elf along a narrow stone corridor and up a spiral staircase cut from the rock, his heart sinking to his stomach. Ellodine was supposed to be his friend and she had left him. Well of course she did. She was the perfect Aesrine, the royal Visrine. She was probably sick of him already. No wonder all the humans lived in the settlement rather than in the perfect city of the Aesir.

Morikend led Henry into a giant chamber with a pointed ceiling high above them. The emerald and gold seams gave off a gentle light and filled the dark-walled throne room with a pale hue. A jet-black throne stood on a dais at the far end.

Morikend sat opposite Henry at a marble dining table in the middle. Henry's eyes darted over the chamber. Other elves who looked and dressed like Morikend were gathered in clusters. There was even a younger group more his own age talking and laughing. They reminded Henry of Forodin.

Another elf carried in a square gold plate filled with steaming hot food and placed it in front of Henry.

"Eat," said Morikend, as the other elf added a bowl of ketchup and a glass of thick, frothy chocolate milkshake.

Henry was starving, but he couldn't.

"It's not poisoned," Morikend laughed. "What would be the point? If I wanted to kill you, I would have done it already. Enjoy."

No arguing with that. He looked at his food - a juicy burger and thick-cut chips. He smelled it. The delicious aroma surged up his nostrils. His empty stomach rumbled and groaned. He stopped. He shot a look at Morikend. Who knew what they had put in it. What if Morikend was lying and it really was poisoned?

"Come on, Henry." Morikend rolled his eyes. "You're in my palace. I can kill you any time I choose. Why go to the effort of poisoning you?"

He had a point. Henry couldn't hold out any longer. He wolfed it down. It was the most delicious food he had ever tasted.

"If there is one thing all elves know, it is how to appreciate and enjoy the many good things the earth gives them. And we love our food."

"You sound like you're all in it together," Henry said through a mouthful of chips, ignoring the manners Mum had drilled into him.

"We share a lot of common traits with the Aesir, as we do with you humans."

"Why are you at war with everyone then?" Henry asked quickly, between swallowing chips and taking another bite of burger.

"Territory," Morikend said simply. "I believe the Arctic elven realm is ours. After all, we were here first. You humans fight for similar reasons all the time. If your governments knew about us, their armies would be marching here right now."

Henry finished his burger. He took a deep breath.

"Did you enjoy that?" Morikend asked.

"Yes. Thank you."

Morikend nodded approvingly.

"Dignity and manners. I like that."

"There's no point kicking and screaming," Henry said. "Who would that benefit?"

"I agree. It's a shame we started off as enemies." Morikend paused and looked at Henry. "Or are we?"

"What do you mean?" Henry asked suspiciously.

"Do you know how Drock found you?"

Henry thought. It suddenly dawned on him.

"The camera," he said. "There must be a tracking device inside it."

"Of course. And you knew it wasn't from Klasodin. But you took it anyway."

"I like cameras." Henry shrugged.

"You wanted one you could show off in public," Morikend said. "And why not? Not that Ellodine or any of your new Aesir friends would understand."

"No," Henry said shortly. "They don't."

"Considering how much time they spend studying humans, their understanding is rather limited, isn't it?"

Henry nodded.

"And after all this time, how many humans actually live in Alvahame?"

"Not many," Henry sighed.

"No matter what the Aesir tell you, only elves belong in Alvahame," Morikend continued. "Even those elves who aren't originally Aesir stand out from the pack, don't they? What chance does a human really have? You and your friend

Ellodine..." Morikend stopped and looked at Henry. "Or are you friends?"

"I thought we were," Henry admitted.

A hollow sick feeling swelled in his stomach.

"It must have been obvious in your short time together how much faster her reactions are, how easily she can throw a snowball or ride a snowboard. She and her classmates, they're better than you at everything."

"What do you want?" Henry shot back. "What's the point in rubbing it all in?"

Morikend held up his hands apologetically.

"I am merely trying to understand your predicament. And I think I've come closer than anyone else. Your foster family isn't much of a fit, is it?"

Henry said nothing. Morikend was right. And it hurt. After all that had happened, he was still alone.

"Being Glondir gives you purpose, a place in life, but how can that be enough?"

Henry could feel his eyes burning. He swallowed, straining to hold back the tears.

"Unless there was a way for you to become more like an elf," Morikend said slowly. "And do all the things we can do. You'd never have to go back to London or live in that ridiculous settlement."

"You want to find a way for me to become one of the Aesir," Henry said hoarsely, staring at the table, trying to stay as calm as he could.

"It's up to you," Morikend replied. "If you were an elf, you would be at home there - or here."

Henry blinked. Morikend looked around him.

"You humans build underground. You like the food. If you are Glondir and have the Affinity for Madjik, you could wield Svaramar just as easily. And don't tell me you don't love the snow."

"Svaramar?"

"The pure Madjik of the Morivari." Morikend looked Henry in the eye. "You would think, after all this time with Klasodin's human helpers, that the Aesir could have found a way for humans to fit in more easily."

"It's not possible."

"Of course it is. I have the solution right here."

Morikend reached under the table and held something up for Henry to see. Henry stared at it.

"But you're working with Omnitec," Henry said. "They want me dead. Why would I trust you?"

"My fight is with the Aesir." Morikend shrugged. "That's it. Do you really think I feel any loyalty towards Omnitec?" He leaned in and lowered his voice. "Do you know the one special talent the Morivari possess?"

Henry shook his head.

"I'll give you a clue." Morikend gestured around him. "None of this magnificent city occurred naturally."

"So you're good at digging and building."

"Exactly," Morikend said enthusiastically. "And once they have served my purpose, Omnitec might just find the ground disappearing under their feet. And with Omnitec gone, you're safe."

Morikend got to his feet, holding the mysterious object.

Henry's eyes were fixed on it, mesmerised by it.

"Follow me young Henry. I'll show you how this works."

CHAPTER THIRTY-FIVE

Henry followed Morikend down the steps of his royal palace and out onto a stone avenue, which ran across the front of the palace and sloped upwards into the darkness between two black, rocky escarpments. They were the tallest cliffs Henry had ever seen.

The palace itself was built into the rock face behind him. Elongated black windows gleamed like black tears among intricate gothic carvings.

Craning his neck, Henry looked up to see roads and walkways tunnelling into the rock face opposite. Bridges arched between the black cliffs high above.

"You dug all this out?" Henry said – not even trying to hide how impressed he was.

"Of course."

Morikend headed left, down the slope. Henry followed. After the palace, stone roads led left and right, carving through the rock and out of sight. At the bottom of the sloping avenue, looming shapes emerged ominously from the shadows. Henry jumped, then realised they weren't alive.

Over an arched opening in the rock, two giant stone warriors stood guard wearing the black of the Morivari and brandishing a scythe and a broadsword. Henry stepped warily under the towering figures and followed Morikend inside.

They stepped out into an amphitheatre hewn out of the black rock and took a couple of steps up onto a large stage. There were stalls, seats and galleries overlooking them. Glistening water trickled from a tiny fissure between two grandstands opposite and gathered in a basin-shaped pool by the stage.

Henry stopped and listened. There was total silence.

"Your city's not very busy, is it?" he said.

"My Morivari are hard at work. But Svaravame isn't like London, where there is noise every minute of every day." Morikend looked around him. "Warriors of all ages compete here. Warriors are made here."

"You have competitions?"

"Every month." Morikend crouched at the water pool, cupped his hands and drank. He beckoned Henry over. "Drink, young Henry, drink. The water is refreshing and very good for you. All Morivari warriors drink together from the pool before competing."

Henry approached warily, his eyes flitting to the item Morikend had placed on the stage behind him.

"We're going to fight?"

"Of course not," Morikend laughed. "You are going to practise being as quick and powerful as an elf. I'm simply here to help. Come. Drink."

Henry's cupped hands delved into the clear pool of water. He sipped. It was good. Refreshing. He gulped down some more. He turned and leapt back onto the stage feeling more energetic and crystal clear.

Morikend picked up the item and showed it to Henry. It was a shiny black breastplate with a stone set into the chest - a fusion of gold, emerald and jet. The colours swirled around inside. Black seemed to be the strongest of the three.

"It's a breastplate like my own," Morikend explained. "But it goes further than your Hafskod or your snowboard. This is

Morivar gold. With it, you will be able to wield Svaramar like Madjik, only you will be an elf. Just as quick, just as powerful."

Henry edged forward. Morikend pointed to his Hafskod.

"Of course, you will have to take that off. They will not work together."

Henry swallowed.

"Once you wear this, the choice will be yours," Morikend said. "You can stay in the Arctic. You can live here or in Alvahame. After all, your friends would never live in the settlement. Ellodine is Aesir royalty. She won't leave Alvahame, will she?" Morikend smiled. "But you would fit right in here if you wanted. You would be closer to me. I could train you personally like a mentor. How many children in your position get to have one of those?"

Henry's head swam. A home. A real one. He blinked, then swallowed.

"But you hate humans."

"I hate my enemies," Morikend said simply. "Who doesn't? All elves know what your kind would do if our existence was discovered. Look at what Omnitec have done. But you have already proven yourself to be a friend of the elves." He held out the breastplate. "To how many humans do you think I have offered such a gift?"

Henry gazed at the breastplate. Power. He could go anywhere. Do anything. Belong anywhere. No more having to sit on the top of the world alone. His eyes swept from the breastplate to Morikend. He was right. Nobody else had offered him such a gift. Just because two sides were at war didn't mean they couldn't both be right or good. The Gold List was in operation. Santa Claus would never give him anything again. He had the camera he wanted. And now something even more special.

The Hafskod came off in Henry's hand. He watched the life die inside it, then shoved it in his pocket.

Morikend placed the breastplate over Henry's head so the thick leather straps rested on his shoulders and strapped it around his waist. Henry felt his shoulders and ribs sag under the weight. The stone in the chest brightened with gold, then it dulled and swelled with jet black Svaramar. Now the breastplate was so light he could barely feel it.

Henry let out a breath. He could feel the power and energy inside him. He grinned up at Morikend, whose eyes gleamed with triumph.

"An elf in that breastplate is one thing, but a Valdir. . . Even I could not define the limits of your capabilities."

A sleek black bow materialised in Morikend's hand.

"You have a ValdFyurring too?" Henry asked, suddenly realising what it meant.

"Every form of elven Madjik has an Epicentre of its own. We have one down here. I might even show you one day." Morikend handed the bow to Henry. It was light, but longer than the Aesir bow. "Show me what you can do."

Morikend turned and paced to the other end of the amphitheatre.

"Are you ready?"

Henry nodded, his heart pounding, the adrenaline pumping through his veins. He wanted to jump up and down, to run around. But he took a few deep breaths and focused on the Morivar bow in his hand.

"This is one trial we use to test our young warriors and their competency with a bow and arrow."

A disk the size of a Frisbee appeared in Morikend's hand. He flicked his wrist and flung it into the air.

Henry reacted like lighting. He pulled back his right hand. The string and bow materialised. He released. The bow zipped through the air and shattered the flying disk in mid-air.

Morikend flung disk after disk. Henry fired, his hands and eyes moving so fast, his brain didn't even try to catch up. He shattered every disk. He reacted quicker and quicker. He struck the disks sooner and sooner, until one broke just after it left Morikend's hand.

"Is that all you can do? Break them? Show me the full extent of your power."

Henry watched, his heart pounding quicker than ever. His hands shook slightly. He brought them under control. He could feel the power. He wanted to burst.

Morikend's eyes gleamed. He flung a disk in the air. Henry reacted and fired. The arrow left a black trail like a shadow. It struck the disk and exploded in a black cloud of Svaramar. Morikend moved to throw again. Henry tossed the bow aside. The disk launched into the air. Henry gathered back his fist and fired. A black flame burst from his hand and obliterated the disk with a bang and a shower of black sparks. A broad smile crept across Morikend's face.

An explosion rang out in the distance.

Henry jumped.

Morikend's smile vanished. His eyes narrowed.

Another explosion. The ground trembled.

"What was that?" Henry said quietly.

Morikend's eyes darted in his direction.

"Our city is under attack."

CHAPTER THIRTY-SIX

Explosions thundered through Svaravame. The booming and showering stone grew louder, coming nearer and nearer to where Henry stood. Feet scrambled. Swords clashed. Screams and shouts rang out.

There was a bang. A flash of gold burst through the entrance. Swords clanged. A blade thrust. There was a grunt of pain. Something heavy slumped to the floor.

Amira appeared, sword in hand, eyes darting from Morikend to Henry. She moved smoothly, her sword aimed at Morikend.

"Come with me, Henry."

Henry said nothing. He stayed where he was. He scowled at Amira.

"Invading our city like this is an act of war," Morikend snapped.

"Herding our children into your city and holding them prisoner is an act of war."

"I'm not your child," Henry blurted.

"Yes you are," Amira shot back. "And so is Ellodine."

"She's not even here."

"Yes. She is. We just broke her out of her cell."

Henry's stomach lurched.

"They imprisoned her near the city wall. We fought our way in here to rescue you and we will not leave without you. Now take that thing off and come with me."

Something burned inside Henry.

"No," he growled. "It's mine."

"That thing is dangerous. You don't know what dark Madjik you're playing with."

"There's nothing wrong with it. You just like to think you're better than me. Now I can do anything you elves can do and more. And you don't like it."

"We like you just the way you are."

"No you don't. Ellodine doesn't."

"The first thing she said when we rescued her was we had to save you. I believe it was the second and third thing she said as well."

Henry glanced at Morikend, who made no effort to argue.

"Look at that," Amira said quietly. "The king of the Morivari is a liar."

"He gave me food and this breastplate."

"We all welcomed you into Alvahame."

"For how long? I saw Mannhame. That's where you send all the humans, isn't it? You all think you're so superior, that you're better than us."

Henry glared at Amira, his blood boiling. He hated her.

Morikend touched his fingers to the sword at his belt.

"Look at you." Amira's dark eyes gazed gently, firmly into his. "That breastplate has corrupted you just like they corrupted Madjik. It's turned black. Now your heart is turning black as well."

"You're lying," Henry snapped.

"I won't tell you again."

"You're not my mum," he shouted.

"Take it off. Now."

"NO."

In a flash Morikend ripped his sword from its sheath. Amira hurled her sword, which tore Morikend's blade from his hand. One, two, three gold arrows flashed from her bow and blew Morikend to the floor.

Henry clenched his fist to fight her off. A flash of gold light struck him in the chest and threw him onto his back. A nauseated, sickened sensation coursed through his head, through his limbs and his chest. He wanted to throw up.

Amira stood over him.

"You see, even now it's fighting you, trying to turn you into him."

Her voice blurred and quietened until it was nothing more than a faintly audible drone, drowned out by the darkness.

Silence.

Black.

Henry passed out.

CHAPTER THIRTY-SEVEN

Gloved fingers lightly slapped his face. Henry came to with a start. He sat bolt upright. He took in a deep breath, aware of his chest expanding and contracting with ease. His head hurt. The breastplate was gone. It lay across the dais in pieces. The Hafskod was back around his wrist.

He looked up at Amira, who crouched over him. A swell of guilt burned through his stomach. He could see and hear himself hating Amira, shouting at her. It was like seeing the memories of another person.

"Sorry," he blurted. "I don't hate you."

"I know." She smiled calmly. "Svaramar had changed you already." She reached out, took hold of his hand and lifted him to his feet. "Come on."

Morikend lay on his side, hanging off the edge of the stage. "Is he . . .?"

"Dead? No. Just out cold."

"Still?"

"He took a couple more hits after you went down."

Amira led him under the stone warriors. Henry frowned. It was so quiet. No shouts, no screams and no fighting. He turned after Amira to head back up the stone avenue carving through the rocks and the cliffs. He stopped dead.

Surrounding them on all sides, spilling out of the palace, on the rocky bridges and walkways above, was an army of

Morivari. Bows and arrows were ready. Swords, scythes, sickles and maces were all aimed at them. But no one attacked.

Henry and Amira climbed into the sleigh where Rodin and Ellodine aimed their bows and arrows up at the walkways. Then Henry saw the huge white shapes lumbering between them and the massed Morivari. Three were on the upper walkways, one was in front of them and the fifth roamed by the steps leading into the palace. Polar bears.

The four reindeer looked around at Henry and Amira. One of them uttered a low growl and the sleigh set off at a gentle pace. The three polar bears up above sprang from the walkways and thudded to the ground. All five fell in step with the sleigh. Grrhdrig lumbered alongside Henry and gave a faint nod of recognition, which Henry returned.

None of the Morivari moved a step, but every weapon trained on them as they slid away on the raw stone, looking up at the towering cliffs on either side of them.

The sleigh took a sharp turn to the left and the road became steeper. It wound left and right as if they were climbing a mountain. They left the last of the Morivar warriors behind and eventually daylight streamed onto the road ahead of them. Their dark, rocky surroundings became gleaming white. Walls of ice flew past and the runners glided over the icy floor. The sleigh left the underground city behind and the reindeer picked up speed. Rodin put down his bow and arrow and grabbed the reins. Henry squinted in the light. He shot a glance back to the tunnel entrance. No one followed or chased them. He breathed a sigh of relief.

The triumphant roar of the polar bears bellowed after the sleigh as it shot over the snow, then took off and flew through the air. Henry was free.

CHAPTER THIRTY-EIGHT

"HE WAS WEARING WHAT?"

Ellodine's face was crimson with rage. Henry sat on the sleigh floor, leaning back against the wall, his arms folded.

"What were you thinking? What is wrong with you?"

"I'm human. That's what's wrong with me." Henry scowled back at her. "I see your face every time I'm not as quick as an elf or don't think the same way as an elf."

"You took their weapons."

"I used them to help us get away."

"You just take whatever you can."

"Why shouldn't I?"

Ellodine pursed her lips. She crouched and thrust her hands into Henry's coat pocket.

"Get off."

Henry tried to shake her off, but Ellodine found what she was looking for and yanked it from his pocket.

"I knew it," she exclaimed.

Amira took hold of her arm.

"What are you doing, Ellodine?"

"In the ice palace, they knew we were there. They were tracking Henry."

"How is that possible?"

"With this." Ellodine held up the camera Henry had found in the star. "You humans and your shiny objects," she snarled.

Amira took it out of her hands. Her expression was grim.

"Where did you get this, Henry?" she said quietly.

"It was in my room this morning."

"Who left it for you?"

"I don't know."

"But you know it's not one of ours."

"One of you must have left it," Henry shot back.

"There is a traitor in Alvahame," said Rodin. "Why would you take it?"

"Why wouldn't I?" he muttered, hugging his knees and staring at the floor. He could feel them watching him.

Amira pulled out the battery and the memory card, then produced a sliver of metal the same size with a tiny red flashing light. She snapped it between her fingers. She gripped the camera in her fist and crushed it, then hurled it away.

"What are you doing?" Henry exploded. "That's mine."

She looked at him, her face grave.

"It doesn't belong in Alvahame."

"Neither do I."

Henry slumped on the sleigh floor. He swallowed a couple of times to stop himself from crying. He wanted to go home, but he had no home. It was the sleigh or Mrs Mcready's house. And he didn't belong in either.

Amira crouched in front of him. Her hand gently touched his. Out of the corner of his eye, he saw Ellodine linger next to Rodin and lean on the front of the sleigh.

"It's alright," Amira said. "Ellodine doesn't understand what it's like to be human any more than you know what it's like to be an elf. It takes time - and watching you through a LagFyurring would never be enough."

Henry nodded his head in agreement, his eyes fixed on the floor.

"In your position, I can't say I would have done any differently," she continued. "But then I wasn't born in Alvahame either."

Henry looked up at her.

"You mean . . . ?"

"That's right," she smiled. "I was born in Svaravame. We left when I was a youngling. My mother didn't make it."

"Sorry."

"She died making sure I got away. Before then I didn't even realise there was something to get away from. I actually liked it down there."

"So did I," Henry admitted. "I think."

"Back in the ice palace," Amira said, changing the subject. "Did you hear anything that might help us?"

"There was gold - Aesir gold inside it, but it's changing to Azmar. They said Grimnir was the one in charge. We think he's an elf."

"There's no elf in Alvahame named Grimnir, Henry."

"He's definitely an Aesr. And a powerful one." Henry looked up at Amira. He thought. His mind raced through the crime dramas and spy films he had seen. "But Grimnir could be a code or an alias - so his real name isn't given away."

"The boy's right," said Rodin, without turning round.

"But Omnitec's ice palace has been there for years," Amira frowned.

"Which means an elf has been working against us for even longer," Rodin replied. "And we still have no idea who it is."

Ellodine took the reins. Rodin handed Henry a hot, steaming mug of Fyoreig. He took the reins back from Ellodine, made her sit down and handed her a mug as well.

"Just sit there, relax and drink it all," said Amira. "You need it."

Henry took a sip. It was like hot life flowing through his insides. He took a deep breath and leaned back.

"Where are we going?" he asked.

"To look for the staff," Rodin answered. "I have a few ideas."

"How did you get out of Alvahame?"

"Rodin talked Gronodin into it – eventually," Amira replied.

"We've already tried Vanahame," said Rodin. "Klasodin wasn't there. He isn't in the Arctic anymore."

"So what happened to him?"

"I'm beginning to think he left Alvahame of his own accord."

"That's not possible," Ellodine exploded.

"If he is no longer in the Arctic, then it is likely he did just that," Rodin continued. "Which means he is hiding somewhere among the humans. And worse still, no one I spoke to remembers seeing his staff since we brought Henry to Alvahame. For all we know, he hid it somewhere so Yohann could not get his hands on it. Either way, Klasodin and his staff are hidden in the world of the humans."

"Where do we go?" said Ellodine.

"I am as familiar with his journeys as any elf. I know of a couple of places."

Henry drank the Fyoreig as quickly as he could. His mind sprang into action. He dug into his pocket and pulled out Klasodin's memoirs. Something told him that if Rodin was right, the answer would lie in the pages.

CHAPTER THIRTY-NINE

Gwendolin found a sumptuous white coat hanging next to her wedding dress on the morning of her big day. It fitted perfectly. No surprises there. Wearing it, she did not feel the cold at all as she led her wedding train up the street, which had been cleared of all snow, but was hardened by a sheet of glittering ground frost.

She caught sight of a bearded figure sitting astride his horse on the mountainside overlooking the town. She smiled to herself. She knew Klasodin would not appear in public, but her newest friend would never forget such an important day, not after he had done so much to bring it about in the first place.

Late at night, after enjoying their first few hours together alone as a married couple, Gwendolin heard the edges of a raucous noise next door. Wrapping herself in her coat, taking her dazed husband by the hand, she headed to her father's home to find him drinking the good health of a visitor with a glass of hot wine - not his first of the day by any means.

She sent Ernest and Ullrich for some more wine.

"Thank you," she said. "For everything."

"You are very welcome," Klasodin smiled.

"Are you really called Saint Nicholas? Is that even the name you told me?"

"The name I gave you was Sin Ni Klas. But I like Saint Nicholas. It sounds more like something you would say."

"Is it your real name?"

"It's more of a title. It means "he who is without nothing". They used my actual name to come up with it."

"Someone invented a title for you? You must be very important."

"I am the king of my people."

She smiled, as if nothing he told her could possibly surprise her.

"Where is your land?" she asked, picturing him as king of some distant country.

"Far north of here," he answered vaguely.

"And what is your real name?"

"My name is Klasodin."

"Not a name I have heard before." She paused. "Are you a wizard?"

"No," he chuckled. "Nothing like that."

"Are you human?"

He smiled. He knew the question was coming - and what answer would follow.

"No. I am an elf. I live in a city called Alvahame."

There was no shock. No surprise. No promise that Klasodin's secret was safe. There was no need of one.

On the morning of the winter festival, Eva awoke to find the food and drink she had left on the window sill was gone, but there was a package wrapped in paper and string, with a tag, which read:

"To Eva, from Santa Claus."

Inside was a thick, warm blanket. Fifty other children awoke to find similar parcels in their open windows.

Klasodin and Slepnir flew back to Alvahame in excitement. Their Purpose was clear.

CHAPTER FORTY

A city-wide party welcomed Klasodin's return. Alvahame itself was slowly crawling its way up the mountains as new houses were built. The tree grew with the city, its very top marking their building progress. At Klasodin's instruction, the Aesir began digging into the tree itself, hollowing out the trunk and carving out spaces around and within the growing crock of gold.

Klasodin spent weeks and months alone with the gold and his staff, fusing them to the Purpose and harnessing their power. Through them, he could feel the connection with every child who had left their window open for him. Every new open window brought a new connection. Soon it wasn't just children doing it either.

By the eve of the winter festival the following year, Klasodin had built himself a sleigh, which he filled with the gifts for his human friends. He gathered his thickest cloak about him. Slepnir's own sense of theatricality meant he wasn't to be outdone either. He took one look at the sleigh and then morphed into the shape of a reindeer.

Klasodin stopped first at Eva's home. He watched her through the open window, her breath billowing in clouds in the frozen air.

"This will not do at all," he said to Slepnir.

Eva's gift in one hand, Klasodin aimed his staff at the food. It vanished - to reappear in Alvahame. There would be far too much for him and Slepnir to consume in one night. The window stretched. The wall around it opened to form a doorway. Klasodin stepped in and closed it behind him.

He added some wood to the fire and had it roaring into life. He placed the empty plates and cups on a table next to it and positioned Eva's gifts by the fireplace. He left how he had entered, shutting the window behind him.

He did the same thing with every house he entered, making sure no one opened their windows to him and the freezing cold.

The next morning, Ullrich pondered the meaning of the sleigh tracks running through the streets of the town and up to his house. Soon the entire town was gathered around the fir tree in the town centre, as talk spread of the generous visitor who had left them gifts during the night.

Klasodin set his elves to work, building the city and making gifts. Every time something new was created, it was given to the ValdFyurring. In turn, it would produce as many duplicates of each item as they needed.

Word spread. By the next winter festival, nearly every house in every town in the area had a plate of food by the fireplace waiting for the generous visitor. Klasodin touched down in his sleigh which was piled high with gifts. He removed all the food with his staff and left gifts by the fireplace.

The fir tree in Ullrich's town, around which all the people had gathered, had been used to celebrate Klasodin's visit. Ernest was the first person to bring a smaller fir tree into his home and leave it in the corner of the room near the fireplace, which nearly everyone copied. Klasodin left their gifts under the tree.

Sliding away after a long night's work, a stone whistled past Klasodin's ear. He turned and caught a second, larger rock hurtling towards his head.

The boy sat on the roof of a tiny house nearby, a pile of stones gathered next to him. He flung them at Klasodin, who caught them and tossed them aside. Slepnir turned and snarled at the boy, who paled and nearly fell off the roof.

"What is your name, boy?"

"Emrick," the boy said sullenly.

"What is your quarrel with me?"

"What is your quarrel with me? You brought all the other children in town a present - just not me."

"Did you leave your window open?"

"No. I have nothing to give you. And I'm cold at night with the window closed."

"I don't leave gifts because people give me something in return. I go where I am needed - or wanted."

"I need things."

"You didn't ask."

"Nobody likes me. It's no surprise you don't either."

"Climb down, young Emrick."

The boy obeyed, his expression still sullen.

"Is throwing stones really the way to catch my attention?"

The boy shrugged.

"But this is how you react to every situation, isn't it? Violence. Unpleasantness. This is why none of the children like you, isn't it?"

Emrick nodded.

"If I'm nicer to people, will I get a present too?"

"You might find the other children like you if you are nicer to them. But my gifts are not deserved or earned. I give out of love. I give to those who want me to. That is all. What would you like?"

"I don't know." Emrick shrugged. "Just something."

"I think we can learn from each other, young Emrick. I never meant to exclude anyone. Now I know I can't just rely on open windows. I need to actively pursue answers, to look for

those who need me. And you shouldn't wait for the children of the town to come to you. You need to be the one who makes friends."

Emrick nodded. Klasodin could tell he believed him. He frowned. Something was happening. He lifted the staff in his hand, which burned with Madjik, fired up by the belief of the boy. He produced a warm blanket and a sledge for Emrick and promised he would return.

The next morning, the ValdFyurring produced an image of a small stone fireplace. Two words had been scrawled on it in chalk:

"Thank you."

By the next winter festival, over a hundred notes and letters to the mysterious visitor had been detected by the growing ValdFyurring. The longest was from Emrick.

CHAPTER FORTY-ONE

"Henry." A voice cut through Henry's state of reverie.

He realised he was reading via the light emanating from the Hafskod. Darkness flew by overhead. Amira looked down at him.

"We're going to land soon," she said.

"Where are we?" he blurted, his mind all over the place.

"Germany."

Henry blinked.

They touched down in thick snow, in a wooded copse surrounded by a thick gathering of silvery fir trees.

"There is Madjik here," said Rodin, vaulting out of the sleigh and landing in snow up to his ankles. "It had better be the staff. We have nowhere else to look."

"We've looked everywhere else already?" asked Henry.

"It's the first trace of Madjik in all the places we've flown over."

"It must be here then."

Henry hauled himself up onto the sleigh wall. He climbed onto his feet and jumped off. He landed in snow up to his thighs. Now he couldn't move.

Behind him, Ellodine collapsed into laughter. Amira giggled. Rodin afforded himself a slight grin, then looked irritable again.

Amira dropped Henry's snowboard in front of him, heaved him out of the snow by his armpits and landed him on it.

A silver flame rose from the Hafskod and floated towards Henry's eyes. It wasn't like the night vision brought by the green flame, but everything was clearer and crystalised in the snow. He slid alongside Ellodine, following the two older elves, who strode gracefully through the snow, picking a path through the trees.

A steep bank dropped down onto a path, which led left into the mountains and right towards a small town of wooden houses with pointed roofs. Henry looked out straight ahead of him, over the path, to fields and mountains in the distance.

Rodin led them towards the little town. Ahead of them on the right, two wooden houses stood side by side, overlooking the left turn onto the snow-covered main road through the town.

Henry stopped in front of the two houses. For some reason, they looked familiar. He looked down the main road. Half way down on the right, the street opened out into a little square bordered by shops. In the middle of the square was a Christmas tree the height of the houses around it.

Suddenly Henry knew where he was. He had just been reading about it. The house on the left had a covered veranda. Henry could imagine Ullrich sitting there at night with a mug of hot wine. The house on his right had a first floor. He could almost see Gwendolin and Ernest at the window.

Rodin crept into what had been Ullrich's home, then emerged thirty seconds later. He opened the door to the house next door, slipped inside, then reappeared.

"Would Klasodin really have left it here?" Amira whispered.

"He trusted his human helpers as much as anyone. If the humans have it, it will be with his first friends or with a

Glondir." Rodin marched past them. "And the first Glondir lived here."

"Gwendolin was Glondir?" said Henry.

"No. It was a boy called Emrick."

Rodin took a sharp left opposite the square. He materialised ahead of them five minutes later muttering under his breath and shaking his head.

"I thought you detected Madjik," said Ellodine.

"I did, but not the staff."

"So where is the Madjik?" Henry asked.

"In the walls." Rodin nodded to Ullrich and Gwendolin's old homes. "How else do you think they stayed up all these years?"

Rodin marched through the snow and out of the town in the direction of where they had left the sleigh.

"Where else can we look?" said Amira.

Rodin shrugged.

Henry slid after them. Ellodine drew alongside him.

"Any ideas?" she murmured.

"This was the place in the book. But there was another girl."

"You mean Eva? We flew over her village on the way here."

"Nothing?"

Ellodine shook her head.

"But where else is there?" Henry said. "How many other Glondirs have there been?"

He looked down at his Hafskod. There were no dancing flames. There seemed to be three in total, all dancing at different times. He thought back to when he had first put it on. There were two flames. Then Klasodin left and there was one. Henry's mind flitted back to when the first noise had awoken him that night. One creak after another. There was the window, the floor. But there was another noise. Something else creaked.

No. That couldn't be it.

His jaw dropped.

He grabbed Ellodine's arm.

"I've got it. I know where Klasodin hid his staff."

"He hid it?"

"Yep. And right where we could find it."

CHAPTER FORTY-TWO

The sleigh touched down on a snow-covered rooftop that Henry knew very well. He looked around him with a strange, happy feeling growing in his stomach.

"Whether we find the staff here or not - that was good work, Henry," Rodin said seriously, vaulting out of the sleigh the second it slid to a standstill.

Ellodine gave Henry a friendly thump on the shoulder. Henry grinned and pushed her back. He climbed out of the sleigh and landed in the snow. Ellodine crunched into the snow next to him and gave him a shove. Henry flicked some snow at her. She squealed.

"Quiet you two," Amira hissed.

Ellodine nudged Henry with her elbow. Henry lifted his right leg and gave her a light kick on the bottom with the outside of his foot. Ellodine snorted with laughter. She aimed a kick back at him, but Henry dodged out of the way.

A scowl from Amira stopped them. Rodin was already on the little balcony outside Henry's bedroom window. Rodin climbed inside. The others followed.

The Hafskod flashed gold light around Henry's attic bedroom. It was immaculate. Henry could tell it had been tidied and the bed had been made since he had left.

He looked at the bedroom that had been his for nearly a year. It almost felt like being home again. He felt a sudden urge to run downstairs and tell the others he was back. They would all be excited to see him. They would want to hear about his adventures.

A thought crossed his mind. His stomach lurched.

"Mrs Mcready knows I'm not here," he hissed. "What if she called the police?"

"You're just thinking about this now?" Ellodine whispered, the indignation etched across her face.

A nudge from Amira calmed her down.

"He asked if they were safe," Rodin whispered. "What else did he need to know?"

"Well, I suppose you had other things to think about," Ellodine said begrudgingly. "I'm sure your foster mother and siblings weren't worried at all."

Amira rolled her eyes.

"Klasodin set everything straight," Rodin reassured them. "Now find the staff."

Henry checked his Hafskod. A flame danced over the face. He knew it. He looked back towards the sash window. Klasodin had hidden it before approaching his bed. He left the others and headed for the two doors near the sash window.

The Hafskod beamed brightly.

Nothing in the bathroom.

He opened the cupboard door. The light from the Hafskod was blinding. Henry screwed his eyes tight shut and groped around with both hands. He reached up towards the top shelf, routing under piles of jumpers Mrs Mcready had bought him from charity shops. Something slapped into the palm of his hand.

A light flashed on inside Henry's head.

He could see thousands of toys and games.

He thought back to his time at the Craft of Creation - to the shelves of toys and games. He could see all of them in the ValdFyurring. There was food. Clothes. Weapons.

He thought back to the inside of the ice palace. He found original designs for flying snowboards, dart guns, crossbows and bows that fired Madjik - all buried in the deepest recesses of the ValdFyurring.

He delved yet further, exploring every part of the ValdFyurring. His mind met what felt like a thick gold curtain. He pushed through it. Now he could see mobile phones, tablets, laptops, games consoles and computer games. The missing designs and gifts.

Slowly, carefully, he pushed the curtain aside and pulled them all out. He found his Hafskod, but left it where it was.

He found the food again and took a good look at the fish. He would need it later.

A hand shaking him vigorously snapped him back to his bedroom. He stared at the staff in his hand, which had shrunk to the size of a wand. No wonder he hadn't found it before leaving for Alvahame.

Ellodine had hold of his arm.

"What did you see?" she urged.

"Everything," he said. "I found the missing designs. I think I brought them back to where the wrappers in Giving can access them again."

Henry held the staff out to Rodin, who shook his head.

"It's yours, Glondir."

Henry stared at the staff in his hands, at the Hafskod.

"I guess I really am Glondir," he said.

"Of course you are," Ellodine replied. "You're only just realising it now?"

"I don't know. It just never seemed real before." He looked around at his three travelling companions. "What do we do now?"

"We have to find Klasodin," Ellodine insisted.

"It's the twenty-third of December," Amira replied. "There's no time."

"We have until the time Klasodin needs to set off from Alvahame," said Rodin. "But where would we look? We don't know of anywhere else."

"Henry, there must be something in Klasodin's journal," Ellodine urged, tugging on Henry's coat sleeve. "Come on, think."

Henry's mind went blank. He shrugged. Ellodine's face fell. Flickers of disappointment crossed the faces of Amira and Rodin. They climbed out of the window. Henry followed them out onto the balcony, shut the window quietly and climbed up after them.

He stood on his favourite spot on the roof, looking out over London, its bright lights and noises radiating up into the night sky. Even now, it was one of his favourite places in the world. It almost felt like home. But then Henry didn't belong there any more than he did in Alvahame. Saving Christmas wouldn't solve anything.

Or maybe it would.

He watched the lights, the spread of the city, seams of traffic surging through it like veins carrying blood through the body. And there Henry was, watching from on high as usual. He'd done it in Alvahame as well.

Funny how Klasodin lived in the star, looking down over the city, looking up at the stars. Living up there, you could feel like you were the only person in the world.

And Klasodin liked his solitude. Henry did too. Wherever Klasodin was, it would be somewhere that gave him peace and quiet and a place to look at the stars.

A laugh erupted from the pit of Henry's stomach. He turned to the elves.

"I think I know where he is. But it's a long way away."

Rodin leapt into the sleigh.

"Let's not wait any longer then."

CHAPTER FORTY-THREE

The city is under attack again. The Morivari are enraged by our making gifts for humankind. They hate humans. They attack our city every year.

One of their kind arrived in Alvahame claiming refuge, carrying a youngling in his arms. His name is Orekend. He claims he ran away with his wife and his young daughter, but his wife did not make it out of Svaravame. He says he saw her die. I do not believe a word he says, but Klasodin welcomed him with open arms. The youngling will be raised as an Aesrine, a raven-haired beauty and a daily reminder of what they really are. Our enemy, the Morivari, are living among us.

Klasodin devotes himself to the fulfilling of The Purpose. He spends most of his time with the ValdFyurring. Some say he should be leading the fight against the Morivari instead, as all elven kings do.

Henry flicked to the next entry, a much shorter one.

The Morivari have found their way inside the city. I do not know how, but they must have had help from within Alvahame. This could be the end for all of us. Klasodin must save us now.

Henry blinked. Dark stains were smeared over the page and the next one. He realised Ellodine was sitting next to him, reading the pages over his shoulder.

"What do you think it is?" he whispered.

Ellodine looked at him, her eyes wide, her face pale.

"It's dried blood."

Henry turned over to the next page. The entry was in different handwriting.

This is the first time I have been able to even look at these pages. Reading it for the first time, I cherish every word. I wish I had been more enthusiastic at the time.

Never again has the Margullring been neglected. Never again have I spent so much time with the ValdFyurring at the expense of time with my kin.

Orek, the Morivar who arrived all those years ago, has flourished and is now the head of the Craft of Creation after Shoffodin, his predecessor, died suddenly in a nasty accident. New developments such as the home computer and the video game will prove a challenge in the years to come, both to the Madgikal power of the ValdFyurring and to our expertise and imagination. We will need Orek more than ever. His daughter, Amira, grew up into the raven-haired beauty Ecromir predicted. Rodin took her under his wing and she has become a fine warrior maiden. Their love remains unspoken.

Larodine, my granddaughter (some generations removed) has removed herself from the responsibility loaded on the shoulders of my descendants. She works hard, caring for this great city, while the boy I know she will marry works equally hard in protecting it.

Henry turned on a couple of pages, looking for something in particular. He found it.

The long-awaited day has arrived. Larodine gave birth to a beautiful Aesrine. She called her Ellodine. The second I saw Ellodine for the first time, I knew it. The special generation this city has been waiting for has arrived.

"Special generation?" Henry whispered.

Ellodine rolled her eyes.

"Klasodin's been going on and on about it all my life."

Henry frowned. He flicked back to the part about Rodin and Amira.

"How long ago was that bit written?" he asked.

"I don't know," Ellodine shrugged. "Twenty, thirty years ago."

Henry nodded over to Amira and Rodin.

"How old are they?" he whispered.

"Amira's nearly fifty. I think Rodin's about a hundred. And they've been in love with each other all that time."

"They're in love?"

"You didn't notice?"

"No. All that time?"

Ellodine nodded.

A thought struck Henry.

"How old are you?" he asked.

"I'm twelve," she said irritably.

"Well, I don't know. You all look young."

"Elf children grow up like you humans," Ellodine explained. "The ageing process slows down once you reach early adulthood."

"So how come they haven't done anything about it? You know, go out with each other, get married or something?"

"They're warriors. When you fight alongside the one you love, you risk getting distracted or making the wrong decision."

Henry nodded. He had seen the same problem on some late night crime dramas he wasn't supposed to be watching.

"So that's it?" he said.

Ellodine nodded.

"It's not because he doesn't like Orek. Or Orek doesn't like him?" Henry pressed.

"No."

"Because if Rodin thinks Orek's a traitor, he wouldn't want to be related to him, would he?"

"Orek is not a traitor," Ellodine insisted. "He left the Morivari to come to Alvahame. His wife was killed."

"So he tells us."

"Orek's great. Next you'll tell me Amira's a traitor."

"It must be Gronodin then," Henry shrugged. "He's got what he wants now."

"He didn't want Klasodin to leave."

"Or so he says."

Ellodine scowled and folded her arms.

"Well someone's a traitor," Henry whispered irritably. "And it's probably someone you know. They've been working against Klasodin since before you were born."

"I like everyone in Alvahame." Ellodine swallowed and stared at her boots. She bit her lip, then took a deep breath. "How could any Aesr betray us like that? What we have is perfect already. Why would you spoil it?"

Henry shrugged, something boiling inside him, waiting to tell her that everything spoils – or it's spoiled already.

But he could see she was hurt and upset. He didn't like it. So he said nothing and edged a little closer instead, wandering what he would do to make sure he never saw her so sad again.

CHAPTER FORTY-FOUR

He wandered further into the grassy meadow, breathing in its sweet aroma. A cold wind flew in from overhead, but the lingering pine trees turned to shield him, allowing just a breeze of fresh pine to waft into his nostrils. Soft, blossom-covered branches coloured in white, pink and blue gently embraced him, showering him in sweet-scented petals. An icy cold wind burst through the trees. Long grasses tickled his face. He realised he was sitting down - on something hard. Was he really in a meadow? But he could still smell something wonderful.

He jolted awake. Wispy clouds whooshed past him in the blue early morning sky. He shifted on the floor of the sleigh. Ellodine had her head rested on his shoulder, her long, blonde hair blowing around him.

He caught Amira's gaze. She was watching him with a faint smile on her face.

"Where are we?" he mumbled.

"Approaching the Antarctic," Amira replied. "You can see it on the horizon."

Ellodine stirred and raised her head, sweeping the hair out of her face. Henry clambered gingerly to his feet, gripping the side of the sleigh for dear life in case his legs suddenly gave way beneath him. He watched the snowy landscape shoot towards him, then fly by under the speeding sleigh.

He checked his Hafskod. Just the one dancing flame. He shot a glance down to the staff lying at his feet.

"We're not near enough yet," he rumbled, several hours of sleep still in his throat. He coughed and spluttered and cleared it.

Ellodine snorted with laughter. He nudged her. She poked him in the ribs.

The reindeer pulled the sleigh through the wintry air over the Antarctic for what seemed like hours until a second, tiny flame burst into life over the watch face on Henry's Hafskod. Rodin steered carefully, reacting to every wax or wane of the dancing flame. Eventually the sleigh lowered into an icy white valley, a flat plain of ice and snow between two cliffs.

Ahead, jutting out from the escarpment and rising out of the snowy plain was a perfectly formed, blade-shaped ice shard. Rodin steered around the shard and pulled up in the corner where it met the cliff. A narrow opening led down inside. The sleigh just fitted down it.

The path curved one way then the other, before opening out into a vast cavern. Its floor was smooth, polished stone and one wall was the silvery surface of the ice shard. There were some chairs and a table near a stove and a fireplace.

A lone figure sat on an armchair in front of the fireplace. He jabbed at it with a poker, making the burning coals crackle and spark, then picked up a mug of steaming hot wine and sipped from it. Slepnir emerged from a shadowy doorway in the opposite corner.

"So you found me," Klasodin said, without turning around.

A blur of blonde flew past Henry and landed on Klasodin's lap. He gave a wry smile and drew his arm around her.

"Why did you run away, Klasodin?" Ellodine asked.

"I didn't run away, my child," Klasodin said. "I simply saw no reason to stay."

"Not even Merrodine?"

"Merrodine will join me here when her work is done."

"She knew?" Ellodine was aghast.

"Of course," Klasodin shrugged.

"But what about Christmas?"

"What about it?"

"Without you it's ruined."

"Christmas will carry on with Gronodin at the helm. And if all else fails, there's always Omnitec."

Klasodin raised his mug and gulped from it. Ellodine climbed off his lap.

"You don't mean that," she said, her voice trembling.

"It's the way the world turns." Klasodin drained his mug, then heaved himself up off his chair, wandered over to the stove, poured himself another hot wine and sank down into his chair again. "The world doesn't care about me. Its children want as much as they can get out of me. Their letters are long, demanding wish lists. Their parents do what they can to further the myth that children can earn my gifts by being better, bribing them into behaving well, when nobody did anything to earn them in the first place. Now the Council of the Aesir has lost faith in the ValdFyurring and in me. My time is over. Long live Omnitec." Klasodin raised his mug again and drank.

Ellodine stepped away from him, looking like she had been slapped in the face, like she was about to cry.

"I don't believe what I'm hearing," said Amira, a dangerous edge to her voice.

Klasodin said nothing.

Amira wheeled around, her eyes burning with fury.

"You two. Leave us," she snapped.

Slepnir gave a grunt and headed towards the corner he came from. Henry and Ellodine followed him without a word, through a narrow doorway and down a couple of steps into a dark room with four bare walls, a pile of supplies in the corner and an unmade bed against the near wall.

A loud, heated argument raged in the cavern behind. The three elves shouted at each other with angry voices.

Slepnir grunted irritably. He found some oats in the supplies and sat with his back to the argument, munching loudly.

Henry could see his photographs in his mind, of his parents, their faces contorted and angry, their eyes hurt and upset. He sat down on the cold floor against the bed, hugging his knees. There was no camera to hide behind. He could still hear them. Their voices just got louder, echoing around the stone walls.

Ellodine was sobbing on the bed behind him.

Henry clamped his hands over his ears. He started to hum to drown out the noise. Two arms reached around and hugged him. Ellodine pressed her head against his, the tears still streaming down her face. Henry squeezed his eyes shut, listening to Ellodine's shaky breaths, hoping the shouting would stop.

CHAPTER FORTY-FIVE

The arguing had stopped. The entire cavern was silent. Ellodine sniffed. She pushed herself up onto her knees and wiped her face dry with her hands. Henry climbed to his feet. Together, they crept out.

Klasodin sat as he was, facing the fireplace, poker in one hand, mug of steaming hot wine in the other. Rodin paced, his face grim. Amira sat on a chair with her arms folded, her expression like granite.

"So you read my journal?" Klasodin said, stabbing at the fire.

Henry stepped forward warily, his hand sweating as it clenched around the staff. He held it out for Klasodin to take, but the elf simply held up a hand to refuse it.

"No. It's yours now. I'll show you how it works." Klasodin's tone was brusque. His jaw set.

Henry opened his mouth to argue, then thought better of it.

"When I first touched it, I saw everything in the ValdFyurring," he said quietly. "Even the missing designs. I put them back."

Klasodin nodded approvingly.

Henry frowned.

"You knew they were there?" he said.

"Of course," Klasodin replied. "But there is nothing they can do about it this close to Christmas. Guard the staff. They will try to take it from you."

"Why can't you guard it?"

"I'm done," Klasodin stated – as if that was the end of the discussion. "You summon gifts from the Sleigh Room like you would anything from the ValdFyurring. Find it. Picture it. Summon it."

"That's how you deliver presents?"

"Now it's how you deliver presents. You will need to accompany Gronodin and summon the gifts for him. I knew every child and every gift, but he won't have a clue."

A thought struck Henry.

"Hang on. How did you know the designs were still in there?"

"I put them there." Klasodin took a calm sip of his hot wine.

"Why?" Henry stared at him in amazement.

"I knew someone was siphoning the ValdFyurring's Madjik and trying to steal the designs. I just hid them." Klasodin gave a chuckle. "They probably thought they'd done it themselves."

"You sabotaged Christmas," Henry accused him.

"I did no such thing," Klasodin snapped. "I simply prevented it from being sabotaged any further."

"Didn't do much good. It's ruined anyway."

"Alvahame will continue. I made sure of that."

"It's ruined. It'll never be the same again. Not that you care." Henry slumped on a chair with his arms folded.

"I care more than anyone," Klasodin growled. "If it weren't for my caring, you wouldn't have received a thing last year. Thanks to your antics at school, you were one of the first on Gronodin's Black List. You tossed my journal aside without a second thought. I made sure you ended up in the best foster home, but you don't want to be there either."

"I don't belong there."

"How would you know?" Klasodin turned on Henry. "You haven't tried. You think you're the only one? You really think every person in that foster home of yours doesn't have their own horror story to tell?"

"And now no presents either," Henry shot back at him. "That'll help. I mean, you're all very good at watching us suffer through the LagFyurring. Now you're going to take Christmas away."

"I'm doing nothing of the sort," Klasodin insisted.

"You're not trying to save it," Henry retorted, getting angrier. "Happy just to watch everything go wrong as usual. You knew about the Valdiri. You knew about Bayne. You knew I was in danger and you did nothing to save us. My parents are dead."

Klasodin leapt to his feet, his face purple with rage.

"THE BLANKET," he roared. "ALL YOU HAD TO DO WAS GIVE THEM THE BLANKET. BUT YOU WANTED A NEW CAMERA BECAUSE THE ONE I GAVE YOU LAST YEAR - THE MADJIKAL CAMERA - WASN'T GOOD ENOUGH. YOU'RE JUST LIKE ALL THE REST OF THEM."

He looked around at the other three elves staring at him aghast. He took a breath and sat down again.

"You humans and your shiny objects," he muttered. "I didn't destroy Christmas. You did. You and your kind have been slowly ruining it for years. I've been fighting a losing battle for as long as I can remember. It never occurred to you that I, like any good parent, don't just give you everything you want. I think about what is good for you. And what thanks do I get? It's no wonder I've given up."

Klasodin drained his mug, levered himself onto his feet and wandered over to the stove. Henry sat in shellshock. He was vaguely aware of Amira marching over to Klasodin and reprimanding him with a pointed finger.

Klasodin wandered back over and sank into his chair.

"I'm sorry, Henry," he said quietly. "That was wrong of me." He sighed. "We spend all this time watching you from afar and we still don't understand you. Life was excruciating for you. Of course you acted out at school."

"I shouldn't have taken the money. Or set off the fire alarm." Henry realised with a jolt that he had just admitted it out loud for the first time.

"No. You shouldn't. But the signs were there. Who else could have done anything about it? You needed me more - not less. That's what we should have learned. Just like I should have foreseen how Yohann would react to not being made Glondir and then you turning up. And what Omnitec would do when a new Glondir was being considered. I just assumed that you would settle in at your new foster home and in Alvahame."

"I'm not an elf," Henry said quietly.

"What does that matter?"

"Humans don't fit in. That's why they all live in Mannhame."

"Alvahame doesn't need another elf, Henry. It needs you. Just the way you are. That's why you fit in."

"But they're better than me at everything."

"Then why do you have the staff?"

Henry had no answer to that.

"No one expected you to be an elf, Henry. We have elves for that."

Henry laughed. Klasodin smiled.

"You're the first Glondir to race around the world on a snowboard and a sleigh to save Christmas," he said. "And it turns out you're not an expert with a bow and arrow. Who'd have thought it?"

"I've seen things in the ValdFyurring I could use instead," Henry suggested.

"I wish I'd thought of that before." Klasodin looked at him. "You know, you don't look like a boy who's having such a terrible time in his foster home."

A smile crept over Henry's face.

"Maybe not. They are nice - even Rosie. My bedroom's cool. And the rooftop's brilliant." Henry stopped and thought. "Some of Mrs Mcready's things are from you, aren't they?"

"Of course."

"I thought you only gave to children."

"Whatever gave you that idea? You've read my journal. Some of my first ever gifts were to grownups."

"My, um, foster family," Henry said. "They wouldn't have much without you."

Klasodin smiled ruefully.

"And if it doesn't happen this year," Henry continued, "it will never happen again."

"I am tired, Henry. I am very tired."

"That's because you're fighting against Omnitec and saboteurs and the Council and making and delivering loads more presents each year."

"Thank you for summing up my pain."

"Isn't it worth fighting to put right?" Henry persisted. "I mean, this is your life's work. You're not on your own. The four of us travelled the whole world to help you. And if you really didn't want to carry on, why leave me your journal, when it leads me right to you? Why give me the staff when you know I can use it? Why hide it at all? And why hide the designs? It's like you were fighting back already."

"No arguing with that," Klasodin conceded.

Henry took a deep breath.

"And if you hadn't given me those gifts last year, where I would be right now?"

CHAPTER FORTY-SIX

The sleigh pulled by Slepnir and Rodin's four reindeer zipped over the Atlantic Ocean. Rodin gripped the reins. Klasodin stood next to him, staff in hand.

"Who wrote your journal?" Henry asked, gripping the side of the sleigh for dear life as the cold, rushing wind beat against his face.

"His name was Ecromir."

"Like the Hall of Ecromir?"

"The very same. I didn't ask him to do it, but he put it upon himself to record as much of my life as he could."

"And the stain on the pages?"

Klasodin took a deep breath.

"Ecromir's last entry details the Morivari attack on Alvahame. They found their way in through the Margullring. I was in the ValdFyurring. Ecromir tried to protect me and fight them off. He died with the journal in his hands."

Klasodin's eyes widened in a look of horror. He blinked and came to again. He shot a sideways glance at Henry, then fixed his gaze on his staff.

"Let's see what shape we're in."

His eyes glazed over and became distant, like he was somewhere else entirely. Henry peered over the side and watched the five reindeer gallop through the sky.

After a while, Klasodin sighed.

"Merrodine found the hidden gifts. Every child should receive something. I've done all I can, which isn't much. Now it's your turn."

He handed the staff over to Henry. It shrank to Henry's size the second he took it. He stared at it, a hollow sense of dread eating away at his stomach.

"Don't try," Klasodin said, his voice calm and relaxed. "Just sit down, close your eyes and see where the staff takes you. Connect."

"With what?" Henry said uneasily.

"With whatever you find."

"Does that help? How do I make the Madjik more powerful?"

"It's not something you have to try," Klasodin explained. "If you possess the Affinity, which you do, it happens naturally. See what you can do."

Henry nodded and sat down on the sleigh floor, leaning against the side. He tried to relax. He closed his eyes.

Nothing happened. He squeezed his eyes tight shut and tried harder.

"He looks like he's doing a poo." Ellodine snorted with laughter.

Amira shushed her.

"Just relax and let your mind wander," Klasodin advised. "Everyone else," his tone darkened, "leave him alone and let him take his time."

Henry sat back, relaxed his shoulders and slowly forgot where he was and who was with him. His mind left the sleigh and travelled by Madjik.

He flitted around the world, from one child to another. Some were awake and too excited to stand still. Some were asleep and dreaming of presents and Santa Claus. He could feel the excitement and the belief course through his body somewhere far away.

He was in the ValdFyurring. He found toys, games, bikes and computers. He found clothes, armour, swords and bows. He found toys and weapons never seen before by any human being. He found the original flying snowboards and Aesir bows designed to fire bolts of Madjik.

He skittered around the ValdFyurring and found every elf wrapping furiously. He flew around the Sleigh Room and found every present.

He flashed like an energy surge around the ValdFyurring and gave a push. Suddenly everything moved much faster, too fast for the human eye to follow. But for Henry's mind, everything could be seen as easily as he wanted. He saw it all - the ValdFyurring, every elf, every gift, every child. Belief flowed like power between each child and the ValdFyurring. He pushed again. Stronger. Quicker. More powerful.

He found an army of Aesir gathered in Hamedall. Fear and dread. Resilience and bravery. The decision to die in battle if need be. Weapons at the ready. Swords. Bows. Shields. Snowboards. He pushed. Madjik coursed through them all.

He flowed out to the protective dome of ice covering the city of the Aesir. There were thin, weak spots everywhere. Little holes were forming. He was so tired. He felt like he could collapse and die any second.

A sharp pain pierced in his brain like a blow with a pick axe. It struck him again and again. Heavy blows hit him like he was being punched in the head. Deadly blades sliced his skin and stabbed his body. Small explosions burned and stung.

He jumped. He remembered he was sitting in the sleigh. He could vaguely hear voices somewhere in the background, wondering what he was doing.

The Margullring. He floated back into it and took more painful hammer blows. He looked outward over the South Passage. Two armies were gathered. The Gaardreng fired steel bolts and blue blasts of Azmar at the ice wall. The Morivari swung and hacked at the Margullring with jagged blades, maces, hammers and sickles.

He braced himself. He pushed. He could feel himself getting stronger. The holes and weak spots filled. He pushed. He was stronger again.

He took a blow to the head. A blast of Svaramar made him see stars.

A hand shook him. He came to. Ellodine was looking at him, her face pale and scared.

"What happened to you?" she said in a quiet voice.

Klasodin, Rodin and Amira were all watching him open-mouthed.

"I did it," Henry breathed. "I made everything stronger and more powerful. But it's not enough. The Gaardreng and the Morivari have joined together and they're attacking outside Hamedall. I can't keep them out. They're going to invade Alvahame."

CHAPTER FORTY-SEVEN

The sleigh left the sea behind and rocketed over the snow.

A barrage of heavy blows made Henry recoil.

"It won't hold out much longer," he grimaced.

"Will he be able to seal the Margullring once they start breaking through?" came Amira's voice, riddled with panic, talking more quickly than usual.

"I don't know." Klasodin's tone was bleak.

Blows pounded. Arrows and darts struck. Svaramar flared. Blue light flashed. It was like being punched, stabbed and poisoned at the same time. Henry tried to push again, but nothing happened.

There was a crack. Pain exploded in his skull. It was like his head had split.

"They're through," he gasped.

He pulled away from the Margullring and climbed gingerly to his feet. He leaned over the side of the sleigh, watching the Arctic snow fly past just metres below. The sleigh touched down. The runners slid over the snow.

The sleigh headed over the snowy peak and shot into the cloud screen. A haze of moisture blew into Henry's face. He wiped his eyes with his hand. His stomach dropped like a lead weight as the sleigh lurched downwards. It found more snow and slid out of the cloud over the white plain towards the line of cliffs towering ahead.

They sped straight at them. It looked like the reindeer were going to crash right into them. At the last second, the steep, snowy path appeared and the sleigh forged up it, past steep walls of rock at either side. It left the cliffs behind and took off into the air.

Henry could feel the Margullring without closing his eyes. Every blow resounded over his head and body.

"It will get better once you're in Alvahame," Klasodin said. "The power you…"

He broke off. A gasp arose from within the sleigh. Angry grunts and roars came from in front of it.

Henry hoisted and levered himself up until he rested on the side of the sleigh on his stomach, his knees hunched up against the sleigh wall, his hands gripping the top to hold himself in place. He saw what the others had seen and nearly toppled over.

Some of the silvery fir trees were on fire. Smoke billowed from them. Smoke. He was flying. He could see himself flying backwards out of his burning home. Mum and Dad weren't going to make it. He wobbled and tipped over. The snowy ground shot up at him. A pair of hands grabbed his ankles and eased him back up. He grabbed the side of the sleigh again and placed his stomach back on the top to steady himself.

"You should come down from there," came Amira's voice.

"It was just seeing it for the first second," he said breathlessly. "I'll be okay now."

Amira kept a hand on his ankle.

The screen of cloud was lifting behind the burning trees, revealing the massive ice screen. A great jagged hole had been smashed in it. Other cracks were creeping and webbing over the surface.

An army crowded around the hole. The Morivari and the Gaardreng hacked at the ice and attacked the Aesir defending Hamedall. Gold arrows of Madjik and black mists of Svaramar flew into the sky. Fists punched. Swords clashed. Blades glinted in the sunlight through a mess of bodies as more and more Aesir, Morivari and Gaardreng piled into the fight by the hole in the ice.

A steel dart shot past his face. A second whistled through his hair. Henry caught a glance at a band of Gaardreng flying at them on their chrome snowboards. Two hands hauled him back into the sleigh and dumped him on the floor.

"Pay attention Glondir." Amira's jaw clenched. She aimed her bow and reeled off a blaze of gold arrows. "You're not much use to us dead."

The Hafskod face was clouding over. Henry blinked. The clouds over the face looked to be blacker than he had seen them before. He made the shield appear over his left arm and took a glance over the side.

Amira took down one flying Gaard after the other. Rodin and Ellodine fired blazing gold arrows into the back of the surging army. A remnant peeled away and fired their arrows and bolts at the sleigh. Some clanged off the base. Madjik glittered from the reindeer's antlers and deflected more away. Most of the attacking army was still fighting towards the growing hole in the Margullring.

Henry picked up the staff lying on the floor and showed it to Klasodin.

"I can use anything in the ValdFyurring, right?" he asked quickly. "Even the things the Aesir don't use?"

"At this point, why wouldn't you?" Klasodin replied.

Henry found what he was looking for.

"How do I do it?"

"Just will it to come to you."

Henry fixed it in his mind. He wanted two of them and he needed them now. Two small, gold curved bows clattered to the sleigh floor. He gave the staff to Klasodin.

He gripped one bow in each hand and with the curves facing him. They shot out into their full size. He aimed them over the side and squeezed. The air blurred in the middle, between the two ends of each one. Two blasts of Madjik erupted and shot to the ground, exploding in the snow. He fired again and again.

A blaze of bright gold ripped from Amira's elven bow. Ellodine fired a stream of arrows. Rodin took down one Gaard after the other.

They were nearing the centre of the battle. They all ducked as a volley of steel darts flew back at them.

More enemy warriors surged inside the Margullring.

"It's not enough," Amira shouted.

"The sooner we get inside, the sooner Henry can seal the Margullring," Klasodin called, grasping the reins with one hand and flinging flaming gold arrows of Madjik from his staff with the other.

"We need to keep them out first," Amira snapped.

"They need another distraction to slow them down." Rodin said it so quietly, Henry wasn't sure if it was even meant to be heard by anyone else.

He watched Rodin throw his bow over his shoulder, then pull his sword from its sheath and study its deadly sharp blade. He looked up, took a deep breath, then leapt up onto the side of the sleigh.

"WHAT ARE YOU DOING?" Amira screamed.

"I'll slow them down," Rodin said calmly.

Amira lunged to grab Rodin, but he stepped out of her reach. He was standing in front of Henry, but his eyes were fixed on Amira.

"I love you."

His voice was calm and gentle. He took a glance down below, then leapt off the sleigh and somersaulted backwards. He plummeted towards the ground, his blade whipping through the air, deflecting arrows and darts.

Rodin hit the snow, the impact rippling through the Gaardreng, creating a ring of snow around him. A mass of Gaardreng gravitated towards him. The steady stream of soldiers charging for the hole in the Margullring slowed. Henry watched the black-clad Morivari ignore Rodin, edge around the side of the battle and push for the entrance to Alvahame.

The sleigh banked suddenly in front of the Margullring. Henry staggered and grabbed the side of the sleigh to keep himself upright. Klasodin struggled with the reins. The sleigh turned around and headed for Rodin. It dipped, aiming for where he fought.

"Turn back," Klasodin shouted.

An angry roar bellowed back at him.

"We have to get inside the Margullring. You know I am right."

Klasodin yanked at the reins. There was an angry yelp. Slepnir let out a howl of frustration. The sleigh banked around the rear of the battle and turned to head over it again. Henry jumped onto the side of the sleigh and landed on his stomach, almost winding himself. He fired down with both hands, sending bright explosions into the mass of enemy warriors. Ellodine fired gold arrows.

Amira's arrows had stopped. Henry turned to see her strap her bow over her shoulder. Before he could react, Amira jumped up onto the side of the sleigh, balancing on the balls of her feet.

"NO," Ellodine screamed.

Amira's face was calm, serene. She looked down at them, the tears streaming down her ivory skin.

"You'll kill yourself," Klasodin shouted.

"Don't do it, Amira," Ellodine pleaded.

"I have to," Amira said quietly. "I love him too."

She glanced down. She turned to them and smiled. Then she simply leaned back, her arms spread, and fell backwards from the sleigh.

Ellodine screamed. Henry watched Amira fall gracefully. Just when he thought she was going to hit the ground, she somersaulted and landed just metres from where Rodin fought. Her Aesir bow blasted the Gaardreng around her.

"TURN BACK," Ellodine screamed at Klasodin.

"No," Klasodin snapped. "We can't help them now."

"TURN BACK."

"You know we can't do that."

"But they'll die."

"Not if we get to them soon enough," said Henry.

He grabbed Ellodine's arm as she moved to fight Klasodin for the reins. The sleigh picked up speed and shot away. Henry was thrown back. Henry grabbed for the side of the sleigh with his free hand. The force slammed his back into the sleigh and Ellodine crashed into him. They toppled to the floor.

Henry and Ellodine scrambled to their feet and leapt onto the side of the sleigh in time to see Rodin and Amira disappear in the fighting crowd.

The sleigh shot through the Margullring. It passed over Hamedall, where Aesir fought with Morivari among the trees. Arrows flew. Madjik flared. Trails of Svaramar billowed. Swords clashed. Appodin's red flailing hair caught Henry's eye in the middle of the battle, fighting savagely with two Morivari. A hail of gold arrows shot into the enemy warriors around him. Appodin waved thanks at Ellodine, who ignored him and kept firing at anything in black.

The sleigh touched down on the edge of Alvahame and kept sliding over the crest of the hill. A group of Morivari were racing down into the city ahead of them. Klasodin leapt out while the sleigh was still moving. Staff in hand, he produced a snowboard, which was ready on the ground before his feet landed on it. He shot down the snowy hill towards Alvahame, firing at the Morivari in front of him.

Ellodine leapt out of the sleigh and fired down the slope. Henry tossed out his bows. He clambered out after her and landed flat on his stomach in the snow. He fired down the hill at the Morivari as Klasodin disappeared down the avenue out of sight. A group of Aesir flew out of the avenue on their snowboards and took down the last two Morivari. They shot right past Henry, heading for Hamedall.

Slepnir shook himself free of his reins. His antlers glittered with Madjik. He threw back his head and roared. It was so loud, it resonated through Henry's skull. Alvahame shook. The trees trembled. Snow rumbled down from the distant mountains.

Something moved in the distance. Herds and crowds appeared from the mountains and forests. Polar bears, caribou, arctic foxes, snow wolves and snow leopards converged on Alvahame and charged over the snow.

Slepnir's eyes blazed with fury. His mouth foamed. He bellowed. He galloped towards Hamedall. Grrhdrig led the crowd of animals racing after him.

CHAPTER FORTY-EIGHT

Henry threw his weapons back in the sleigh and hauled himself up with his hands, pushing with his feet, until he could heave himself over the side and back in. Ellodine dropped in next to him. Henry grabbed the reins. All four reindeer looked back at him as if expecting orders of some kind.

"I need to get to the Margullring," he said.

The sleigh shot off. Henry clung onto the reins to stop himself being thrown to the back. They flew through the trees, following the trail of destruction left by Slepnir and the animals of Alvahame. Ellodine released a blaze of arrows into a crowd of Morivari running straight at them. Appodin leapt in and did the rest.

More Gaardreng poured through the jagged hole in the Margullring. Aesir warriors gathered and ran behind the sleigh. Ellodine fired a volley of flaming gold arrows from her bow at the Gaards bursting through the hole.

Henry handed the reins to Ellodine. The reindeer slowed. He scrambled up the side of the sleigh and dropped into the snow.

"Stay here," he said.

"No," Ellodine snapped.

She flicked the reins. The sleigh shot off and disappeared through the Margullring.

"COME BACK," he screamed after her.

It was too late.

Henry ran to the Margullring, which gently curved up and over the city of the Aesir. He touched his hands to the ice. It was colder than any ice he had touched before. The icy cold darted up his arms and through his veins.

Then the cold didn't matter. It all flashed through his mind. He could see dark, silhouetted figures smashing at the Margullring without even looking at them. He pushed. He pushed again. The ice crackled. The hole slowly closed up. The weak points in the ice thickened and strengthened. He pushed. The Margullring blew attacking warriors back in the snow.

Then an idea struck him. He didn't know why, but he had to do it. Henry stepped into the Margullring.

He stopped, embedded completely within the ice. A chill surged through his mind and body, but not from the ice. There was someone else inside the Margullring. There were many of them. Their voices began as whispers. They became more distinct.

"Release us. Let us help you."

They were all around him. One edged nearer to him than the others.

"The power of ice and fire," he said. "This power is yours."

Henry stepped out onto the snow outside the Margullring. The battle raged around him. He knew what to do. He placed his left palm against the ice wall.

"Rise up," he said quietly. "Defend your city."

He could sense them moving inside, sinking downwards under the ice. He watched as the ice-white figures rose up through the snow along the Margullring. All elves. All drew their gleaming white swords.

"The power of ice and fire," the elf next to him said. "Remember them both."

A band of black-clad Morivari charged at them. The ice elf next to him stepped in, knocked one back and ran one through.

A sword of ice slid through the ribs. The Morivar froze, then thudded to the ground like he was made of stone.

Henry closed his fist around his gold bow. It froze over. He squeezed it. Darts of ice flew from it and pushed the Morivari back. The ice elves fought the Morivari, turning them to blocks of ice, blowing ice and snow to repel their Svaramar.

Henry watched Grrhdrig beat a path through the Gaardreng. Darts and arrows bounced off him, but a barrage of blue flashes repelled the advance of the polar bears. Omnitec armour deflected the Madjik of the Aesir. Henry's eyes scanned the battle. He picked out Appodin's red hair, leading a charge out of Hamedall. Perrodin was firing arrows so quickly, he didn't need a sword, even at close range.

He couldn't see Rodin or Amira. He couldn't see Ellodine.

He knelt and touched his bow to the snow. The ground around him crackled and froze to ice. He watched several Gaards lose their footing and the advantage in their fights.

"The Gaardreng are prepared to fight the fire," the ice elf said. "Not the ice. There is a gap in the Margullring. We don't know where, but we can feel it. Alvahame will be in danger until you find it."

Henry nodded. The ice elf turned away and flung an ice dart at a Gaard on a flying snowboard, shooting him out of the sky. More Gaards flew at the ice elves. A polar bear leapt from the fray and clawed one out of the air. The Gaards' darts and arrows shot through the ice-elves pure white torsos without leaving a hole. The ice elves launched knives and spears, sending the Gaards flailing to the ground.

Henry wanted to find his friends, but he didn't dare leave the Margullring without his protection. Time to try something. He touched his bow to the Margullring and swept it over the surface. Spikes of ice shot out from the base.

That should do it.

He gripped his ice bow. He ran. He followed the path smashed through the battle by Grrhdrig, heading for the centre, where Aesir and Gaardreng converged in a mess of blades and arrows. He could no longer see any Morivari. He wondered if they had retreated. Polar bears and snow wolves tore savagely into any Omnitec warrior in their path. The caribou lowered their antlers and stampeded through the Gaardreng.

A band of Omnitec's soldiers rose on their chrome boards. Their steel darts rained down on the chaos below them. They bounced off Grrhdrig like he was bullet proof. Henry aimed his bow and sprayed the Gaardreng with his deadly ice darts. The flying Omnitec warriors fired back at him. Their darts deflected off his shield. He ducked down so his shield covered him. He swept his fingers over the surface of the ground and sent snow and ice blowing up from the ground. It whipped up into a thick, blustery storm. The darts stopped coming. The Gaards swerved through the flying snow. Polar bear claws swiped two out of the air. A couple of arctic foxes snatched at another.

Henry got to his feet. A Gaard plummeted to the ground straight at him. There was a whoosh. Something shot over the snow behind him. An arm hauled him onto a snowboard and clamped over his chest to stop him falling off. They sped away, accelerating so quickly, Henry's stomach nearly leapt into his throat. Behind them, the Gaard hit the ground where he'd been standing.

"I'll steer, you fire," came Forodin's voice in his ear.

Without waiting to be asked where to go, Forodin shot through the crowds towards the polar bears. Henry aimed and fired ice arrows, creating a path in front of them. Appodin launched into three Gaards stepping out of Henry's way. Some Gaards peeled off the battle and slid away over the snow.

Forodin wound his way around Grrhdrig and whoever else was still in the middle of the fight. Henry picked off more

Gaards. Forodin veered right suddenly as one of Grrhdrig's polar bears leapt into a band of Omnitec warriors.

More Gaards turned and fled for their lives. Grrhdrig stood on his hind legs and gave a roar. The Gaardreng fled. Slowly, the battle thinned.

Slepnir stood in the middle, his eyes darting around him, his teeth long and sharp, guarding two stricken figures. Forodin slid closer.

Rodin lay on his back in the snow. Amira knelt over him, her long, jet black hair hanging down like a black curtain, hiding Rodin's face. The closer they slid, the louder her sobs sounded.

Henry could see from the way Rodin's stomach heaved in and out that he was still breathing, but his eyes were glassy, staring into nothing.

"I don't know what to do," Amira whimpered.

She held her bloodied hands over the wounds on Rodin's chest.

Henry stared at them, frozen to the spot, watching the life ooze from the elf's body, from his friend's body. He felt sick. There had to be something. Or someone.

"I know," he said suddenly. "Ellodine..." He stopped. He looked around him. "Where is she?"

CHAPTER FORTY-NINE

Henry spun around, his eyes sweeping the battlefield, over elves, humans and animals. Some dead. Some tending to their wounds. The ice elves stood guard at the Margullring with Balnir, Zadira and Rimida close by, trying to bandage a wound on Raiodin's shoulder.

A mournful groan from a reindeer caught his ear. He wheeled around. Beyond what was left of the battle lay an overturned sleigh, the four reindeer still harnessed to it. Vega was trying to bite through his harness. The other three had given up and lay in the snow.

Henry ran to the sleigh and rounded it to see inside, his stomach turning, hoping it wasn't bad. He stopped and stared at what he saw. The sleigh was empty. Ellodine was nowhere to be found.

A group of Aesir warriors ran over and turned the sleigh the right way up. Rodin was lifted into it and taken through the Margullring, back to Alvahame.

Rimida had managed to bandage Raiodin's arm.

"See?" she said. "Takes the skill of a wrapper to bandage this whiny idiot."

"I'm fine," Raiodin insisted.

He winced as Rimida poked him with her finger.

"Where's Ellodine?" Zadira asked.

"You haven't seen her either?" Henry said.

No one had.

"Alvahame's enemies are still in the city," said the ice elf who had spoken to Henry before. "Start there. We will stand guard until every last one of them is gone."

"How will you know?"

"We can feel their Madjik. Now go."

They left the ice elves standing guard and slid back into Alvahame. Groups of Aesir flew over the snowy avenues on their snowboards. Henry spotted Appodin running over the rooftops and scouring Alvahame's skyline.

They flew down the avenue to Iddrassil. Larodine stepped out of the Craft of Care and stood in front of them. They all skidded to a halt.

"You shouldn't be flying around Alvahame in your condition," she said firmly. "Raiodin. Look at the state of you."

"I'm fine."

"I know you're not," Larodine insisted. "I've heard all about it. Now into the Craft of Care with you. All of you."

Henry opened his mouth to tell her they were looking for her daughter, then thought better of it.

"We're fine," Balnir insisted.

"Yeah, only Raiodin was stupid enough to get himself hurt," Zadira laughed.

"Hey!"

"I'm faster than a speeding arrow."

"I took down two of them and look at me."

Larodine stood in the middle of them, hands on her hips, her jaw set.

"You are all coming with me. Now."

The others all argued, but they weren't going to win. Larodine wasn't so mild mannered any more. She sounded like Ellodine.

Henry took his chance. He shot down the avenue and out of earshot. He flew around the trunk and into the stable. He ran past Equodin feeding and preparing the eight reindeer for their journey and entered the base of the Hollow. He stood there, looking up, trying to work out where to head next.

Ullnir from the Craft of Creation appeared and strode towards him, the same impassive expression on his face.

"I am pleased you survived the battle in one piece," the gadget specialist said - with no emotion at all.

"I'm looking for Ellodine. She's missing."

"Really?" Ullnir replied. "I saw her only a few minutes ago, heading down to the Hall of Ecromir. She was with someone, but I didn't notice anything untoward."

Henry ran for the stairs.

"Thanks, Ullnir."

The Hall of Ecromir buzzed with activity. Every elf was hard at work, wrapping so fast, it made Henry dizzy just trying to watch. He stood at the top of the stairs, his gaze sweeping the spherical chamber. No sign of Ellodine.

He hurried down the stairs towards the gold tree and made for the same giant gift as before. He stepped into it.

His legs were dangling in the air. Henry concentrated and held himself up in the same spot, floating at the top of the Sleigh Room. His eyes traced every gift in the long column next to him, which stretched all the way down to the floor far below. Every column he could see was full. If there were gaps to be filled, he couldn't see any.

The Sleigh Room was silent.

Henry's heart pounded. Something was wrong.

Staying close to the wall circling the Sleigh Room, Henry slipped from one column to the next, stopping at each one to take a good look around him.

When he had followed the circumference of the room and reached the column he had started from, Henry floated slowly downwards, staying hidden behind the column of presents. He couldn't hear or see anyone.

He touched down on the floor. His eyes scanned the walls, ceiling and floor. They flitted over every column, every present. He stood, watched and waited.

"Henry. What are you doing here?"

Salvodin emerged from behind a column at the far end with a smile on his pale features.

Henry felt a stab of panic through his stomach.

"I just wanted to see it all again before the presents go," he replied, his gaze sweeping the room, then resting on the blond-haired toy designer, whose piercing silver blue eyes seemed to be studying every move he made.

"You didn't want to wrap presents?" Salvodin said.

"Merrodine wouldn't let me," Henry grinned.

"She is a perfectionist, isn't she? Likes everything just so."

"What brings you down here, Salvodin?" Henry asked as casually as he could.

"Well, with all of Alvahame being in such a hurry, I wanted to quality check some of the designs that were brought back into circulation," Salvodin replied. "I should have done it before, I know, but who has the time? Seeing as my wrapping skills were not required, here I am."

"Did you have to unwrap them to examine them?" Henry probed.

"That's right."

"Did you wrap them back up again?"

"I did. I was able to take my time down here."

"So you brought Sellotape and scissors with you? I don't see any."

Salvodin gave a flat, humourless smile. His pale features were cold. His piercing eyes seemed cruel. There was nothing friendly about him.

"You are quite the detective, aren't you, Henry? And not a bad spy either. Worthy of your CSI and James Bond combined. I almost believed you."

Salvodin whipped out a crossbow from under his green cloak. He aimed it at Henry's head. Morikend emerged from behind a column. A second Morivar followed. Yohann ambled into view, looking very pleased with himself.

Henry's blood boiled.

"What are you doing here, Yohann?" he blurted.

"I'm here to watch you suffer," Yohann said smugly.

"They'll probably just kill you later anyway," Henry retorted.

"Certainly not." Morikend placed his arm around Yohann's shoulders. "Yohann and I are the best of friends."

"Yeah. Look what he gave me."

Yohann opened his coat with a grin to reveal the black breastplate Henry had worn in the city of the Morivari.

"You have already met Morikend," Salvodin said casually. "Ivrakend was also very keen to make your acquaintance."

Ivrakend was a Morivar warrior. He was bigger than Morikend. He brandished a sword with a curved, jagged blade.

"And you know Yohann. Proven to be quite a waste of space has Yohann. But I believe Morikend has found a solution to that particular problem." A cruel smile crept over Salvodin's face. "And then there's the girl."

Henry's blood ran cold.

"What a surprising gift she turned out to be."

Ellodine emerged from behind a column, her hands tied behind her back, Bayne's hand clamped over her mouth, his sword held at her throat.

Bayne shoved Ellodine towards Henry. She stumbled and fell face down on the floor. Henry helped her to her feet. He touched his ice cold Hafskod to the rope and caught a glance at the ice crawling over it.

"You?" Ellodine exploded. "You're Grimnir? Why? How could you betray us all?"

"After decades of being ignored and overlooked, watching my genius go to waste while my human competitors enjoy immense riches?" Salvodin replied. "Very easily. And it turns out the Aesir can't spot a traitor if their city depends on it."

"So you enjoy feeling cleverer than anyone else then?" said Henry.

"I'm used to it. And this last part has just been too easy." Salvodin surveyed Henry with cold eyes. "I needed to isolate you, to get you alone. You did all the hard work for me. Ellodine charged into battle alone and you came to look for her. It was just a case of convincing her mother you were all hurt, then having you come down here instead of going up to the star, where Klasodin would have been all along."

Henry flashed back to Ullnir finding him in the Hollow and sending him downstairs.

"What do you want with me?" he said.

"I don't need you at all," Salvodin laughed. "There is nothing remotely special or interesting about you. If you were anything other than plain and ordinary, you would have seen through the camera I left for you. And you would have realised that the Hafskod Klasodin gave you has one very important function. You see, without the Hafskod, Klasodin can't deliver all the presents."

Salvodin stepped forward, his bow aimed at Henry's chest.

"And he's not going to."

Henry and Ellodine took a step back.

Bayne aimed his Azmar bow at Henry. Yohann aimed his breastplate at him. Morikend and Ivrakend advanced, brandishing their swords.

"Try sinking or flying and we'll kill at least one of you," Salvodin growled. "Now take off the Hafskod."

"No," Henry uttered.

"Take it off. Or I'll kill you both and prise it off your cold, dead body."

CHAPTER FIFTY

Salvodin's crossbow was aimed at his chest. Henry ran through his options in his mind. His Hafskod was ice cold. He wondered if it would work if he wasn't wearing it. What would he be able to do without it? He had two bows tucked under his coat. He had a snowboard on his back. That was it.

"Now," Salvodin snarled.

"No," Ellodine pleaded. "You can't."

A black and gold flash burst from Yohann's breastplate and struck Ellodine. It blew her to the floor. She climbed to her feet gingerly, her face pale, her eyes wide with shock, as if she couldn't believe he'd really done it.

An idea swelled in Henry's mind.

"Fine," he snapped.

Yohann sniggered.

"I just didn't realise Yohann only liked to fight girls."

"I'll fight you any day," Yohann shouted.

He lurched forward – but Ivrakend hauled him back by the scruff of the neck.

"The Hafskod," Salvodin growled through gritted teeth. "Resist me again and I will shoot her myself."

"Fine," Henry muttered. He turned to Ellodine, his left hand on her shoulder while his right slipped a bow into her pocket. "Just making sure she's okay."

He pulled her behind him, then turned to face Salvodin. He fumbled with the ice cold Hafskod, moving slightly so Salvodin stood between him and the others, blocking their path to him. He held the Hafskod up while he poked at it, picturing in his mind what he wanted to happen. He could feel the Hafskod recognise it.

Salvodin's eyes blazed with fury.

"GET ON WITH IT."

The Hafskod reacted on its own. The blast of ice struck Salvodin in the face. Henry hit him again.

Ellodine fired a gold flash. It struck Ivrakend and knocked the Morivar warrior on his back.

Bayne already had his weapon aimed.

The shield burst out of Henry's Hafskod and covered his arm. He edged towards Ellodine, wishing he could give her a shield as well.

A blue flash from Bayne's bow shot at Ellodine.

A shield materialised on her arm and deflected it. She stared at it in amazement, then threw her arm in front of her face.

Another blue flash exploded onto her shield and hurled her backwards.

A black swirl of Svaramar blew at Henry. It took him off his feet. He landed on his back. A black and gold flash shot at him. He threw his shield in the way.

Ellodine leapt to her feet and ran for Henry. She hauled him to his feet. Henry fired an icy blast at Ivrakend. They ran for cover. Ellodine leapt behind a column. Henry dived after her. A black and gold flash exploded into the wall behind him.

Salvodin swore violently. He sank into the floor and vanished.

Silence.

Henry peered around the column. A blast of Svaramar blew at him. Ellodine yanked him out of the way by his coat. They ran to the next column. Nobody in sight. They ran to the next.

"I wouldn't go anywhere," came Morikend's voice.

They crept to the next column, then the next.

Henry could see Morikend standing calmly in the open space. Ivrakend paced, sword in hand, eyes darting around the Sleigh Room. Yohann edged nearer to Morikend, his expression fearful.

"What are you going to do?" Ellodine called.

"I am going to burn the gifts. I am going to burn the tree to the ground with every elf inside it."

Ellodine choked back a sob.

Henry felt his blood run cold. His face was numb. He realised he couldn't see Bayne and had no idea where he was.

He looked around him. No sign of the YotunMens.

"And if you're wondering," Morikend continued. "Salvodin will get his as well. I will not share the Arctic with anyone."

Something hard jabbed into Henry's back. He froze.

"Looking for me?" a voice rasped.

He glanced behind him. Bayne grinned down at them.

"Get moving."

Henry moved out towards Morikend, Ellodine next to him.

Morikend swirled a black, cloudy mass around in each hand. Slowly, the Svaramar rose from his hands and spread over the floor and walls like a thick, black mist.

"I know what you're thinking," said Morikend. "That your pyjamas saved your life, so no human or elf in Aesir clothes could ever die in a fire. But a fire fuelled by Svaramar will kill everything. The clothing will simply prolong the agony."

The Svaramar spread over the walls of the Sleigh Room and swirled around the columns of wrapped gifts. Morikend clenched his fists. It burst into flames. Fire flared around the Sleigh Room.

Ellodine ran forward to beat the flames away. A gold and black blast hit her in the chest and blew her to the floor.

Henry helped her to her feet. Her breaths were shaky. Every part of her face looked like she had been hurt. Henry didn't like it.

"You okay?" he murmured.

Ellodine nodded.

The smug grin on Yohann's face made him boil inside. He took another look. Yohann brimmed with the arrogance of someone who thought he had all the power the world. Henry thought back to when he had tried on the breastplate. He would have blown Ellodine through the wall - or blasted her into a million pieces. Yohann was not a Valdir.

Flames swept over the walls and spiralled around the columns of gifts.

"You can't," Ellodine sobbed. "How can you hate us doing so much good?"

"Good?" Morikend's voice lowered to a snarl. "There's nothing good about what you do. Humans. They're like rats, spreading their disease. You devote yourselves to giving them gifts they don't deserve. You live in secret, because you know they would destroy you if they ever found out you existed."

Henry watched the flames rise. What could he do?

"They are all Omnitec," Morikend snapped. "By coming here and claiming the northern elven realm as your own, you Aesir are just like them. You deserve what's coming to you."

Henry's hand gripped his bow, still made of ice. He knew what he needed. He'd been around so much of it, he had some left. There was more. It was everywhere. He found it. He felt it happen. He had to wait.

"I almost want to watch you burn in the fire," said Morikend. "But then Bayne would miss out. He has new ways of inflicting agonising pain to show you."

"Well, it's not like he can do much else," Henry sneered. "He's not an elf."

He watched Bayne's face darken with anger.

Snow started falling from the ceiling. Ice spread over the walls and the floor. The flames hit them and turned to steam. It mixed with snow falling from the ceiling and swirled together around the gifts, attacking the fire and putting it out. The black and purple flames surged and raged against the ice. The ice covered the walls and thickened. Steam billowed.

Morikend shot a murderous glance at Henry and Ellodine.

"Deal with them," he instructed Bayne. "Those gifts will burn if it takes me all night."

A cruel grin crept over Bayne's face. His ears bore fresh scars. His eyes burned with hatred. He pulled out a gun, which changed into his sword. Ivrakend advanced, wielding his sword with its curved, jagged blade. Yohann aimed the breastplate at Ellodine.

An icy snowball struck Yohann in the face. A second knocked him off his feet. Snowballs bulleted down. Arrows zipped at the four enemies of Alvahame. Ellodine released a blaze of gold blasts. Morikend disappeared from view. The flames flared around the room.

Bayne ran across the room right at them. He dodged the arrows. A snowball grazed his face, but he kept running. He fired from his Azmar bow. A blue flash blew at them. Henry and Ellodine dived for cover. Bayne advanced. Ivrakend sliced at a snowball with his jagged blade and bore down on them.

Balnir, Forodin, Raiodin, Zadira and Rimida dropped to the ground in front of Ellodine and Henry. Amira landed in front of them.

"Take care of the fire, Glondir," said Balnir, drawing his sword. "We've got this."

"Something I can throw would be good," Rimida murmured.

CHAPTER FIFTY-ONE

Ellodine and Zadira bombarded Bayne with arrows. Amira leapt at Ivrakend. Yohann climbed to his feet, his face clouded with anger. Forodin shot over the floor and knocked him off his feet.

Henry pushed. The ice crawled and thickened over the walls. It slid under his feet. He made it rise and bubble around Rimida. He made the ice and snow gather at the ceiling of the Sleigh Room. He lifted into the air to get a better view and soared up to the gathering ice.

It was hot up there. The fire blazed around the columns of gifts. Smoke billowed into his face. He pushed. Snow and ice rained down. The ice closed around the Sleigh Room. Henry fired blasts of ice from the bow and from his Hafskod. The fire died in lingering wisps of steam.

Svaramar and flames flared from one source down to his right. He surveyed the battle scattered over the floor below him. Amira fought Ivrakend. Raiodin, Balnir and Forodin took on Bayne with Ellodine and Zadira's arrows holding him at bay. Rimida pelted anyone in her eye line.

There was only one thing for it. Henry aimed at the source. He fired ice at the billowing Svaramar. He pushed at the ice coming into the Sleigh Room and growing around the walls. He made it rise up in columns next to the columns of gifts. He made it gather at the source, pushing back against Morikend.

He sank, edging towards Morikend. Something in the back of his mind quivered, telling him to stay out of danger, but he couldn't. There was no one else to save his friends. He fired ice. He pushed harder. He could make out the silhouetted figure of Morikend through a screen of Svaramar. He took a breath. He dived.

He flew down at Morikend, firing blasts of ice from both weapons. Morikend recoiled. The Svaramar shrank back around him. Morikend retreated. Henry plummeted downwards. He shot straight at Morikend. The ice flared at him. It struck the Svaramar and blew in every direction. Morikend dived out of the way. Henry flew over him. Morikend turned and blew a flurry of Svaramar back at him. Henry threw his Hafskod in the way. The force of the two Madjiks colliding flung him back up in the air like a catapult. He braked before he shot into the clump of ice on the ceiling.

Way below him, Amira fought viciously with Ivrakend. His young Aesir friends held off Bayne. Yohann was climbing to his feet, lingering, looking for a chance to hit someone.

Bayne ducked an arrow. He deflected a flash of Madjik at Raiodin, throwing him off his feet. Yohann fired a blaze of black and gold. Zadira dived for cover. Bayne whipped his blade at Balnir and Forodin. Amira stabbed at Ivrakend. He caught her blade in the jagged points of his sword and twisted, throwing her off balance.

Henry sent the ice on the walls surging at Morikend. Svaramar flared back at him. He hurled an ice storm at Morikend.

Morikend retreated and aimed another blast. A blade flew from behind Henry and caught Morikend in the shoulder, sending him reeling. Rodin landed and hurled another. Morikend fired back at him.

Henry took his chance. He fired. An icy blast burst from the Hafskod. It struck Yohann's breastplate and shattered it, hurling Yohann across the room. He fired at Ivrakend, who swung his sword wildly to deflect it. Amira took her chance and thrust at him, forcing him back. Bayne advanced on the stricken Raiodin. Henry sent an icy blast at him. Bayne swung at it with his sword. Henry touched down on the icy ground and made a line of spikes shoot up over the floor. Ivrakend dived out of the way. An ice spike ripped through Bayne's sleeve. He turned to fire back. Henry fired his bows. Bayne dived for cover. Yohann scrambled after him. Bayne grabbed Yohann's arm. They flew up the Sleigh Room and disappeared.

Morikend blew Svaramar at Rodin, who retreated behind a column. Morikend turned and fired more Svaramar at the gold floor, blazing a hole in the middle. He and Ivrakend dived into the hole. It sealed up after them.

Appodin appeared through the ceiling and floated to the floor.

"Did Morikend just do what I think he did?" Appodin demanded. Without waiting for an answer, he disappeared through the floor after the Morivari.

Rodin lumbered towards them, then dropped to his knees. His face was deathly white. Blood seeped through the bandage over his chest. Amira cried out and dropped to the ground next to him.

Balnir and Forodin were helping Raiodin to his feet.

"Larodine can't do any more for him," Amira sobbed. "Why did he come here?"

Henry nudged Ellodine. She elbowed him back. He took hold of her hand and gave it a gentle squeeze.

"Maybe Klasodin's right," he whispered.

She turned on him, her eyes swimming with tears.

"What?"

"What if Klasodin was right? What if this is the special generation?"

She shook her head.

"You know what you can do," Henry urged. "You have to try."

"No." Ellodine shook her head. "He's wrong."

"No other elf can do what you did for me when those snowballs hit my face."

She shrugged, her eyes fixed on the floor.

"You'll regret it if you don't and Rodin dies," he whispered.

"How can you say that?" she hissed.

Henry pointed at Raiodin, who looked pale, his hand clutching his shoulder.

"You can help Raiodin too. I know something will happen if you try."

She looked him in the eye and squeezed his hand back.

"Come with me," she breathed.

They knelt down either side of Rodin. Ellodine placed her hands over Rodin's wounds. The room fell silent. Nothing happened.

"It's not working," Ellodine wept.

"Keep going," Henry urged.

She took a breath. Her brow furrowed in concentration.

Suddenly Rodin's eyes shot open. He sat bolt upright. He grimaced and rubbed his ribs. He looked at Ellodine, a stunned expression on his face.

"Finally," he said. "I was wondering how long it was going to take you."

"FINALLY?" Ellodine screamed.

"I was lying there for an age waiting for you to pull yourself together."

"But . . ."

"Don't tell me you were just going to let me lie there and die?"

Ellodine turned crimson with rage.

"I just saved your life you . . ."

Rodin roared with laughter and took her in his arms.

Amira gently peeled them apart. She pointed to Raiodin, who was swaying on his feet with Forodin, Balnir and Zadira holding him up.

"I think Raiodin needs her too."

They lay Raiodin on the floor.

Amira helped Rodin climb to his feet.

"Did you have to tease her like that?" she scolded him.

"Of course. How long have we been waiting?"

"Even so."

"You knew she could do that?" Henry asked.

"I saw her heal an injured caribou when she was five," said Rodin. "It's been a very long wait."

"Even for you?" Henry grinned.

"Yes. Why?"

"Well, you're about a hundred, aren't you?"

"Thank you, Henry."

"I think what Rodin was trying to say is that we've always known you and your friends were the generation Klasodin was waiting for," Amira explained.

Henry frowned. They were looking at him.

"Yes, Henry," Amira smiled. "That includes you. There was always going to be a human in there."

Henry felt himself smile. He had never thought it might include him.

Raiodin sat up like a shot. He looked around him wild-eyed.

Appodin sprung through the floor, a scowl on his face.

"They're not in the Council Chamber. Must have left the way they got in."

"What about Bayne?" said Henry. "Did he get away?"

A wide grin creased Appodin's features.

"Not likely. He's lying out cold in the Hall of Ecromir. Or he was when I left."

"What happened?"

"Never interrupt Mrs Claus while she's wrapping," Appodin said with a glint in his eye. "I'm already in there as part of our sweep. Bayne emerges with Yohann. Before I can move, Merrodine shoves me aside and punches him out. Then she just goes back to her wrapping as if nothing's happened."

Appodin collapsed into laughter, the tears rolling down his face. He stopped, cleared his throat and stood straight up.

"Maybe not the right time. Do we know who our traitor is?"

"Salvodin is Grimnir," said Ellodine. "He went the same way."

"So they've all run off?"

"No," Henry decided out loud. "He wasn't running away. He left this room, because he thought Morikend had us. There's more to his plan." He paused and thought back to what had happened. "He's not the only one. Ullnir sent me down here."

"Ullnir told Larodine we were all hurt," Zadira added. "He's in on it too. Ullnir's working with Salvodin."

CHAPTER FIFTY-TWO

Salvodin, Morikend and Ivrakend had vanished. The Council Chamber beneath the Sleigh Room was empty. The door behind Klasodin's chair, which he had disappeared through during the Council meeting, led up some spiralling stairs. Henry and his friends pounded up them and came out in an opening in the north side of Iddrassil's trunk.

Henry reached the top of the stairs last. He looked up the steep avenue leading to the Northern Route.

"I don't think they came this way," said Zadira, her brow furrowed.

"There are lots of footprints here," Henry answered.

"But no fresh ones."

"You can tell?"

"When you live in snow all year round, you can tell all kinds of things about it."

"Wow."

"The footprint thing's just you," Forodin said lazily, jumping on his snowboard.

Zadira blinked.

"Really?"

"You've never noticed it's only you who does that?"

"No."

"But other elves . . ."

"No."

"You all. . ."

"No."

"Is there another way out of there?" said Henry.

"Just this one," Balnir replied.

"So where are they?" Raiodin demanded.

It was subtle, but Henry felt it. He gave a slight shiver. He was sure he must have felt it before, but hadn't been aware of it at the time, because something else had grabbed his attention. It had happened as the Margullring had been bombarded outside Hamedall.

"Something weird just happened," he said. "In the Margullring."

"Like what?" asked Balnir.

"I don't know. But I'm sure I've felt it before. I think it happened before when they were all trying to get through it into Alvahame, I just wasn't aware of it because I was trying to keep them out."

"We can't see it from here," Raiodin said irritably. His eyes lit up. He punched Balnir on the arm with a grin on his face. "Follow me."

They raced up a nearby branch, shot up and across The Hollow, ran along the branch and down the stairs to their classroom. Raiodin dived down through the trapdoor and stood in front of a LagFyurring.

Alvahame appeared as if they were looking down on it through the glass floor.

"Start on the north," Balnir advised.

"Why?"

"The Aesir army is focused on the south."

The view zeroed in on the Margullring at the start of the Northern Route. Beyond it, two tiny black figures flew away over the snow and disappeared out of sight.

"I only saw two of them," said Rimida.

"Morikend and Ivrakend," Forodin replied.

"So where's Salvodin?"

"He isn't trying to escape," said Henry. "We're the only ones who know it's him. He's got one last chance to stop Klasodin and destroy Christmas."

The view in the LagFyurring swept to the centre of Alvahame and up the avenue leading to the South Passage. Crowds of elves lined the avenue. More leaned out of the windows of houses overlooking Klasodin's route out of Alvahame, which wound its way through Alvahame's maze of streets and out at the top.

More Aesir lined the path leading through Hamedall.

Perrodin stood at his usual post.

Beyond Perrodin and out of Hamedall, a hooded figure slid on a chrome snowboard towards the Margullring. Salvodin stepped out from behind a tree, jumped onto an identical board and together they flew over the snow, through the Margullring.

"They're going to lie in wait for him," Ellodine shouted.

They shot down the empty Hollow. Henry flew downwards at lightning speed, then braked just before the floor. His stomach lurched up towards his throat.

They slid down the street-sized branch joining the avenue, as Klasodin emerged on his sleigh from the crowd at the base of Iddrassil.

He shook hands with Gronodin.

"Looks like they've made up," said Zadira.

"I don't think Gronodin had much choice," Balnir replied.

"Don't be so cynical," Rimida reprimanded him. "They're old friends. They left Vanahame together."

Klasodin gave Merrodine a kiss on the cheek.

Henry slid onto the avenue as Klasodin's sleigh set off. He saw Henry and slid to a halt in front of him. Henry opened his mouth to tell him everything, but Klasodin waved it all away. He pointed to the Hafskod.

"Do you need it?" Henry said, moving to take it off.

"No," Klasodin replied. "But I need you to do something for me."

"We didn't catch him. He's out there. It's…"

"I don't have time," Klasodin interrupted. "I have to get going and I need the Hafskod for one vital task. I use it to slow down time."

Henry opened his mouth, then shut it again.

"Slow down time?"

"Of course. How else would I do it?"

"So when it feels like Christmas Day is taking ages to come, that's because it is?"

Klasodin nodded.

"And in Alvahame, while I am gone, Christmas Eve lasts about three weeks. Although I will only actually be gone a few hours. Now, take hold of the bezel and turn it ninety degrees anti-clockwise. Do it now."

Henry touched his fingers to the bezel around the watch face. He turned it slowly. He was suddenly aware of the bright light blazing all around him. He could hear the crowd of voices swelling somewhere beyond him. He could hear Ellodine screaming at Klasodin to stop. His eyes fixed on the Hafskod. He turned the bezel ninety degrees and the light died out.

Nobody else seemed to have noticed.

Klasodin's sleigh set off, picked up speed, left the snow and soared over Alvahame. It shot through the Margullring and out of sight.

The crowd dispersed, a large number hurrying back to the Hall of Ecromir.

Ellodine turned to Henry, the tears streaming down her face.

"What do we do?"

"Wait there," Forodin commanded them.

He shot down the avenue. A minute later a sleigh led by four familiar reindeer and driven by Forodin skidded to a halt in front of them.

"You drive a sleigh as well?" Henry exclaimed.

"Of course I do," Forodin shrugged. "Jump in."

CHAPTER FIFTY-THREE

Henry clung to the side of the sleigh as it shot over the snow, leaving the cloud screen behind. The darkened snowy landscape whizzed by. He opened his mouth to say something, caught a large gulp of air and lowered himself carefully to the floor.

"How does he get reindeer to go faster?" he gasped.

Ellodine sat down next to him.

"Adult Aesir always drive with control and care. Forodin can go at maximum speed and he knows he won't crash."

"So even elves have limits?"

"Apart from Forodin."

Ellodine eased herself up and looked about her.

"This isn't right."

"What do you mean?"

"Klasodin starts in the east and heads west. We're heading south." She scrambled to the front of the sleigh. "We're going the wrong way."

"No," Forodin said shortly.

"Klasodin never goes this way first."

"He did this time," Zadira answered. She pointed to the sky, as if that would answer every question. "One sleigh, seven reindeer and two... No. Wait."

The sleigh left the Arctic behind and bulleted over the sea.

"It's a bit late to be getting it wrong now," Forodin complained.

"I didn't get it wrong," Zadira said irritably. "There were two riders on snowboards following the sleigh, but now there are more. They met just before we left the coast."

"How many are there now?"

"Ten joined them."

"So twelve."

"Yes, that's right, Forodin. Twelve."

"There are twelve of them?" Rimida said in alarm. "But we're just younglings. There are only seven of us."

An angry grunt came from the front of the sleigh.

"Fine. Eleven. But they are Gaards. They have all kinds of modern weaponry."

"Madjik is better," Ellodine said flatly.

"Well, we don't have a lot of that, do we?" Rimida snapped.

"We have all the weapons we need," Forodin said calmly.

"He's right," Raiodin agreed, placing himself between Ellodine and Rimida, who were still glaring at each other. "Glondir can get us all the weapons we need."

"He doesn't have the staff," Balnir said quietly.

"We don't need it," Ellodine insisted.

The sleigh started to descend.

"It looks like he's gone to ground somewhere in Norway," Zadira reported.

"Why Norway?" said Rimida.

"He likes Europe," Henry thought out loud. "Maybe it's like playing at home in football."

"He knows there's a fight coming and he wants to gain the advantage," Balnir agreed excitedly.

The sleigh touched down and followed tracks in thick snow covering a path leading through thick forest. The Madjik glittering from the reindeer's antlers lit their way.

Forodin slowed the reindeer right down and veered the sleigh into the forest, then brought it to a stop between bunched trees. The Madjik disappeared from the reindeer's antlers. Darkness.

"What are you doing?" Raiodin demanded.

"The tracks get messy up ahead," said Forodin, looking about him. "We can't just slide headlong into a fight."

"Right. We need an advantage," Balnir agreed. "What happened up there?"

"I'd say the snowboarders all stopped together, then went off in different directions," said Zadira.

"What weapons do we have?" Balnir asked.

"Our elven bows," Ellodine replied. She pulled out the small bow, which fired blasts of Madjik. "And this."

"And another one." Henry held his up.

"Where did you get those?" Raiodin's eyes gleamed.

"They're hidden in the ValdFyurring," Henry replied.

"That's all we have?" Balnir demanded.

"Add anything Rimida can throw and four reindeer spoiling for a fight," Forodin grinned, his teeth showing in the darkness.

Henry glared down at his Hafskod. Why couldn't it help?

The Hafskod glowed in the darkness as if it recognised him.

Henry felt the hairs stand up on the back of his neck. A black cloud closed around the edge of the watch face, thickening, closing in on the centre.

"Come on. Do something," Henry muttered.

"He's talking to it," he heard Raiodin say.

"He does that," Ellodine replied. "It usually works."

"Bows and crossbows can reload. Rodin's sword can summon a new blade. We need weapons. Something," Henry breathed.

The Hafskod's Madjik flashed over the sleigh.

"That won't give us away at all."

"You know Forodin, sarcasm's a human trait. If you didn't watch so much of their television when you think nobody can see you."

"Really, Zadira? How would you know…What the?"

The light subsided.

Every elf in the sleigh with Henry wore the same Hafskod. Green flames rose from them.

"What's it doing?" Rimida breathed.

"It's fine. Just let it."

Suddenly Henry could see in the dark like he had at home when the Gaardreng attacked. Every pair of eyes flashed with green light.

A gold shield materialised at every left forearm.

Madjik bows and crossbows clattered on the sleigh floor.

"I need a Ferrari," came Forodin's voice.

"I think I just felt it laugh," Henry grinned.

"I thought only Glondir got these," said Rimida.

"We're the special generation, remember?" Zadira laughed.

"They're copies of mine," Henry said, suddenly knowing the answer. "They don't work without this one."

"Better than nothing," Forodin grunted. "Mine's covered in a dark cloud."

"Mine too," said Rimida.

Henry's eyes flitted to the forest. He could make out five dark shapes floating through the trees towards them. He looked the other way. Five more.

"They know we're here," he hissed.

All seven ducked down.

Silence.

"We're surrounded," Balnir whispered. "We should…"

The night air filled with blinding blue flashes. Something hit the sleigh hard and threw it up into the air.

Henry was flung from the sleigh. He flew through the air and landed on the snow with a crunch.

CHAPTER FIFTY-FOUR

Henry lay on his back, looking up at the night sky and the silhouette of overhanging tree branches. He had been thrown clear of the sleigh.

He eased his head up. The sleigh was upside down. The reindeer had broken loose and were wandering around it.

Gaards advanced from the forest over the track to Henry's left.

He couldn't see anything to his right. He was hidden by the trees. Torchlight flitting over the snowy ground told him more Gaards neared. He rolled to his right and slid downwards into a ditch.

There was a movement in front of him. He jumped.

"It's me," Ellodine breathed.

She slid down into the ditch next to him.

The Gaards advanced on the sleigh.

The reindeer's antlers glittered with Madjik.

The Gaards surrounded them.

Henry strained his ears for sounds coming from under the sleigh. None came.

A heavy footstep crunched in the snow behind him. A boot rested on his foot. Something metal jabbed in his leg.

Henry twisted his body around to see Salvodin standing over him, one Azmar bow aimed at his leg, a second aimed at Ellodine.

"Get up," he snarled.

Henry and Ellodine scrambled to their feet. Salvodin herded them to the track and next to the sleigh.

"I found two more. Good thing I was here to do your jobs for you." Salvodin glared at his Gaards. "I don't have time for this. Just as well we planned where we want him."

A thought struck Henry.

Salvodin jumped on his chrome snowboard.

"Kill them all."

Henry's blood ran cold. He took a breath to regain his composure.

"I'm surprised you have the time to be here at all," he said calmly.

Salvodin's eyes flashed angrily at him.

"I mean, you are Grimnir, aren't you? The head of Omnitec?"

A cruel smile crossed Salvodin's face.

"I started the company."

"You've been betraying us all that time," Ellodine sobbed. "How could you?"

"What choice did I have? Nobody would listen to me. My best work and greatest designs were going to waste. My human contemporaries, less talented than me, were being handsomely rewarded. I even killed my predecessor to clear my path."

Ellodine gasped.

"You killed Shoffodin?"

"Of course," Salvodin laughed. "But then a Morivar turned up, gave Klasodin a sob story and he bought it. I couldn't kill another Head of Craft and get away with it. So I tried another venture. Very successful it has been too. Now there is only one competitor in my way. Or at least there is for another half hour or so - or however long it takes us to kill the old wretch once and for all."

Henry stayed calm.

"Really?" he said. "That's all you have left to contend with?"

"Yes," Salvodin said. "I have thought of everything. I have the humans and even the Morivari working for me."

"Oh." Henry pursed his lips. "Well, I met Morikend, as you know. He doesn't seem like someone who works for anyone else."

"We struck a deal to destroy the Aesir."

"But he hates humans as well."

"Now no elf will be giving them anything for free."

"Or selling them anything."

"That is precisely what I will be doing," Salvodin replied.

"But not from your ice palace," Henry answered casually.

"What are you doing, you little human vermin?" Salvodin snarled.

"Morikend doesn't like you or Drock or Omnitec. He wants to destroy you all. He knows where your ice palace is. He's been inside it and knows how it works. He can get inside without any of your Gaards knowing."

"He can't."

"He did it when I was there. And when he realised he couldn't burn Iddrassil down, he escaped. He left in a hurry."

"He ran off." Salvodin scowled. "I knew it."

"But where was he running to?" Henry said knowingly.

"I know what you're doing."

"But do you know what he's doing. I mean, I was in Svaravame. There are loads of Morivari. They should fill the city, but it didn't look that busy. We got in and out pretty easily. So if they weren't in Svaravame, where were they?"

Henry could see it dawning on Salvodin.

"Morikend told me himself," he continued, enjoying the tortured look on Salvodin's face. "If the Morivari are good at one thing, it's digging. Your factory is built on a bed of ice. He doesn't like you or what you do. He's probably there right now, watching it slowly collapse into the ice."

Salvodin's eyes were wide with fear. He turned his snowboard around.

"Kill them," he growled through gritted teeth. "And leave the human until last."

With that, he shot off into the night.

"Nicely done," Ellodine murmured. "You have anything for the rest of them?"

Ten Gaards bore down on them.

CHAPTER FIFTY-FIVE

The reindeer weren't doing what Henry had expected. They were war reindeer, yet not even Vega had made a move. Instead they stood next to the sleigh. They had all turned to face the Gaards coming from the left, ignoring the five from the right. Tiny scattered fragments of Madjik glittered in their antlers, but nothing more.

What were they doing?

Henry's eyes fell on the overturned sleigh. He hadn't heard or seen anything from his friends since a blast of Azmar had struck it and thrown Henry from it.

Were they unconscious? Dead?

Henry's stomach felt hollow and sick. They were his friends. He was starting to fit in, without needing Morikend's breastplate.

One burly Gaard stepped forward brandishing an Azmar bow.

"You think they are dead under there?" he grinned.

Ellodine sobbed.

He ushered five Gaards forward.

"Lift it and look," he ordered them.

The reindeer shifted. Vega bristled, as if he was ready for something.

The Hafskod felt warm - like it was ready too.

"We'll have to bury them deep," the Gaard gloated. "We can't have their kind being discovered now."

They gripped the side of the sleigh.

A whispered command came from under the sleigh.

A bright flash of Madjik.

The sleigh launched sideways, knocking five Gaards on their backs.

The reindeer's antlers glowed. They ran at the other five.

A blitz of Madjik and gold arrows blazed from six young Aesir and one human, forcing the Gaards back into the forest.

"Grab the sleigh," Balnir urged.

All seven of them grabbed it and hauled it back in the direction Henry came from, over the ditch and in the cover of the trees. The reindeer ran after them.

Bolts, arrows and Azmar zipped and flashed around them.

Forodin strapped the reindeer back to the sleigh.

Steel arrows whistled past Henry's ears. He ducked for cover.

He fired his Madjik bow.

Ellodine sent a string of bright gold arrows firing through the trees.

Henry glanced over his shoulder. Rimida kept the five behind them at bay, pelting them with rocks and snowballs, while Zadira and Balnir fired their arrows.

"We can't do this forever," Zadira grated. "We can't even get in the sleigh."

Something flew past overhead. Henry ducked.

Two shadows dropped through the trees to Henry's left. A stream of gold arrows and a flying blade sent the five Gaards retreating into the trees.

Amira and Rodin turned and aimed at the five in front of them. Henry and his friends joined in, forcing the Gaardreng back into the forest.

"Jump in the sleigh," came Forodin's voice.

Henry scrambled up and clambered over the side. He dropped to the floor. Ellodine landed next to him.

Forodin landed in the front. He hauled Henry forward, then handed him the reins.

"What are you doing?"

"We have to hold them here," Forodin said. "Go and find Klasodin. Head for the Fjords. That's where he'll go. Look for Stavanger if you can't find him."

"I know where to go," Ellodine said confidently.

Forodin waited a few seconds, then dived out of the sleigh.

"Away," Ellodine called.

The sleigh accelerated. Henry tumbled and hit the back. The sleigh lifted into the air. Henry scrambled to his knees, levered himself up and peered over the back.

A stream of bolts and arrows fired through the trees, as five young elves, each with a glowing gold band around their arms, pinned back five shadowy figures hiding among the trees. Over the path, Rodin and Amira fought with swords in hand. Two Gaards were no longer moving.

The sleigh shot through the night sky. Henry fixed his eyes on the trees until they disappeared in the night.

He scrambled to the front of the sleigh, then clung to the front as they rose majestically in the moonlit sky. He peered over the side to look at the view below.

"Wow."

Long, frozen fjords stretched in every direction, carving through cliffs and ravines, past meadows, fields and forests. Towns and villages were scattered around them. Henry and Ellodine flew high, scanning one stretch of water after the other.

"I can't see them," Ellodine said, her voice riddled with panic.

Henry checked his Hafskod. No dancing flames.

Ellodine took the sleigh over a ravine and up towards the mountains.

Two flames flickered over the watch face.

"He's close. Keep going."

The flames danced.

A gold flash in the distance caught Henry's eye.

The sleigh shot down towards it.

CHAPTER FIFTY-SIX

Klasodin's sleigh tore down the mountain side, carving a path through banks of thick snow. The nine reindeer galloped and pulled the sleigh faster. A blaze of Madjik ripped from Klasodin's staff and shot at the armoured figure on the chrome snowboard who zigzagged in and out of the fir trees to his left.

Steel bolts fired from the snowboard and collided with the sleigh. Some were blown into the air by the Madjik glittering from the reindeer's antlers. Blasts of Azmar burst from the gloves of the armoured elf, exploding in the snow around the sleigh, forcing it to veer one way, then the other.

The sleigh carrying Henry and Ellodine swooped behind them and landed with a bump on the snow. Ellodine thrust the reins at Henry, who grabbed them and watched his sleigh hurtle down the mountainside.

A blaze of gold arrows from Ellodine's elven bow fired at the snowboarder, throwing him off course. He returned fire. Rockets of blue Azmar exploded at both sleighs and sent snow flying. Henry's sleigh jolted and swerved violently. Steel bolts battered the side of his sleigh and collided with the shield at Ellodine's arm.

A volley of Madjik arrows from Klasodin and Ellodine sent the snowboard spinning out of control. It fired rockets and bolts, which blasted into the snow. The sleigh veered violently. Snow sprayed Henry and Ellodine.

"I can't see," Henry shouted.

The sleigh left the snow and soared into the air. The snow cloud cleared. They had flown off the end of a cliff and over a fjord. Klasodin's sleigh was right in front of them. They were going faster. They were going to collide. The snowboarder shot straight at them and crashed into the side of the sleigh.

The sleigh landed on hard ice and bounced. The reins were wrenched from Henry's hands. The sleigh skidded on the ice and turned over. Henry was thrown from it. He glided over the ice and slowly came to a stop, lying on his back.

Silence.

He could hear himself breathing. He could see his breath billowing in the night air above him. He carefully moved every body part, from his toes to his nose. Everything moved. Nothing hurt. He was still alive.

How have I managed to be thrown from a moving sleigh twice and still be alive?

He sat up with a start. Ellodine. Klasodin.

Ellodine was closest to him. She levered herself onto her elbows with a groan.

The armoured elf scrambled to his feet and ran to grab his snowboard. A blast of Madjik blew it over the frozen fjord and out of reach.

What sounded like a snort of laughter rumbled from the pit of Slepnir's stomach. He opened his mouth and guffawed.

A blue flash from the elf's armour shot at him. Klasodin deflected it with a swing of his staff.

"All of you stay out of the way," he ordered.

Klasodin put his staff away and produced a sword with a gold hilt and a long, double-edged blade.

"I am going to kill you in front of them," the elf sneered from behind a chrome helmet. "Then I will slaughter all your little helpers - reindeer, elf and human alike."

Vega gave a snort of derision.

The others pawed at the ice.

It sounded like Slepnir was laughing.

"Remove your helmet and face me," Klasodin growled.

The helmet came off.

Ullnir stared back at Klasodin with the same robotic, emotionless expression on his face.

Then his features contorted into an angry snarl.

"You have no idea how long I have waited to do this."

The gadget specialist clenched his fists, both decked in chrome gauntlets. Flashes of Azmar ripped from them. He fired again and again. He bombarded Klasodin.

Klasodin moved like lightning. He deflected every bolt. He advanced on Ullnir with every stroke.

Ullnir drew his sword. He swung and brought his blade down. He hammered at Klasodin's blade. He swung wildly. Klasodin deflected his swing, knocked his blade aside and punched him to the floor.

He stood over him calmly, waiting for Ullnir to get up.

"You all seem to forget that I used to be a warrior." He glanced over at the two children, as if that was aimed at them as well. "Why are you so desperate to kill me, Ullnir? I have felt nothing but fondness for you. And your father."

"MY FATHER," Ullnir roared, jumping to his feet. "You never gave a damn about him. He WORSHIPPED you. He devoted his life to you. He died for you. AND YOU BARELY NOTICED."

Ullnir's face was crimson. His eyes bulged. His jaw clenched. His body and arms shook with fury. He circled Klasodin, aiming his sword at him.

"You never do," he spat. "It all revolves around you. The Great Santa Claus. But there's nothing great about you. I have been dreaming of this since the day he died."

"I was very fond of Ecromir," Klasodin said quietly.

"You never showed it," Ullnir screamed. "He died serving you - and for what? You named a room after him. He died for you. He spent his life writing about you. And you gave him a room. I'm sure he's really grateful for that now."

"It was meant as an honour."

"It is an insult. You spit in the face of my father. I want to vomit every time I hear it. It just makes me want to kill you more. I hate your entire family. When I'm done with you and your spawn, I will return to Alvahame. They will let me in without questioning where I have been and I will butcher every elf related to you."

Ullnir foamed at the mouth. His eyes flared wildly. He ran at Klasodin swinging with all his might. Klasodin repelled every stroke. He knocked Ullnir to the floor. Ullnir screamed with fury. He leapt at Klasodin. Klasodin stepped back.

Something rose from the ice between Ullnir and Klasodin. At first it looked like a shard of ice, then a mound. Then it started to take shape. It looked like a snowman. Then it looked like an elf made of ice. A face formed. There was long hair. Pointed ears. The same prominent cheekbones. An ice elf. The same ice elf who had spoken to Henry at the Margullring. He nodded in Henry's direction, then turned to Ullnir and Klasodin.

Both looked like they had seen a ghost.

"Father."

"Ecromir."

"I'm here to avenge you, Father. Watch as I slay him once and for all."

Ullnir raised his sword.

Ecromir calmly held out a hand. Ullnir froze.

"That is enough," Ecromir said. "Ullnir, my son. Your actions here disturb my spirit more than any fate that may have befallen me while I was alive."

He turned to Klasodin, a warm smile on his face.

"I am sorry, old friend," Klasodin said, his voice hoarse. "He is right. I never appreciated your work. It is my fault you were killed. I meant the renaming of the hall as an honest tribute - and out of guilt. I have borne it to this day. I always will."

"Klasodin," the elf said gently. "I forgive you. In my spirit, I forgave you the second I passed away. There was no need to carry the burden with you all this time. I believed in The Purpose. I believed in you as our King. That was all. The fact you have kept my work and used it was all I needed." The elf turned his head towards Henry and Ellodine. "You were right. The generation you so eagerly awaited has arrived. Without them, there would be no Christmas."

Klasodin nodded in agreement.

"You have appreciated my work, Glondir?" Ecromir asked.

"I couldn't have done all this without it," Henry replied.

The elf smiled.

"Be at peace, Klasodin. Continue in your Purpose."

"I will. Thank you, Ecromir."

"Goodbye Klasodin. Henry. Ellodine."

"Father. This is…"

"Enough."

Ecromir stretched out his hand and touched Ullnir's face with it.

Ullnir's eyes filled with alarm.

"No. I…"

The ice spread over his face, his head, his body, until he looked like Ecromir. Slowly, they both sank into the ice and vanished.

CHAPTER FIFTY-SEVEN

"Is he dead?" a voice rang out over the ice.

Henry wheeled round, his bow aimed at the top of the cliff. A sleigh and five familiar figures on snowboards touched down on the ice.

Klasodin didn't seem to have noticed them. He stood with his eyes closed, taking in slow, deep breaths.

"Was it good to see him again?" Ellodine asked.

"Yes. Very good."

"Is he dead or not?" Raiodin demanded, sliding to a stop over the spot where Ecromir and Ullnir had just vanished.

"Who was that with him?" said Forodin.

"Is he dead?"

"Ullnir. I never thought it would be him."

"Ecromir was his father. Was that Ecromir?"

"Ecromir died ages ago."

"What's he doing so far from Alvahame?"

"I can't see anyone down there."

"Is he dead?"

Klasodin held up his hands to silence them.

"Your friends can answer your questions once I am gone."

They harnessed the sleigh and the Elf King climbed in, pulling his fur-lined red coat about him. The sleigh shot over the ice and flew into the night sky. Henry stood and watched Santa Claus and his sleigh disappear into the distance. He realised he still had no idea if he and his foster family would receive any presents. Somehow, after all that had happened, it didn't seem to matter if he got any Christmas presents or not. But he hoped the others in his foster home did.

He climbed into the sleigh with the others and let Ellodine field most of the many questions fired at them on the way back to Alvahame.

The ice elves stood guard around the Margullring. Henry was sure there was one more than there had been before.

"So they're all spirits of dead elves?" he asked.

"Aesir spirits rarely go far," Rodin replied. "But I have never seen them before."

"They were just there in the Margullring. I think only Ecromir spoke."

"His was the spirit with something to resolve."

Henry had seen enough spy films to know what to look for once the initial search of Salvodin's home revealed nothing. He found a hidden door in the wood-panelled wall of his basement and led the party down to the hidden room below, which was filled with computers and screens. There was a trapdoor in the floor, hiding stone stairs leading deeper underground. With Rodin and his friends right behind him, Henry led the way along a tunnel, which headed under the city and up towards the north-west edge. As the tunnel rose, a bright blue screen barred his way, covering the entire height and width of the tunnel.

He thought back to seeing Bayne and Yohann in the Sleigh Room. No way had they sneaked through the Hall of Ecromir. He stepped into the blue screen.

He found himself standing in snow, staring up at the forests outside the city of Alvahame on the north-west edge. He turned, expecting to see a blue screen, but just saw a wall of ice. He stepped to the side. There was a screen of ice in front of the Margullring, roughly the size of a door. Looking closer, it looked like a thin blue screen sandwiched between sheets of ice to hide it from anyone not looking too closely. He stepped into the ice screen and found himself back in the tunnel, looking up at Rodin, his friends all gathered behind him.

"It's a portal, like the gifts into the Sleigh Room," he reported. "It goes just the other side of the Margullring."

"Then we destroy it," the warrior elf replied.

Arrows of Madjik had no effect. But a blast of ice from his bow disintegrated it and Henry could walk the rest of the tunnel to the Margullring and lead the others through it to destroy the outer portal. Then they slid around the Margullring to where it joined the South Passage. The ice elves were gone.

CHAPTER FIFTY-EIGHT

There was a deep blue night sky overhead. Alvahame was lit up in bright lights lining every avenue and covering every tree. Music was playing. Elves were eating, drinking and dancing. There were races around the city on snowboards, sledges and sleighs which everyone took part in - except Forodin, who had already been banned from entering any more races until next Christmas.

Henry slept when he was too tired to stay awake any longer. At least twice he remembered being somewhere in Iddrassil, then found himself in bed several hours later. Officially, only two hours had passed, but Henry was certain he had slept nearly twenty times. After every breakfast, he loaded sacks of fish and meat into a sleigh and took it up into the forests with Forodin and Ellodine for Grrhdrig and the other animals. Grrhdrig's sharp, black eyes always carried the same expression, but Henry was sure Grrhdrig at least thought of him as a comrade now.

In Alvahame, he spent a lot of time with his new friends, eating and drinking and enjoying the party atmosphere. He took part in some races and managed to only crash a few times. He received archery lessons from Perrodin and sword training from Appodin and was getting much better at both. He hadn't seen much of Rodin or Amira at all. He went to the Craft of Creation with Forodin to test bikes and games. The holographic computer games were his favourites.

It was his twentieth sleep when Ellodine woke him up more excited than usual. She'd done it every time like a very effective and accurate alarm clock, never letting him sleep for longer than she decided he needed.

"It's the Feast of Rains," she announced. "Hurry up."

They took the food to the animals in the forests as usual. By the time they had made their way back, crowds were gathered around Iddrassil and lining the central avenues. Aesir children chattered excitedly, clutching baskets and bags.

Henry gathered near the stables with his friends, who looked just as excited as the younger children.

"It means Klasodin's nearly done," Rimida explained. She jigged around on the snow, looking up at the sky. "Come on. Hurry up."

"He can't eat all the food people leave for him," Zadira continued, rolling her eyes. "So he collects it all and sends it here. You'll see."

A murmur of excitement arose. Everyone was looking up.

A gold light appeared above the star and spread over the sky, as if part of the Margullring was turning gold.

Then it started to rain. Lots of little objects fell and landed in the snow. Some dropped in the branches. Some bounced off the trunk or dropped onto the roofs of nearby houses and slid to the floor. Every elf rushed to pick them up. Henry followed Ellodine and Rimida as they ran to grab some.

He picked up a few and realised he was looking at a chocolate chip cookie, a bourbon, a digestive and a chocolate hobnob.

He could hear thuds and grunts of delight coming from the stable. Inside, the floor was covered in carrots and oats. Vega was gulping from a vat of milk, which was filling up as he drank it.

Soon they were sitting on a branch a couple of storeys up, eating their haul, watching the food fall and children still gathering.

"Amateurs," said Balnir. "It keeps falling for ages yet. You have to work in shifts. Collect. Eat. Collect. Eat."

Henry was full when he had finished his haul. Ellodine stayed with him as the others all scrambled up and raced to find more.

"They're on a sugar high," she grinned.

She nudged him, then pointed to a branch further up with a smirk on her face. Two elves emerged from a house built into the trunk, wandered over the branch and stood to watch the fun below. They were holding hands. It was Rodin and Amira.

"You know it's Aesir tradition that on Christmas Eve night, an elf declares his true love," she said quietly.

"And then you party again for all of January?"

"It's the season for Aesir weddings as well."

"They declare their love in December and get married in January?"

"What's the point in waiting? If you're destined to be together."

"But how would you know?"

"An elf knows. We don't do dating like you humans, trying one, then another. It's very romantic - once they actually get around to declaring. Warriors are only good at fighting. They usually need a push. The hot wine always helps." She shot Henry a sly look. "They say an Aesrine knows who she will marry before she leaves school."

She leaned over and kissed him on the cheek.

"You're my friend," she stated plainly. "But one day, when I want a boyfriend, it's going to be you."

A fusion of nerves and excitement exploded in Henry's stomach.

"Just like that?" He looked up towards Rodin and Amira. "That's going to be us?"

"One day. Klasodin always said I'd marry a human. And I knew it too. You're going to be here in Alvahame a lot, but I'm telling you this now so you don't start chasing after any human girls."

"Okay."

"Not that you'd want to. I mean, I don't want to sound superior or anything, but you've seen Amira and how time works here. I'm going to be a beautiful young Aesrine for a very long time. And you don't want to miss out on that now, do you?" She leaned in again and kissed him on the cheek, then jumped to her feet and ran off. "Come on. I want more cookies."

Henry stared into the distance, too stunned to move. He heard raucous laughter from above. Rodin and Amira were waving to him.

After four more sleeps and a lot of partying, Henry and Ellodine gathered among the crowds surrounding Iddrassil and lining its avenues to watch for Klasodin's arrival. They found a spot on a low branch with their friends and sat down to watch, tucking into the remainder of their Rains.

The second and third flames burst into life on the face of Henry's Hafskod. The cheers sounded further out in the city. They all jumped to their feet. Nine reindeer emerged pulling a sleigh driven by Klasodin, Santa Claus. Alvahame shook with the noise of the shouts and cheers.

"Come on," Ellodine said suddenly.

She led them off the branch and onto the bottom of the avenue under Iddrassil. Everyone else seemed to be doing the same thing.

The bezel on the Hafskod was turning. It stopped back in its usual position.

The night sky was lifting. Bright morning sunlight streamed into the city. The baubles on the tree were changing colour.

Suddenly they were more like TV screens. Henry could see a boy and his little sister tearing down the stairs and diving into a pile of presents under their Christmas tree. The boy tore open the paper and pulled out a remote control helicopter and a fire engine. His sister found a teddy bear and skateboard. Every bauble showed a different family and different children. He looked around him. The eyes of every elf were fixed on a screen.

A hand laid on his shoulder. Klasodin smiled down at him.

"There's nothing quite like it, is there?" he said.

"No," Henry agreed.

Klasodin took in a deep breath.

"I haven't actually been down here to watch the present opening for more years than I can remember. I might make it a habit."

"Can we see London?" Henry said hopefully.

"Too early. Give it a couple of hours." Klasodin studied Henry, a thoughtful expression on his face. "Keen to get back?"

Henry thought about it.

"I don't want to leave here, but yes, I think so."

"Well, well. Left London with no family and you're about to return with two of them."

"I suppose you're right," Henry laughed.

After seeing children in a couple of familiar-looking towns in the mountains, Henry climbed into the sleigh with a sack full of presents, some for him, some from him to the others in the house. Everyone shook his hand and hugged him. Ellodine and his friends piled in with him. He waved goodbye. The sleigh set off, shot over the snow and flew into the air, heading for home.

The End

A GUIDE TO ALVAHAME

Aesir (ez-EER): The race of elves in Alvahame led by Klasodin.

Aesr/Aesrine (EZ-ur / EZ-reen): An elf (male/female) belonging to the Aesir.

Affinity for Madjik: The potential ability of certain human children to wield Madjik.

Alvahame (ALV-a-hame): The city of Santa Claus and his elves.

Amira (a-MEE-ra): Aesrine warrior. Orek's daughter.

Appodin (APP-o-din): Aesir warrior and sleigh driver.

Azmar (AZ-maar): The product of fusing Madjik with human technology.

Balnir (BAL-neer): Elf in Henry's class in Alvahame. Talent for tactical thinking.

Bardag (BAR-dag): Reindeer.

Bayne: Leader of the Gaardreng and a Yotunmens.

The Black List: The naughty list.

Blaze: Reindeer.

Ecromir (ECK-ro-meer): The elf who wrote Klasodin's memoirs.

Ellodine (ELL-o-deen): Henry's classmate and best friend in Alvahame. Klasodin's direct descendant. Talent for healing, which she tries to keep quiet.

Elven Realm: A realm on Earth hidden from everyone except elves and those possessing elven Madjik.

Epicentre: Every form of Madjik comes from one and needs one. Every race of elves has its own Epicentre, which is made of a combination of precious stones or metals.

Equodin (ECK-wo-din): Looks after the reindeer in Alvahame and manages the stables.

The Five Crafts: Everything the elves of Alvahame do falls under one of the Five Crafts:

    The Craft of Care: Looking after elves, animals and nature.

    The Craft of Creation: Designing and making toys and gifts.

    The Craft of Education: School and learning. Studying humans and the wider world.

    The Craft of Giving: Reading Christmas lists. Wrapping and delivering gifts.

    The Craft of War: Warriors defending Alvahame.

Forodin (FOR-o-din): Henry's classmate. Talent for speed.

Fyoreig (FYOR-egg): Nourishing hot drink made from the sap of Iddrassil.

Fyur: The purist form of Aesir Madjik.

Gaard: Member of the Gaardreng.

Gaardreng: Armed mercenaries doing Omnitec's dirty work – such as sabotage and murder.

Glondir (GLON-deer): The name given to Klasodin's chosen human helper.

The Gold List: An idea for desperate times. You have to be good enough to earn your place on the Gold List. Only those on the Gold List receive a present from Santa Claus.

Gratall (GRA-tal): Reindeer.

Grimnir (GRIM-neer): Codename of the traitor, the elf working against Klasodin from inside Alvahame.

The Great Santa Claus: Sarcastic name and insult aimed at Klasodin by Grimnir.

Gronodin (GRON-o-din): Klasodin's second-in-command and his oldest friend.

Grrhdrig (GURR-drig): Polar bear. King of his tribe.

Hafskod (HAFF-skod): The Madjikal gold wristband worn by Glondir. It looks like a watch and possesses Madjikal powers.

Hamedall (HAME-daal): Village on the edge of Alvahame, inside the Margullring. The elves living there are guards protecting Alvahame.

Henry Frey: Our hero. An orphaned boy living in a London foster home.

The Hollow: The massive space inside Iddrassil.

Iddrassil (ID-ra-sill): The Great Tree at the centre of Alvahame.

Ivrakend (IV-ra-kend): Morivar warrior.

Klasodin (KLAAS-o-din): Santa Claus. The King of Alvahame. The great warrior who led the Aesir from Vanahame.

LagFyurring (LAG-fyur-ring): Hovering gold globe used by the Aesir to watch humans.

Larodine (LAR-o-deen): Ellodine's mum. Head of the Craft of Care.

Leglodin (LEG-lo-din): Head of the Craft of Education.

Madjik (magic): The magic of the elves.

Mannhame: The settlement close to Alvahame inhabited mainly by half-elves and humans who've spent time in Alvahame.

Margullring (MAAR-gull-ring): The dome of ice surrounding Alvahame. A Madjikal shield protecting the city.

Merrodine (MERR-o-deen): Klasodin's wife. Head of the Craft of Giving.

Monira (mo-NEE-ra): Henry's school teacher in Alvahame.

Morikend (MOR-i-kend): King of the Morivari.

Morivar (MOR-i-vaar): Elf belonging to the Morivari.

Morivari (mor-i-VAA-ree): Race of elves living in the underground city of Svaravame in the elven realm. Mortal enemies of the Aesir.

Nerivari (ner-i-VAA-ree): Savage race of elves living much deeper underground than the Morivari. Rarely seen above the surface.

Omnitec: Massive world-conquering multinational intent on world domination, controlling the world's toy market and destroying Santa Claus in the process.

Orek (O-reck): Head of the Craft of Creation. Amira's father.

Pellodin (PELL-o-din): Warrior and guard. Lives in Hamedall.

The Purpose: One of the Three Foundations. The Purpose is Alvahame's primary reason for existence – Klasodin's role as Santa Claus.

Raiodin (RYE-o-din): Henry's classmate. Talent for warcraft.

Rimida (ri-MEE-da): Henry's classmate. Talent for throwing.

Rodin (ROE-din): Warrior. Head of the Craft of War.

Salvodin (SALV-o-din): Toy designer in the Craft of Creation.

Shoffodin (SHOFF-o-din): Former Head of the Craft of Creation.

Slepnir (SLEP-neer): Klasodin's white eight-legged horse who changes into a reindeer.

Svaramar (SVAR-a-maar): Dark Madjik wielded by the Morivari.

Svaravame (SVAR-a-vame): Underground city of the Morivari hidden in the elven realm.

The Three Foundations: The three rules governing and defining life in Alvahame:

> **The Equality of all Elves.**
> **The Purity of Madjik.**
> **The Purpose.**

Ullnir (ULL-neer): Gadget specialist in the Craft of Creation.

ValdFyurring (VALD-fyur-ring): The Epicentre of Aesir Madjik. Made of pure gold. It sits in Iddrassil's roots.

Valdir (VAL-deer): One of the human children with the Affinity for Madjik.

Valdiri (val-DEE-ree): The chosen human children with the Affinity for Madjik. Klasodin selects one of them to become Glondir, his human helper.

Vanahame: Klasodin's old home. The city he and the Aesir originally came from. Klasodin led a group of elves from Vanahame. They built the city of Alvahame and became the Aesir.

Vega: Reindeer.

Visr/Visrine (VIZ-ur) (VIZ-reen): The Aesir term (male/female) for "Your Royal Highness".

Yohann: The human boy helping Klasodin, but not officially named Glondir.

Yotunhame (YO-tun-hame): Home of the ice giants in the Antarctic.

Yotunmens: Half-elf.(Half elf, half human). Bayne is a half-elf.

Zadira (za-DEE-ra): Henry's classmate. Talent for working with snow and ice.

Zander Drock: CEO of Omnitec.

Printed in Great
Britain
by Amazon